Teen
Smi

MAY − − 2013

P9-CRB-343

THIS
IS WHAT
HAPPY
LOOKS LIKE

Carn

THIS IS WHAT HAPPY LOOKS LIKE

JENNIFER E. SMITH

poppy

Little, Brown and Company
New York   Boston

Also by Jennifer E. Smith:

The Statistical Probability of Love at First Sight
The Storm Makers
You Are Here
The Comeback Season

Poppy

Hachette Book Group
237 Park Avenue, New York, NY 10017
For more of your favorite series and novels, visit our website at www.pickapoppy.com

Poppy is an imprint of Little, Brown and Company.
The Poppy name and logo are trademarks of Hachette Book Group, Inc.

The publisher is not responsible for websites (or their content) that are not owned by the publisher.

First Edition: April 2013

Library of Congress Cataloging-in-Publication Data

Smith, Jennifer E., 1980–
This is what happy looks like / Jennifer E. Smith. — 1st ed.
p. cm.
Summary: "Perfect strangers Graham Larkin and Ellie O'Neill meet online when Graham accidentally sends Ellie an e-mail about his pet pig, Wilbur. The two 17-year-olds strike up an e-mail relationship from opposite sides of the country and don't even know each other's first names. What's more, Ellie doesn't know Graham is a famous actor, and Graham doesn't know about the big secret in Ellie's family tree. When the relationship goes from online to in-person, they find out whether their relationship can be the real thing"— Provided by publisher.
ISBN 978-0-316-21282-3
[1. Online dating—Fiction. 2. Love—Fiction. 3. Actors and actresses—Fiction.
4. Maine—Fiction.] I. Title.
PZ7.S65141Thi 2013   [Fic]—dc23   2012028755

10 9 8 7 6 5 4 3 2 1
RRD-C
Printed in the United States of America

To Mom, with love

PROLOGUE

From: GDL824@yahoo.com
Sent: Thursday, March 7, 2013 10:18 PM
To: EONeill22@hotmail.com
Subject: (no subject)

Hey, we're running pretty behind here. Any chance you could walk Wilbur for me tonight?

From: EONeill22@hotmail.com
Sent: Thursday, March 7, 2013 10:24 PM
To: GDL824@yahoo.com
Subject: Re: (no subject)

I think you have the wrong e-mail address. But since I'm a dog owner too, and I don't want poor Wilbur to be stranded, I thought I'd write back and let you know...

From: GDL824@yahoo.com
Sent: Thursday, March 7, 2013 10:33 PM
To: EONeill22@hotmail.com
Subject: Re: (no subject)

Ah, sorry about that. New phone, so I'm typing in the address.

Looks like I forgot a number. Wilbur and I both thank you. (And by the way, he's actually a pig.)

From: EONeill22@hotmail.com
Sent: Thursday, March 7, 2013 10:34 PM
To: GDL824@yahoo.com
Subject: Re: (no subject)

A pig! What kind of pig goes for walks?

From: GDL824@yahoo.com
Sent: Thursday, March 7, 2013 10:36 PM
To: EONeill22@hotmail.com
Subject: Re: (no subject)

The very sophisticated kind. He even has his own leash . . .

From: EONeill22@hotmail.com
Sent: Thursday, March 7, 2013 10:42 PM
To: GDL824@yahoo.com
Subject: Re: (no subject)

Some pig!

From: GDL824@yahoo.com
Sent: Thursday, March 7, 2013 10:45 PM
To: EONeill22@hotmail.com
Subject: Re: (no subject)

Oh, yeah. He's terrific! Radiant! Humble!

From: EONeill22@hotmail.com
Sent: Thursday, March 7, 2013 10:47 PM
To: GDL824@yahoo.com
Subject: Re: (no subject)

Wow, a pig owner *and* a fan of *Charlotte's Web*. You must be either a farmer or a librarian.

From: GDL824@yahoo.com
Sent: Thursday, March 7, 2013 11:01 PM
To: EONeill22@hotmail.com
Subject: Re: (no subject)

I dabble in both.

From: EONeill22@hotmail.com
Sent: Thursday, March 7, 2013 11:03 PM
To: GDL824@yahoo.com
Subject: Re: (no subject)

Seriously?

From: GDL824@yahoo.com
Sent: Thursday, March 7, 2013 11:04 PM
To: EONeill22@hotmail.com
Subject: Re: (no subject)

No. Not seriously. What about you?

From: EONeill22@hotmail.com
Sent: Thursday, March 7, 2013 11:05 PM
To: GDL824@yahoo.com
Subject: Re: (no subject)

I'm neither a farmer nor a librarian.

From: GDL824@yahoo.com
Sent: Thursday, March 7, 2013 11:11 PM
To: EONeill22@hotmail.com
Subject: Re: (no subject)

Let me guess then. You're an underemployed dogwalker who's been sitting by the computer in the hope that someone might ask you to walk something more exciting than a poodle?

From: EONeill22@hotmail.com
Sent: Thursday, March 7, 2013 11:12 PM
To: GDL824@yahoo.com
Subject: Re: (no subject)

Bingo. Guess this is my lucky day . . .

From: GDL824@yahoo.com
Sent: Thursday, March 7, 2013 11:13 PM
To: EONeill22@hotmail.com
Subject: Re: (no subject)

Really, though. What's your deal?

From: EONeill22@hotmail.com
Sent: Thursday, March 7, 2013 11:14 PM
To: GDL824@yahoo.com
Subject: Re: (no subject)

. . . asks the random stranger from the Internet.

From: GDL824@yahoo.com
Sent: Thursday, March 7, 2013 11:15 PM
To: EONeill22@hotmail.com
Subject: Re: (no subject)

. . . says the girl who's still writing back.

From: EONeill22@hotmail.com
Sent: Thursday, March 7, 2013 11:17 PM
To: GDL824@yahoo.com
Subject: Re: (no subject)

How do you know I'm a girl?

From: GDL824@yahoo.com
Sent: Thursday, March 7, 2013 11:18 PM
To: EONeill22@hotmail.com
Subject: Re: (no subject)

Easy. You quoted *Charlotte's Web*.

From: EONeill22@hotmail.com
Sent: Thursday, March 7, 2013 11:19 PM
To: GDL824@yahoo.com
Subject: Re: (no subject)

So did you!

From: GDL824@yahoo.com
Sent: Thursday, March 7, 2013 11:24 PM
To: EONeill22@hotmail.com
Subject: Re: (no subject)

Yeah, but my parents are teachers.

From: EONeill22@hotmail.com
Sent: Thursday, March 7, 2013 11:26 PM
To: GDL824@yahoo.com
Subject: Re: (no subject)

So does that mean you're not a girl?

From: GDL824@yahoo.com
Sent: Thursday, March 7, 2013 11:27 PM
To: EONeill22@hotmail.com
Subject: Re: (no subject)

Nope. Not a girl.

From: EONeill22@hotmail.com
Sent: Thursday, March 7, 2013 11:31 PM
To: GDL824@yahoo.com
Subject: Re: (no subject)

Does that mean you're a creepy old Internet predator using your pet pig as an excuse to stalk 16-year-old girls?

From: GDL824@yahoo.com
Sent: Thursday, March 7, 2013 11:33 PM
To: EONeill22@hotmail.com
Subject: Re: (no subject)

Busted.

No, I'm only seventeen, which I think lands me pretty solidly outside of creepy-old-man territory.

From: EONeill22@hotmail.com
Sent: Thursday, March 7, 2013 11:38 PM
To: GDL824@yahoo.com
Subject: Re: (no subject)

Fair enough. Though, unfortunately, I'm still not available to walk Wilbur tonight. And even if I was, you'd probably have to find someone a little bit closer, since I doubt you live anywhere near me.

From: GDL824@yahoo.com
Sent: Thursday, March 7, 2013 11:39 PM
To: EONeill22@hotmail.com
Subject: Re: (no subject)

How do you know?

From: EONeill22@hotmail.com
Sent: Thursday, March 7, 2013 11:40 PM
To: GDL824@yahoo.com
Subject: Re: (no subject)

I'm from Middle-of-Nowhere, Maine.

From: GDL824@yahoo.com
Sent: Thursday, March 7, 2013 11:42 PM
To: EONeill22@hotmail.com
Subject: Re: (no subject)

Oh, then I guess you're right. I'm from Middle-of-Everything, California.

From: EONeill22@hotmail.com
Sent: Thursday, March 7, 2013 11:43 PM
To: GDL824@yahoo.com
Subject: Re: (no subject)

Lucky duck.

From: GDL824@yahoo.com
Sent: Thursday, March 7, 2013 11:44 PM
To: EONeill22@hotmail.com
Subject: Re: (no subject)

Lucky pig, actually.

From: EONeill22@hotmail.com
Sent: Thursday, March 7, 2013 11:48 PM
To: GDL824@yahoo.com
Subject: Re: (no subject)

Right! Hey, weren't you running behind with something?

From: GDL824@yahoo.com
Sent: Thursday, March 7, 2013 11:51 PM
To: EONeill22@hotmail.com
Subject: Re: (no subject)

Yeah, I should probably be getting back to it...

From: EONeill22@hotmail.com
Sent: Thursday, March 7, 2013 11:55 PM
To: GDL824@yahoo.com
Subject: Re: (no subject)

Okay. Nice talking to you. And sorry I couldn't come through for

Wilbur.

From: GDL824@yahoo.com
Sent: Thursday, March 7, 2013 11:57 PM
To: EONeill22@hotmail.com
Subject: Re: (no subject)

He'll forgive you, I'm sure. He's a very magnanimous pig.

From: EONeill22@hotmail.com
Sent: Thursday, March 7, 2013 11:58 PM
To: GDL824@yahoo.com
Subject: Re: (no subject)

I'm relieved to hear that.

From: GDL824@yahoo.com
Sent: Friday, March 8, 2013 12:01 AM
To: EONeill22@hotmail.com
Subject: Re: (no subject)

Hey, E?

From: EONeill22@hotmail.com
Sent: Friday, March 8, 2013 12:02 AM
To: GDL824@yahoo.com
Subject: Re: (no subject)

Yes...G?

From: GDL824@yahoo.com
Sent: Friday, March 8, 2013 12:03 AM
To: EONeill22@hotmail.com
Subject: Re: (no subject)

What if I e-mail you again tomorrow?

From: EONeill22@hotmail.com
Sent: Friday, March 8, 2013 12:04 AM
To: GDL824@yahoo.com
Subject: Re: (no subject)

I don't know. I'm not exactly in the habit of trolling the Internet
for pen pals...

From: GDL824@yahoo.com
Sent: Friday, March 8, 2013 12:05 AM
To: EONeill22@hotmail.com
Subject: Re: (no subject)

But?

From: EONeill22@hotmail.com
Sent: Friday, March 8, 2013 12:07 AM
To: GDL824@yahoo.com
Subject: Re: (no subject)

But I'm also terrible at good-byes.

From: GDL824@yahoo.com
Sent: Friday, March 8, 2013 12:08 AM
To: EONeill22@hotmail.com
Subject: Re: (no subject)

Okay then. I'll just say hello again instead.

From: EONeill22@hotmail.com
Sent: Friday, March 8, 2013 12:09 AM
To: GDL824@yahoo.com
Subject: Re: (no subject)

I like that better. And I'll say: Good morning!

From: GDL824@yahoo.com
Sent: Friday, March 8, 2013 12:10 AM
To: EONeill22@hotmail.com
Subject: Re: (no subject)

But it's not morning...

From: EONeill22@hotmail.com
Sent: Friday, March 8, 2013 12:12 AM
To: GDL824@yahoo.com
Subject: Re: (no subject)

It is in Maine.

From: GDL824@yahoo.com
Sent: Friday, March 8, 2013 12:13 AM
To: EONeill22@hotmail.com
Subject: Re: (no subject)

Ah, right. Then: Howdy!

From: EONeill22@hotmail.com
Sent: Friday, March 8, 2013 12:14 AM
To: GDL824@yahoo.com
Subject: Re: (no subject)

How very western of you. Greetings!

From: GDL824@yahoo.com
Sent: Friday, March 8, 2013 12:15 AM
To: EONeill22@hotmail.com
Subject: Re: (no subject)

Are you an alien invader? Ni hao.

From: EONeill22@hotmail.com
Sent: Friday, March 8, 2013 12:17 AM
To: GDL824@yahoo.com
Subject: Re: (no subject)

You definitely just looked that one up.

From: GDL824@yahoo.com
Sent: Friday, March 8, 2013 12:19 AM
To: EONeill22@hotmail.com
Subject: Re: (no subject)

You don't think I'm proficient in Chinese?

From: EONeill22@hotmail.com
Sent: Friday, March 8, 2013 12:20 AM
To: GDL824@yahoo.com
Subject: Re: (no subject)

I do not.

From: GDL824@yahoo.com
Sent: Friday, March 8, 2013 12:21 AM
To: EONeill22@hotmail.com
Subject: Re: (no subject)

Fair enough. Then, salutations! (That one was from Wilbur, of course.)

From: EONeill22@hotmail.com
Sent: Friday, March 8, 2013 12:24 AM
To: GDL824@yahoo.com
Subject: Re: (no subject)

Of course. Until tomorrow...

From: GDL824@yahoo.com
Sent: Friday, March 8, 2013 12:25 AM
To: EONeill22@hotmail.com
Subject: Re: (no subject)

Wait, is that your way of saying good-bye without really saying good-bye?

From: EONeill22@hotmail.com
Sent: Friday, March 8, 2013 12:27 AM
To: GDL824@yahoo.com
Subject: Re: (no subject)

No. Actually, I'm not sure I'm quite finished saying hello yet.

From: GDL824@yahoo.com
Sent: Friday, March 8, 2013 12:30 AM
To: EONeill22@hotmail.com
Subject: Re: (no subject)

Me neither. Hello.

From: EONeill22@hotmail.com
Sent: Friday, March 8, 2013 12:31 AM
To: GDL824@yahoo.com
Subject: Re: (no subject)

Hi.

From: GDL824@yahoo.com
Sent: Friday, March 8, 2013 12:33 AM
To: EONeill22@hotmail.com
Subject: Re: (no subject)

Good morning.

From: EONeill22@hotmail.com
Sent: Friday, March 8, 2013 12:34 AM
To: GDL824@yahoo.com
Subject: Re: (no subject)

I already said that one.

From: GDL824@yahoo.com
Sent: Friday, March 8, 2013 12:36 AM
To: EONeill22@hotmail.com
Subject: Re: (no subject)

Yeah, but it really is.

PART I

From: EONeill22@hotmail.com
Sent: Saturday, June 8, 2013 12:42 PM
To: GDL824@yahoo.com
Subject: Re: hi

Don't you hate it when people use smiley faces in their e-mails?

From: GDL824@yahoo.com
Sent: Saturday, June 8, 2013 12:59 PM
To: EONeill22@hotmail.com
Subject: not really

☺

From: EONeill22@hotmail.com
Sent: Saturday, June 8, 2013 1:04 PM
To: GDL824@yahoo.com
Subject: Re: not really

I'm going to ignore that.

I read once that in Russia, they usually end the salutation of a letter with an exclamation point. Isn't that funny? It must always seem like they're shouting at each other. Or that they're really surprised to find themselves in touch.

From: GDL824@yahoo.com
Sent: Saturday, June 8, 2013 1:07 PM
To: EONeill22@hotmail.com
Subject: not a chance

Or maybe they're just really happy to be writing to that person . . .

Like I am: ☺!

From: EONeill22@hotmail.com
Sent: Saturday, June 8, 2013 1:11 PM
To: GDL824@yahoo.com
Subject: Re: not a chance

Well, thank you. But that's *not* what happy looks like.

From: GDL824@yahoo.com
Sent: Saturday, June 8, 2013 1:12 PM
To: EONeill22@hotmail.com
Subject: Re: not a chance

What does it look like, then?

From: EONeill22@hotmail.com
Sent: Saturday, June 8, 2013 1:18 PM
To: GDL824@yahoo.com
Subject: what happy looks like

Sunrises over the harbor. Ice cream on a hot day. The sound of the waves down the street. The way my dog curls up next to me on the couch. Evening strolls. Great movies. Thunderstorms. A good cheeseburger. Fridays. Saturdays. Wednesdays, even. Sticking your toes in the water. Pajama pants. Flip-flops. Swimming. Poetry. The absence of smiley faces in an e-mail.

What does it look like to you?

1

It was not all that different from the circus, and it came to town in much the same way. Only instead of elephants and giraffes, there were cameras and microphones. Instead of clowns and cages and tightropes, there were production assistants and trailers and yards upon yards of thick cables.

There was a sense of magic in the way it appeared as if from nowhere, cropping up so quickly that even those who had been expecting it were taken by surprise. And as the people of Henley showed up to watch, even the most jaded members of the film crew couldn't help feeling a slight shiver of anticipation, a low current of electricity that seemed to pulse through the town. They were used to filming in locations like Los Angeles and New York, cities where the locals gave them a wide berth, grumbling about the traffic and the disappearance of parking spots, shaking their heads at the huge lights that snuffed out the darkness. There were places in the world where a movie shoot was nothing more than a nuisance, a bothersome interruption of real life.

But Henley, Maine, was not one of them.

It was June, so the crowds that had gathered to watch the men unload the trucks were fairly large. The size of the town rose and fell like the tides. Through the winter, the full-timers rattled around the empty shops, bundled against the frost coming off the water. But as soon as summer rolled around, the population swelled to four or five times its usual size, a stream of tourists once again filling the gift shops and cottages and B&Bs that lined the coast. Henley was like a great hibernating bear, dozing through the long winters before coming back to life again at the same time each year.

Most everyone in town waited eagerly for Memorial Day, when the seasons clicked forward and the usual three-month frenzy of boaters and fishermen and honeymooners and vacationers invaded. But Ellie O'Neill had always dreaded it, and now, as she tried to pick her way through the thick knots of people in the village square, she was reminded of why. In the off-season, the town was hers. But on this blisteringly hot day at the start of June, it belonged to strangers again.

And this summer would be worse than ever.

Because this summer, there would be a movie too.

A few seagulls wheeled overheard, and from some distant boat a bell began to clang. Ellie hurried past the gawking tourists and away from the trailers, which now lined the harbor road like a gypsy caravan. There was a sharp tang of salt in the air, and the smell of frying fish was already drifting out of the town's oldest restaurant, the Lobster Pot. Its owner, Joe Gabriele, was leaning against the doorframe, his eyes trained on the flurry of activity down the street.

"Kind of crazy, huh?" he said, and Ellie paused to follow his gaze. As they watched, a long black limo glided up to the main production tent, followed by a van and two motorcycles. "And now photographers too," he muttered.

Ellie couldn't help frowning as she watched the explosion of flashes that accompanied the opening of the limo door.

Joe sighed. "All I can say is, they better eat a *lot* of lobster."

"And ice cream," Ellie added.

"Right," he said, nodding at the blue T-shirt with her name stitched to the pocket. "And ice cream too."

By the time she reached the little yellow shop with the green awning that read SPRINKLES in faded letters, Ellie was already ten minutes late. But she didn't have to worry; the only person inside was Quinn—her very best friend and the world's very worst employee—who was hunched over the ice-cream counter, flipping through the pages of a magazine.

"Can you *believe* we're stuck in here today?" she asked as Ellie walked in, the bell above the door jangling.

The inside of the shop was wonderfully cool and smelled

like spun sugar, and as always, there was something about it that made the years recede for Ellie, peeling them back one at a time like the layers of an onion. She had been only four when she and her mom moved here, and after the long drive up from Washington, D.C.—the car heavy because of all they'd taken with them and silent because of all they had not—they'd stopped in town to ask for directions to the cottage they'd rented for the summer. Mom had been in a rush, eager to finish the journey that had started well before the ten-hour drive. But Ellie had walked right through the front door and pushed her freckled nose against the domed glass, and so her first memory of their new life would always be the black-and-white tiles, the cool air on her face, and the sweet taste of orange sherbet.

Now she ducked beneath the counter and grabbed an apron from the hook. "Trust me," she said to Quinn, "you don't want to be out there right now. It's a total zoo."

"Of course it is," she said, twisting around and then hoisting herself up so that she was sitting beside the cash register, her feet dangling well above the floor. Quinn had always been tiny, and even when they were younger, Ellie used to feel like a giant beside her, tall and gawky and entirely too noticeable with her red hair. The Bean and the Beanpole, Mom used to call them, and Ellie always wondered how it was fair that the only thing she'd inherited from her father was his ridiculous height, especially when her only goal in life was to stay under the radar.

"This is probably the biggest thing that's ever happened

here," Quinn was saying, her eyes bright. "It would be like something out of the movies if it wasn't *literally* a movie." She grabbed the magazine and held it up. "And it isn't some little dinky art-house film either. I mean, there are huge stars in this thing. Olivia Brooks and Graham Larkin. *Graham Larkin.* Here for a whole month."

Ellie squinted at the photo being dangled in front of her, which showed a face she'd seen a thousand times before, a dark-haired guy with even darker sunglasses, scowling as he muscled his way through a group of photographers. She knew he was right around their age, but there was something about him that made him seem older. Ellie tried to picture him here in Henley, dodging paparazzi, signing autographs, chatting with his beautiful costar between takes, but she couldn't seem to make her imagination cooperate in that way.

"Everyone thinks he and Olivia are dating, or will be soon," Quinn said. "But you never know. Maybe small-town girls are more his type. Do you think he'll come in here at all?"

"There are only like twelve shops in the whole town," Ellie said. "So the odds are probably in your favor."

Quinn watched as she began rinsing the ice-cream scoops in the sink. "How can you not care about this stuff at all?" she asked. "It's *exciting.*"

"It's a pain," Ellie said without looking up.

"It's good for business."

"It's like a carnival."

"Exactly," Quinn said, looking triumphant. "And carnivals are fun."

"Not if you hate roller coasters."

"Well, you're stuck on this one whether you like it or not," Quinn said with a laugh. "So you better buckle up."

Mornings were always quiet at the shop; the real rush didn't start until after lunchtime, but because the town was so busy today, a few people trickled in to buy bags of penny candy from the jars on the shelves, or to cool off with an early cone. Just before the end of her shift, Ellie was helping a little boy pick out a flavor while Quinn made a chocolate milkshake for his mother, who was busy on her cell phone.

"What about mint chip?" Ellie suggested, leaning over the cool glass as the boy—probably no more than three years old—stood on his tiptoes in an effort to survey the various flavors. "Or cookie dough?"

He shook his head, his hair falling across his eyes. "I want pig."

"Pink?"

"Pig," he said again, but less certainly.

"Strawberry?" Ellie asked, pointing at the pink container, and the boy nodded.

"Pigs are pink," he explained to her as she scooped some into a small cup for him.

"That's true," she said, handing him the cup. But her mind was already elsewhere; she was thinking about an e-mail she'd gotten a couple weeks ago from—well, she didn't quite know *who* it was from; not really, anyway. But it had been about his pig, Wilbur, who had apparently, to his horror, gotten hold of a hot dog during a barbeque.

My pig, the e-mail had read, *is now officially a cannibal.*

That's okay, Ellie had written back. *I'd be surprised if there was any real meat in that hot dog at all.*

This had been followed by a lengthy exchange about what exactly *was* in hot dogs, which had then, of course, spun off into other topics, from favorite foods to best holiday meals, and before she knew it, the clock was showing that it was nearly two in the morning. Once again, they'd managed to talk about everything without really talking about anything at all, and once again, Ellie had stayed up way too late.

But it was worth it.

Even now, she could feel herself smiling at the memory of those e-mails, which felt as real and honest as any conversation she'd ever had face-to-face. She was practically on California time now, staying up late to wait for his address to appear on her screen, her thoughts constantly drifting across the country to the other coast. She knew it was ridiculous. They didn't even know each other's names. But the morning after that first e-mail went astray, she'd woken up to find another note from him.

Good morning, E, he'd written. *It's late here, and I just got home to find Wilbur asleep in my closet. He generally stays in the laundry room when I'm out, but his "dogwalker" must have forgotten to shut the gate. If you'd been nearby, I'm sure you'd have done a much better job...*

Ellie had only just gotten out of bed, and she sat there at

her desk with the morning light streaming in through the window, blinking and yawning and smiling without quite knowing why. She closed her eyes. *Good morning, E.*

Was there any better way to greet the day?

Sitting there, thinking back to the previous night's correspondence, she'd felt a rush of exhilaration. And though it seemed odd that she still didn't know his name, something kept her from asking. Those two little words, she knew, would inevitably set off a chain reaction: first Google, then Facebook, then Twitter, and on and on, mining the twists and turns of the Internet until all the mystery had been wrung out of the thing.

Maybe the facts weren't as important as the rest of it: this feeling of anticipation as her fingers hovered over the keyboard, or the way the lingering question mark that had pulsed inside her all night had been so quickly replaced by an exclamation point at the sight of his e-mail. Maybe there was something safe in the not knowing, something that made it feel like all the mundane questions you were usually required to ask were not all that important after all.

She considered the screen for another moment, then lowered her hands to the keys. *Dear G,* she'd written, and so it had gone.

Theirs was a partnership of details rather than facts. And the details were the best part. Ellie knew, for example, that GDL—as she'd taken to thinking of him—once cut open his forehead while attempting to jump off the roof of his family's van as a kid. Another time, he'd pretended to drown in a neighbor's pool, and then scared the hell out of everyone when they tried to rescue him. He liked to draw buildings—high-rises and brownstones and skyscrapers with rows upon rows of windows—and when he was anxious, he'd sketch out entire cities. He played the guitar, but not well. He wanted to live in Colorado someday. The only thing he could cook was grilled cheese sandwiches. He hated e-mailing most people, but not her.

Are you any good at keeping secrets? she'd written to him once, because it was something she felt was important to know. It seemed to Ellie that you could tell a lot about someone by the way they carried a secret—by how safe they kept it, how soon they told, the way they acted when they were trying to keep it from spilling out.

Yes, he'd replied. *Are you?*

Yes, she'd said simply, and they left it at that.

All her life, secrets had been things that were heavy and burdensome. But this? This was different. It was like a bubble inside her, light and buoyant and fizzy enough to make her feel like she was floating through each day.

It had been only three months since that first e-mail, but it felt like much longer. If Mom noticed a difference, she didn't say anything. If Quinn thought she was acting funny, she made no mention of it. The only person who could probably tell was the one on the other end of all those e-mails.

Now she found herself grinning at the cup of pink ice cream as she handed it to the boy. Behind her, there was a loud click and a sputter, followed by a thick glugging sound, and when Ellie spun to see what was happening, it was to find the aftermath of a chocolate milkshake explosion. It was everywhere, on the walls and the counter and the floor, but mostly all over Quinn, who blinked twice, then wiped her face with the back of her arm.

For a moment, Ellie was sure Quinn was about to cry. Her entire shirt was soaked with chocolate, and there was more of it stuck in her hair. She looked like she'd just been mud wrestling—and lost.

But then her face split into a grin. "Think Graham Larkin would like this look?"

Ellie laughed. "Who doesn't like chocolate milkshakes?"

The boy's mother had lowered her cell phone, her mouth open, but now she dug for her wallet and placed a few bills on the counter. "I think we'll just take the ice cream," she said, shepherding her son out the front door, glancing back only once at Quinn, who was still dripping.

"More for us," Ellie said, and they began to laugh all over again.

By the time they'd gotten the mess cleaned up, Ellie's shift was almost over.

Quinn glanced up at the clock, then down at her shirt. "Lucky you. I've got two more hours to stand around looking like something that crawled out of Willy Wonka's factory."

"I've got a tank top on underneath," Ellie said, peeling off her blue T-shirt and handing it over. "Wear mine."

30

"Thanks," Quinn muttered, ducking into the tiny bathroom near the freezers in the back of the store. "I think I've even got chocolate in my ears."

"It'll help you survive the noise when things start getting busy," Ellie called back. "Want me to wait with you till Devon gets here? I can be late for Mom's."

"That's okay," Quinn said, and when she emerged again, she was wearing Ellie's shirt as if it were a dress. "It's a little long," she admitted, trying to tuck in all the extra material. "But I'll make it work. I can stop by the shop when I'm done to give it back."

"Great," Ellie said. "See you then."

"Hey," Quinn called, just as Ellie was about to walk out the door, her shoulders now bare except for the thin straps of her tank top. "Sunscreen?"

"I'm fine," she said, rolling her eyes. It was just the second week of summer vacation and already Quinn had a deep tan. Ellie, on the other hand, was only ever one of two shades: very white or very pink. When they were little, she'd landed in the hospital with a bad case of sun poisoning after a trip to the beach, and ever since then, Quinn had taken it upon herself to enforce the liberal use of sunblock. It was a habit that Ellie found simultaneously endearing and annoying—after all, she already *had* a mother—but nevertheless, Quinn was unrelenting in her duties.

Outside, Ellie paused to study the movie set being assembled down the street. There was less of a crowd now; people must have grown tired of watching the teams of men in black shirts rushing around with heavy trunks of equipment. But just as she was about to head up toward the gift shop, she noticed a guy in a Dodgers cap approaching the ice-cream parlor.

His head was low and his hands were in his pockets, but everything about his casual posture suggested a kind of effort; he was trying so hard to blend in that he ended up sticking out all the more. Part of her was thinking that he could be anyone—he was, after all, just a guy; just a boy, really—but she knew immediately that he wasn't. She knew exactly who he was. There was something too sharply defined about him, like he was walking across a billboard or a stage rather than a small street in Maine. The whole thing was oddly surreal, and for a moment, Ellie could almost see the magic in it; she could almost understand why someone might fall under his spell.

When he was just a few feet away from her, he glanced up, and she was startled by his eyes, a blue so deep she'd always half assumed they were touched up in the magazines. But even from beneath the brim of his cap, they were penetrating, and she pulled in a sharp breath as they landed on her briefly before sliding over to the awning of the shop.

The thought occurred to her with surprising force: *He's sad.* She wasn't sure how she knew this, but she was suddenly certain that it was true. Underneath all the rest of it—an unexpected nervousness, a hint of caution, a bit of wariness—there was also a sadness so deep it startled her.

It was there in his eyes, which were so much older than the rest of him, and in the practiced blankness of his gaze.

She'd read about him, of course, and seemed to recall that he wasn't one of those celebrities always in and out of rehab. As far as she knew, he didn't have financial troubles or nightmare parents. He hadn't been brought up as one of those poor child stars either; his big break had happened only a couple of years ago. She'd heard he celebrated his sixteenth birthday by flying the entire cast of his last movie to Switzerland to go skiing in the Alps. And he'd been linked to several of the most sought-after young actresses in Hollywood.

There was no reason Graham Larkin should be sad.

But he is, Ellie thought.

He'd come to a stop outside the ice-cream parlor and seemed to be weighing something as he stood there. To her surprise, his eyes drifted over to her one more time, and she smiled reflexively. But he only gazed at her for a long moment, his face unchanged beneath the low brim of his cap, and the smile slid from her face again.

As she watched, he squared his shoulders and stepped up to the door of the shop, and Ellie's eyes caught Quinn's through the window. She mouthed something that Ellie couldn't make out, her face a picture of disbelief, and then turned her attention back to the entrance as the bell rang out and Graham Larkin made his way inside.

It was only then that the photographers appeared, seemingly from nowhere, six of them, with enormous black

33

cameras and bags strung over their shoulders, each of them rushing to press against the window, where they began to snap photos with frantic intensity. From inside the store, Graham Larkin didn't even turn around.

Ellie stood there for another moment, her eyes flicking between the window, where Quinn was smiling behind the counter as he approached, and the photographers, who were jostling one another for better angles. Those milling around in the streets nearby started to drift closer, drawn to the scene by some sort of magnetic pull, an irresistible mixture of celebrity and spectacle. But as the crowd grew, Ellie took a few steps backward, making her escape around the side of the building before anyone could notice she was gone.

From: GDL824@yahoo.com
Sent: Sunday, June 9, 2013 10:24 AM
To: EONeill22@hotmail.com
Subject: Re: what happy looks like

Visiting new places.

Graham had been visualizing this moment for weeks now. And so the way it was all unfolding—the town looking just as he'd imagined it, the rows of shops and the salty breeze at his back—almost made it feel like he was in a dream.

The sun was gauzy behind a thin film of clouds, and his head was pounding. He'd taken the red-eye to Portland and, as usual, hadn't slept at all. Graham had never flown when he was growing up, and even with things like first-class seating and private jets, he was still restless and anxious in the air, unaccustomed to the rhythms of this type of travel, no matter how much of his life seemed to be spent on a plane.

But it didn't matter now. As he walked to the shop, he felt more alert than he had in ages, wide awake and burning with conviction. It had been a long time since he'd felt this way. In the past two years, as his life had become increasingly unrecognizable, Graham had grown as malleable as a piece of clay. He was now accustomed to being told what to do, how to act, who to see, and what to say when he saw them. Casual-seeming conversations on the couches of talk shows were pre-scripted. Dates were set up for him by his people. His clothes were chosen by a stylist who was forever trying to wrangle him into V-neck shirts and skinny jeans, things he'd never have been caught dead in before.

But *before* felt like a million years ago.

And this is how things were in the *after*.

If someone had told him two years ago that he'd be living on his own at seventeen—in a house three times the size of the one he'd grown up in, complete with a pool and a game room and the necessary precaution of a state-of-the-art security system—Graham would have laughed. But like everything else that came on the heels of his first movie role and the unexpected feeding frenzy that followed it, this just seemed like the next logical step. There had been a momentum to the whole chain of events that struck him as inevitable. First there was a new agent, then a new publicist; a new house and a new car; new ways of acting in public and new tutors to help him finish high school while filming; new rules for social engagements; and, of course, new and previously unimagined possibilities for getting into trouble.

Even his parents were different. Now, whenever he stopped by, they were both oddly strained, choosing their words carefully, as if they were all on camera. Every once in a while, Graham would do something that used to drive them nuts—leave his dirty dishes on the counter or his shoes strewn in the middle of the hallway—but instead of barking at him like they used to, they'd only exchange an unreadable look and then pretend not to see it. The whole thing was so disconcerting that Graham had, for the most part, stopped going home at all.

He thought this must be what whiplash felt like. It wasn't long ago that he was just a high school sophomore acting the part of Nathan Detroit in the dim auditorium, after having tried out on a lark for the same reason he did most things: to impress a girl. A few days later, he'd been shocked to actually discover his name on the casting list.

His school was located in a suburb so affluent that Graham often felt like a visitor to some strange and well-groomed planet, but its proximity to L.A. meant that most of his classmates, and certainly those in the drama club, dreamed of Hollywood. They'd spent their lives at dance lessons and voice lessons and acting lessons. They studied *Variety* to keep up a certain level of industry knowledge, and they viewed shopping as an important opportunity to cultivate their image.

But then Graham, lanky and off-key and a little bit awkward, had sauntered onstage with a goofy grin directed at some girl he'd never even spoken to, and somehow, he'd managed to get the part. And yet, nobody else seemed to find this odd. That's just the way things had always worked for him. He'd never had a problem making sports teams or the honor roll, collecting awards for everything from Most

Valuable Player to Exemplary Citizen. For better or worse, he'd always been that guy.

And so there he was on opening night, plowing his way through the lyrics in a costume that was perhaps a size too small, his eyes watering from the glare of the lights, feeling less certain about his plan to ask the girl playing Adelaide to the spring formal afterward. As it turned out, he didn't have the chance. A classmate's father was trying to cast an unknown to play a teenage magician in a movie—not the lead, but the one who makes the love interest doubt her feelings for the hero—and afterward, he cornered Graham to discuss the possibility of his coming in for some screen tests. His parents, as clueless as he was about just what it might mean if he got the part, agreed that it could be a good opportunity, a fun experience, maybe even something to put on his college applications—and if things worked out, to help foot the bill.

Later, all the magazines would describe his emergence as a star in ways that made him sound like a cartoon character, how he'd been "plucked from obscurity" or "skyrocketed to fame" or "catapulted into the limelight." And that was sort of how it felt. He enjoyed the acting part of it more than he thought he would, and at first, he found the world of Hollywood intriguing, a welcome distraction from the smaller melodramas of high school.

But what nobody ever told him was that once something like this happens to you, there's no going back. In hindsight, this seemed like it should have been obvious, something he might have realized before everything was already in motion, but there was a slow inertia to the whole process that made it feel less like a catapult and more like a tumble down a hill. And as with most cartoon characters, once the ground ran out beneath him, he continued to hang there in midair, legs churning, hoping that if he just kept moving, maybe he wouldn't fall.

It was lonelier than he ever could have imagined. There were agents and managers and directors, costars and tutors and wardrobe specialists, publicists and hairstylists and image consultants. But none of them seemed quite real to him, and when the cameras stopped rolling, they faded away like opportunistic ghosts. He tried to keep up with his friends from high school, but something had shifted between them, and in this strange and uncharted territory, they didn't know how to act around him anymore. He'd drifted too far beyond the world of curfews and homework and soccer practice, and once he stopped offering up his house for parties, there was little reason for them to see one another anymore.

It was the same with the new people he met at events and parties, and with the girls he met pretty much every-where. Before, he'd been the guy everyone wanted to be around because he was funny, and because he knew how to have a good time, and because underneath it all, he was actually pretty decent. But now he was the guy everyone wanted to be around because he was good-looking and famous and had a nice house, or because they wanted those things too, and thought he might be the key.

So when he wasn't working, he holed up and read the scripts his agent sent, trying to fill his days. He went to parties only occasionally, usually to meet some hot new director or a writer he'd been hearing good things about, and when the photographers inevitably showed up, he smiled grimly and left as soon as he could slip away. He read more books than he ever had in school. He ordered more pizza than he thought was possible. He played video games with depressing enthusiasm. He adopted a pig and the two of them spent most of their days out by the pool.

Then one of his e-mails found its way to her.

And just like that, he understood the power of the Internet. There was something intoxicating in the anonymity of it all. Suddenly, he had a clean slate. He was as much a mystery to her as she was to him, no longer Graham Larkin, but just GDL824. And GDL824 could be anyone, a hundred different brands of seventeen-year-old guy: the kind who lived for football or who won awards for playing chess, the type who smoked on the bike path behind school or who was one of those geniuses already in his second year of med school. He might be a guy who collected butterflies or baseball pennants or girlfriends. He could be a fan of rock stars or tennis stars or the countless stars in the sky. He could be a fan of Graham Larkin, for all it mattered.

The point was, he could be anyone.

For weeks, as he reported for preproduction on his newest movie—a love story, this time, to showcase his more sensitive side—he struggled to keep his attention on the

42

studio in L.A. But his mind was all the way on the other side of the country. Ever since she first mentioned she was from Maine, Graham had found himself reading up on the state as if it were some sort of exotic land.

Did you know that the wild blueberry is the state berry of Maine? he wrote to her one night. *And, more important, that the state treat is the whoopie pie?*

I don't even know what a whoopie pie is, she'd written back. *And I work in a sweet shop. So I have a feeling you're making that up.*

I'm not, he responded. *In fact, I imagine that all towns in Maine are paved with whoopie pies.*

Not Henley, she'd said, and like a coal miner grasping about in the darkness, he was suddenly presented with the tiniest crack of light.

Just a few days earlier, the location scout for the film had been fired after it was discovered that the North Carolina town where they were meant to be shooting for the first month of the summer was under attack by a swarm of cicadas. The director was furious that she'd managed to overlook a bug infestation that showed up every thirteen years like clockwork, but Graham had been secretly pleased.

He'd suggested changing the location to Henley, pointing out that it had everything they were looking for: the quaint shops, the scenic harbor, the rough stretch of beach. He spoke of it as if he'd been there many times, and the truth was, he'd thought about the place so often recently that, in a way, it felt like he had.

43

Still, it took some convincing, and in the end, Graham had been forced to act the way everyone always seemed to expect him to act anyway: he was petulant and demanding and condescending. He made threats and waved his phone around menacingly. And to his surprise, it had worked. New scouts were sent ahead and reported back that it was indeed a perfect location. Permissions were obtained and papers were signed. The second unit went out early to start collecting B roll. And Graham and his costars were slated to spend four weeks at the Henley Inn, which was just three-tenths of a mile from the only sweet shop in town.

Even if his love life weren't a newsworthy topic, and even if he weren't constantly wary of the potential for gossip and rumors, Graham still wouldn't have told anybody the real reason he was so desperate to go to Henley. At best, it made him sound a little crazy. At worst, it made him seem like a stalker.

But the truth was, he was pretty sure he was falling for a girl he'd never met before, a girl whose name he didn't even know.

He realized that it was ridiculous. If someone had handed him a script with this exact story line, he'd have told them it was completely unrealistic.

But that didn't change what he felt.

He supposed it might have been easier if he'd just asked to meet her. But what if she wasn't feeling the same way about him? What if she was only looking for a pen pal? This way, at least he had an excuse for being there.

After all, they had to film the movie *somewhere*.

Graham wasn't scheduled to begin shooting his scenes until the next day, and when he'd told Harry Fenton, his rapidly balding manager, that he wanted to get there early, the older man had looked confused.

"You're *never* early," he said, but Graham only shrugged.

"I'm supposed to have lived there all my life, so I think it's important to fully immerse myself," he told him, parroting back something he'd once heard his pompous costar on the Top Hat trilogy say. He realized he was getting as good at playing Graham Larkin as he was at playing all these other roles.

He slowed a bit as he drew near to the ice-cream shop. He could sense the photographers lurking somewhere behind him, stealthy as a school of sharks. The sun was hot on his shoulders, his shirt already sticking to his back. He passed a willowy girl with long red hair, and when he glanced up at her, there was a look of silent rebuke in her green eyes. Graham had been so fixated on getting to the town of Henley that it had never occurred to him that the town of Henley might not be as thrilled about having him. He looked over again, and this time, she smiled, but he felt it as a kind of appraisal, a summing up of something about himself he wasn't sure he wanted to know.

But it was too late to worry about that now. He paused in front of the shop and squinted at the glass storefront, but the light was thrown back at him. He was desperate to see what she looked like, though he knew it shouldn't matter. It had been a long time since he'd felt this way about anyone. Being famous was like carrying around some kind of magic key; you could say something stupid or boring or you could say nothing at all, and the girls still liked you anyway. But rather than making him more confident, this just seemed to shake his resolve, since it meant there was never a way to gauge how anyone *really* felt about him.

Until now. Because whoever this girl was, Graham was pretty sure that she liked him. Not the movie-star version of him, but the real him.

And he liked her too.

When he pushed open the door, he was rattled by the sound of the tiny bell, and he ducked his head so his face was hidden by the brim of his cap. There were no other customers in the shop, and he kept his eyes trained on the black-and-white tiles of the floor until he was nearly to the counter. It had been a long time since he'd been afraid to look at a girl, but he was inexplicably nervous now, and it took him a moment to force his eyes in her direction.

When he finally did, he was relieved to see that she was quite obviously beautiful, with almond-shaped eyes and long dark hair. But he barely took the time to register that. He was too busy looking at the word sewn onto the pocket of her shirt.

Ellie, he thought, finally pairing a name with the initial. *Ellie O'Neill.*

She was watching him anxiously, her expression halfway between shock and delight. He nodded at her, then slid over to the display of ice-cream flavors and pretended to be deciding. But what he was really doing was thinking back to a conversation they'd had a few weeks ago, when he'd jokingly sent her one of those e-mails that asks you to answer questions about your favorite things.

There's no way I'm filling this thing out, she'd replied. *You can't be that desperate to know my favorite ice-cream flavor.*

Are you kidding? Graham had said. *You'd be surprised how much it says about you.*

Let me guess, she'd written. *If I say rocky road, it means I'm going through a hard time. If I say vanilla, it means I'm boring...*

Something like that, he'd responded. *I'm a sherbet guy myself. What does that say about me?*

That you've got great taste, she'd written back. *That's my favorite too.*

He watched now as she moved down along the opposite side of the counter to lean over the glass at him. "Can I help you with anything?" she asked, and he was startled to hear a familiar note in her voice, the same sugary tone used by so many publicists and managers in L.A. He gave her a half smile, but said nothing, and she giggled. Graham's stomach twisted.

He pointed at the glass. "I'll have the rainbow sherbet," he said, venturing a look in her direction, waiting to see if she'd put things together. But she simply nodded and turned to grab a cup, and he realized that it wasn't enough; of course it wasn't enough. He tried to think of other ways into the conversation—casually mentioning something else they'd already discussed over e-mail, some other inside joke—but over his shoulder, there was a sharp bang as a photographer got too close to the window with his camera, and Graham realized that maybe this wasn't the right moment after all.

"You're going to like it here," she was saying as she handed over his ice cream. "It's a great place to spend the summer."

Her tone was light as air and quite obviously flirty, and Graham had to remind himself that it was unfair to assume she'd be so different from all the other girls. Once she realized who he was—who he *really* was—then everything would click into place, but until then, it was pointless to be surprised by the way she tossed her hair as she spooned out the ice cream.

"Oh yeah?" he said, placing a ten on the counter and then waving away the change. "Where's a good place to grab dinner?"

"The Lobster Pot," she told him, smiling a bit coyly. "It's my favorite."

Graham nodded. "Well, in that case," he said, "would you like to go with me tonight?"

"Me?" she asked, looking at him with genuine surprise. "Really?"

"Really," he said, smiling his million-dollar smile, the one that in his previous life had never seemed to hold any extraordinary charm, but that now had the curious ability to make hordes of teenage girls go wobbly at the sight of it.

"I'd love to," she said, her voice an octave too high.

He nodded, and an awkward pause followed. It took him a moment to realize he was supposed to suggest a time. "Should we meet there at nine?"

She looked embarrassed. "I think it might close at nine."

"Ah," Graham said. "Seven thirty, then?"

She nodded, then handed over a spoon. It took him a moment to reach for it; the sleepless plane ride must have been catching up to him, because he felt suddenly weary. A spreading disappointment filled his chest, though he wasn't sure why. This was exactly what he'd wanted. This town, this girl. She was not only cute, but perfectly nice, and apparently eager to go out with him. What more had he hoped for?

He jabbed the spoon into the ice cream, which was already melting, and then lifted his cup in a little salute as she waved good-bye. When he turned around, he was greeted by the dizzying flash of the cameras at the window, and for a brief moment, he closed his eyes. But the lights refused to go away, and all he could see were stars.

From: EONeill22@hotmail.com
Sent: Sunday, June 9 2013 11:11 AM
To: GDL824@yahoo.com
Subject: Re: what happy looks like

The change of seasons.

It seemed to Ellie that walking into the Happy Thoughts Gift Shop was a little bit like stepping inside her mother's brain. There was no sense of organization whatsoever, nor was there an obvious theme to the store's contents. Eight years ago, when Mom first bought the shop, it had been known for selling mostly furniture and home decor, and was filled with elegant displays of candles and napkin rings and vases of all kinds. The previous owner was now happily retired in Florida, having long since given up on the Maine winters, but Ellie was pretty sure that if she were ever to see what had become of the place, she'd be horrified.

There was simply no rhyme or reason to it now. The whole store was no bigger than a large classroom, but it was so crammed with stuff that it tended to feel even smaller. They still sold place mats and pepper grinders, lamps and pillows and other assorted furnishings, but now there were also books and vintage toys and bins full of saltwater taffy. There were greeting cards and postcards, T-shirts and swimsuits, beach toys and board games.

And, of course, there were lobsters. Not real ones—though Ellie wouldn't have been terribly shocked to stumble upon a fish tank in all the confusion—but lobster teacups and kettles, key chains and bookmarks and wind chimes. There was even a giant plush lobster that had been sitting in the back of the shop for years now. It was the size of a large ape, and with its black marble eyes and oversize antennae, it had, on more than one occasion, startled an unsuspecting kid who came wheeling around the corner a bit too fast.

Quinn was always itchy to organize the place, but Ellie loved its chaos. She'd basically grown up in this shop, and it felt almost like an extension of the house, a messy closet or treasure-filled basement. Mom had been hoping to expand for years now, lingering each morning at the dusty window of the adjacent storefront, a former real estate office that had been empty for ages. But there was never the money for it. At this point, there was hardly even enough to keep their house from falling to pieces all around them. And so the clutter in the shop only continued to grow. But the customers didn't seem to mind, and neither did Ellie.

She'd spent countless afternoons here, doing her homework with lobster-shaped pencils, balancing on the old antique sea captain's trunk while waiting for Mom to close up, sitting at the window and listening to the waves crash into the rocks just down the street. But her favorite part of the shop was the collection of picture frames lining the shelves in the far back corner. They came in all shapes and colors and sizes, some of them silver and some of them wood, while others were made of sea glass or had delicate designs along the edges. And in each and every frame, instead of a glossy photograph, there was a poem.

Years ago, on a winter day when the snow drifted high against the window and the shop was empty and quiet, Mom had left Ellie alone to trek down the street for some hot chocolate. While she was gone, Ellie found herself studying the framed photographs, black-and-white images of happy families smiling their toothy grins. There were couples gazing into each other's eyes, parents holding the hands of their kids, families on picnics and boat rides and walks in the woods. As her eyes skipped over the display, Ellie realized there were exactly four pictures of fathers with their daughters perched on their shoulders, and exactly zero pictures of mothers and daughters.

She was eight that winter, old enough to understand that they weren't ever going back to D.C., but too young to keep a firm grip on the memory of her father's face, which slid in and out of her mind like a slippery fish. And so when she'd looked at all those happy faces tiling the wall of the shop, something inside of her split clean open.

By the time Mom returned, a steaming cup of cocoa in each hand, Ellie had systematically removed every single one of the photos, sliding them from their frames and ripping each one neatly before throwing it into the garbage.

Mom stood in the doorway, her cheeks pink from the cold, a look of confusion in her eyes, and then she set down the cups and unwound her scarf. Without a word, she crossed the shop and grabbed a new pack of crayons from one of the hooks in the toy section, handing them over to Ellie.

"I have a feeling you can do better anyway," she said.

For years after that, the frames housed Ellie's construction-paper drawings, brightly colored sketches of trees and boats and lobsters. And when she was older, she switched to poetry, filling them with her favorite stanzas, each one scrawled in her tiny handwriting. Customers began to linger in that corner, perusing the shelves, lost in the words, and they became as much a draw as anything else in the shop. The ones with poems about Maine were scooped up by the tourists almost as soon as they were set out, and once, when Ellie went to a party hosted by one of her classmates, she saw that the frame his mom had bought months ago was still empty of a family photo. But it was there in the foyer anyway, featuring a poem by W. H. Auden, Ellie's favorite.

As she walked into the shop this afternoon, Mom was opening a brand-new carton of frames, and when Ellie was close enough to get a look, she began to laugh.

"Those aren't—"

"I know," Mom said with a groan. "They sent us the wrong ones."

"Maybe some gift shop in Maryland can use them."

"Who'd want a picture frame with a crab on it?"

Ellie rolled her eyes. "Who'd want one with a lobster?"

"Hey," Mom said with a grin. "Don't knock the lobsters. They're our bread and butter. So to speak." She began to pack up the frames again, wrapping them in tissue paper. "How come you're late? Were you busy gawking at movie stars like everyone else in this town?"

Ellie hesitated, then shook her head. "Quinn had a little milkshake mishap just as I was leaving, so I helped her clean up."

"See," Mom said, sweeping aside the box. "That's why you should only be working here. We're nothing if not tidy."

Ellie raised her eyebrows pointedly at the mess of inventory, the random items strewn about so that the whole shop felt like a maze, and they both laughed. But it was clear she was only partially joking about the second job. When Ellie had started taking shifts at Sprinkles a few months earlier, Mom wasn't thrilled about it.

For as long as Ellie could remember, money had been an issue. When she was younger, it had never seemed to matter. They had everything they needed, the two of them. But this fall, she'd be starting her last year of high school, which meant that college—and the staggering cost of tuition—was looming ever closer. Ellie didn't want to go to a state school; she had her heart set on the Ivy League, and so they'd already started talking about loans, the paperwork piling up on Mom's desk, columns of numbers and percentages, line after line of fine print. This, alone, was enough to make Ellie feel guilty, enough to set her heart beating fast with worry whenever the subject came up.

But a few months ago, she found out she was accepted into a summer poetry course at Harvard. The program was impossible to get into, and Ellie had only applied on a whim after seeing a flyer taped to the bulletin board of her English classroom, never thinking she might be chosen. There were only fifteen high school students from across the country who would get to spend the first three weeks of August studying poetry while staying in the Harvard dorms. But the program cost just over two thousand dollars, and there were no scholarships or financial aid.

The night she told Mom about it, she'd seen the hesitation in her eyes.

"It sounds like a great opportunity," she began, choosing her words carefully. "And I'm so proud of you for getting in. But—".

Ellie didn't let her finish. She couldn't bear it. "And they gave me a scholarship too," she found herself saying, relieved to see the light go back on behind Mom's smile, the worry replaced by a look of pure pride.

"Of course they did," she said, giving her a hug. "I'm so happy for you."

Ellie had needed to let them know she was coming by the end of May. At that point, she had exactly $178.24 in her savings account, and no plan whatsoever for how to make up the balance by the time the course started and the payment was due. But she sent back the form anyway, a check mark in the box beside the words "Yes, I will attend!"

The job at Sprinkles helped. But even with that and her pay from Happy Thoughts, Ellie's calculations showed that at the end of the summer she was still going to be short by half. Quinn had offered to lend her some of it, and as much as Ellie appreciated the gesture, she knew not to count on that. Money had a habit of slipping through Quinn's fingers pretty quickly, her paychecks usually disappearing the same day she got them; a few hours of online shopping and *poof*, they were gone.

But she dreaded having to give up her spot in the course to some trust-fund kid who'd spent her summer lying by the pool at a country club. There was no way she couldn't go, and there was no way she could ask Mom to help make up the difference when they were just getting by as it was. It only made it worse that Ellie knew she'd say yes. It didn't matter what she needed to do—sell the shop, donate a kidney, rob a bank—Mom would make it happen, which was precisely why Ellie could never, ever ask her.

Since school had let out, she'd started to become more desperate, working all day at one job or another, and then babysitting at night. She could see that Mom was worried about her new industrious streak, the way that work was taking over her summer.

"You're sixteen," she said. "You should be out getting into trouble."

"I'm fine," Ellie told her, again and again.

Now, as they stood there on opposite sides of the counter, the wind chimes tinkling in the breeze from the window, Ellie was sure they were about to stumble into the discussion once again, the same one that had lately been running on an endless loop like a bad recording. But there was a reluctance in Mom's eyes that matched Ellie's own. Neither of them wanted to talk about this; neither of them wanted to argue.

So when the door banged open, Ellie whirled around with a rush of relief. It took a moment for Quinn to emerge from between the T-shirts that were hanging near the register, and when she did, Ellie could see that her face was flushed.

"Okay," she said, her hands held up as if she were about to perform a spell. "Okay, okay, okay."

Mom leaned forward and turned to Ellie. "Is she having a nervous breakdown?"

"This is serious, Mrs. O," Quinn said, sinking onto a blue beanbag chair. "This is, like, a dire emergency."

"Is everything okay?" Mom asked, still looking relatively unconcerned. Ellie and Quinn had been best friends since they were five, and if the O'Neills had learned one thing in that time, it was that Quinn had a flair for the dramatic. Her definition of an emergency was a little more flexible than everyone else's.

"*Okay?*" Quinn said, her eyes widening. "I have a date with *Graham Larkin.*"

There were a few beats of silence as this announcement

60

settled over them. The moment Quinn said his name Ellie was surprised to be reminded of those eyes of his, and she blinked hard to shake loose the memory. Just behind her, Mom was shrugging her shoulders, mystified.

"Who's Graham Larking?" she asked, and Quinn gave her a stern look.

"Graham *Larkin*," she said, "is only one of the biggest stars in the world."

Ellie laughed at the expression on Mom's face, which was still utterly blank. "He's in those magician movies," she explained, "and now he's the star of whatever they're filming here."

"And you're going out with him?" Mom said to Quinn, who raised and then lowered her chin. "I haven't been outside all day. Are there movie stars just wandering around town looking for dates?"

"He was in Sprinkles," Ellie explained. "And he must have thought Quinn was at least as irresistible as the ice cream. By the way, who's watching the shop?"

Quinn waved a hand in the air, as if this were a matter of little importance. "I left Devon there," she told them. "He said he could handle it on his own. I need your help to get ready."

Ellie couldn't help feeling sorry for poor Devon Alexander, who'd been in love with Quinn for years now, and probably had no idea he was covering their busiest hours alone so she could get ready for her date with a movie star.

"Well," Mom said, grabbing a red rubber ball from the

jar beside the register and tossing it absently from one hand to the other, "you've come to the right place. I'm proud of my daughter for a great many things, but most particularly for her fashion sense..."

"Very funny," Ellie said, glancing down at what she was wearing: a jean skirt, a plain white tank top, and black rubber flip-flops, which was pretty much her summer uniform.

"I really just need her for moral support," Quinn said, hopping to her feet. "Is it okay if she knocks off early?"

"I just got here..." Ellie began, but Mom was nodding.

"It's okay," she said, still juggling the red ball. "Really. We can't send Quinn off on a date with a major celebrity without a little help, can we?"

There was a teasing note in her voice, but Quinn was too distracted to pick up on it. "Exactly," she said, rocking back on her heels. Everything about her was wound too tight, and she couldn't stop fidgeting. "I mean, it's a big deal. You should've seen all the cameras at the shop this afternoon. I can't imagine what it'll be like tonight..."

Mom fumbled the ball, which fell to the floor, glancing off a bin full of snorkeling gear and then rolling off into a corner. "Cameras, huh?"

"Yeah, tons of them," Quinn was saying, while Ellie remained frozen, her gaze focused on the wooden floor in an attempt to avoid Mom's eyes. "They're all camped out by the set right now, but I'm sure they'll be following him around later." She paused, not noticing the strained look on the faces of her audience. "Paparazzi in Henley. Crazy, right?"

"Yeah," Ellie said, looking sideways at Mom. "It is."

"Too bad I don't want to be an actress. Or a reality-TV star or something," Quinn said. "This would be such a great opportunity."

"Yes," Mom said, regaining herself. "It's a terrible shame you only want to be a marine biologist. I suppose it would be much more useful to have been asked out to dinner by a whale."

Quinn laughed. "They're terrible conversationalists, though."

"Then I guess you'll have to make do with the movie star," Mom said with a smile. "Just be careful of those photographers, okay?"

"I will," Quinn said. "I've read enough gossip magazines to know not to wear my skirt too short."

"That's not quite what I meant," Mom said. "But you're right. Better go find something appropriate to wear. Your wardrobe specialist is officially free for the afternoon."

"Thanks, Mrs. O," Quinn said, grabbing Ellie's wrist and pulling her toward the door, already rattling off all the things they'd need to do to get ready for the evening. But just before they stepped outside, Ellie broke away and trotted back over to the register.

"Thanks, Mom," she said, giving her a quick hug.

"Sure thing," Mom whispered as she pulled back. "I'm just glad it's not you."

Ellie thought once more of Graham Larkin's eyes, so guarded and sad, and of the way he'd paused in front of the store, his shoulders hunched and the brim of his cap pulled low as the photographers crept up behind him, as patient and certain as snipers. She glanced over at Quinn, who was practically dancing from one foot to the other, and it struck her how complicated this was, all of it, not just the cameras and the movie trailers, but the way someone could look at you, how it could feel like a question without an answer. Suddenly, all she wanted to do was go home and write an e-mail, to send her thoughts across the country like a message in a bottle, like the poems in the frames.

She turned back to Mom with a little nod.

"I know," she said. "Me too."

From: GDI.824@yahoo.com
Sent: Sunday, June 9, 2013 3:02 PM
To: EONeill22@hotmail.com
Subject: Re: what happy looks like

Meeting new people.

The light off the water was golden in the last hours of the day. Graham took the long way to dinner, cutting over to the beach, where he paused every now and then to pick up a stone, weighing it in his hand before letting it fall back to the ground. All day, the smell of the ocean had been calling to him.

A couple of sunburned tourists walked by with beach chairs under their arms, but neither of them bothered to look up at him as they passed, and Graham felt a little shiver of delight. After the first movie came out, it had been the opposite; each time someone recognized him in public, it was like a benediction, like in some strange way he was being knighted: Graham Larkin, Somebody. But now—now it was the lack of recognition that made his heart thump in his chest, that small thrill of anonymity, which had become such a rare thing these days.

He glanced at his watch, realizing he would soon be running late, but instead of heading back up to the road, he turned to face the ocean squarely, watching the light skip off the water. There were still a few boats on the horizon, silhouettes against the sun, and Graham had a sudden longing to be out there too.

He remembered a fishing trip he'd taken with his father when he was only eight, the two of them bobbing in the little rowboat, their necks lost in the orange lifejackets. For three days, they'd tied their bait and cast their lines and caught nothing. Dad kept apologizing, like it was his fault the lake refused to offer anything up, and as the last afternoon began to wear thin, he only looked more miserable. This had been his idea, the kind of bonding trip he'd taken with his own father, and he'd been telling Graham for months now about all the fish they'd surely catch.

"Salmon?" Graham had asked, and Dad shook his head.

"Probably not," he said. "They're tougher to find. But trout. Lots and lots of trout. You'll see."

They hadn't brought anything else for dinner—he was that certain—and so the previous night, they'd eaten beef jerky and string cheese out on the cabin porch, swatting away the mosquitoes and listening to the thrum of the crickets. They were close to giving up that last afternoon when it occurred to Graham to tie some of the beef jerky to the end of the line. Dad had sat forward, the little boat rolling back and forth, and his eyes brightened.

"That's not a bad idea," he'd said, breaking off a piece.

Graham was the first one to get a bite, a rainbow trout that flopped and jerked on the line as Dad helped him reel it in. After that, it was easy. Dad pulled in three more trout, and then Graham caught a small carp. The light was fading and the water was getting dark all around them, but neither of them wanted to stop. It was like magic, like they'd conjured three days' worth of fish, a whole weekend's worth of memories, into that last hour of daylight.

When he felt one final tug on his line, Graham reeled it in to find a small salmon on the end, silvery and sleek in the dusky light.

"I guess you proved me wrong," Dad said with a grin. He sat back in the rowboat, his face all lit up, and held up the empty package of beef jerky. "Looks like the wrong kind of bait can get you the right kind of fish."

Graham was thinking about that now as he turned and cut up toward the town, leaving the fishing boats behind. Maybe that's what it was like with Ellie. He'd cast his e-mail out into the world in search of a trout, and what he'd found instead was a salmon. He couldn't help smiling at this, though he suspected a girl like Ellie might object to being compared to a fish.

He smoothed the front of his shirt as he passed the movie trailers, now dark and silent. They'd already shot a few scenes on a soundstage in L.A., but there was an air of excitement about being on location, especially in a place like this, and Graham couldn't help getting caught up in it. He'd spent the past two years playing the same character and working with the same actors, so it was refreshing to be doing something different. The new director, the new script, the new costar—all of it helped him remember why he enjoyed acting in the first place. It was the challenge of it all, being set down in the middle of someone else's life like a tourist and feeling your way through it.

The Lobster Pot wasn't far from the beach; Graham could see it as he made his way up the street. It was just after seven thirty, which meant Ellie was probably already in there. Outside, there was a knot of photographers, their dark clothing giving them away, even as they tried to look casual among the tourists. A few motorcycles were parked nearby; on more than one occasion, Graham had been chased by paparazzi as he tried to slip out of some restaurant or club. There was a breathless absurdity to these pursuits, and though he understood that they had a job to do, he had little respect for the way they did it, and even less for the people who were so desperate to read what they reported. The truth was, he wasn't really worth reading about. He was a better-than-average-looking seventeen-year-old guy who occasionally took a pretty girl to dinner and who played a part decently well, but who mostly sat around at home reading books with his pet pig.

As he approached, the photographers began hoisting their cameras and calling out his name. He ducked his head as they gathered around him. There were fewer than earlier, only four or five; the rest probably had the sense to go get some dinner, or to stay behind and watch TV in their hotel rooms. Those who had stuck it out clicked away like mad, though, the flashes popping as they peppered him with questions, each more relentless than the one before.

"Who's this girl, Graham?" asked one of them, a brick wall of a guy with a diamond earring and a head so pale and bald that it reflected the last of the day's light. "Was that the first time you'd met? What does Olivia think? Are you two official?"

He ignored them all, shoving his way past, and when he reached the door of the restaurant, he was greeted by a thick man with enormous arms and a trim beard.

"Joe Gabriele," the man said, extending a meaty hand. "I'm the owner. Listen, you like lobster?"

Graham nodded, surprised by the question.

"Good," said Joe. "You eat enough lobster while you're in town, and I'll keep these clowns out of here. Deal?"

"Deal," he said, looking past him to see if Ellie had arrived yet. The walls of the restaurant were covered with well-worn buoys and old maritime clocks, fish netting rigged like bunting and framed paintings of schooners and lobsters and whales. At a seat in the corner, beneath a huge iron anchor that appeared to have come straight off a fishing boat, Graham recognized the back of her head, her dark hair pulled up into a low ponytail. All around her, the other tables were empty, and he was grateful to Joe for clearing the way. There was nothing worse than trying to have a private conversation with the faint click of camera phones going off at every angle.

Joe waved toward the table, in case Graham wasn't sure where to go, and then headed off to the kitchen. But Graham remained where he was, suddenly frozen with uncertainty. It wasn't that he was disappointed. How could he be? She was unquestionably beautiful. But ever since leaving the ice-cream shop that afternoon, Graham had been trying to work out his feelings about tonight. After all this time, and all those e-mails, shouldn't he be more excited? Shouldn't he be overjoyed? Shouldn't he be... something?

Maybe the problem was that he'd been forced to read too many scripts with happy endings. Maybe he'd been in Hollywood for too long already. Graham had never been in love before, so he had no idea what to expect. Maybe this was it: you strike up a long-distance conversation with a girl, you enjoy talking to her more than anyone ever before, then you show up and she's gorgeous, and you count yourself lucky.

But still, he thought there'd be something more. He thought that when he saw her, when their eyes first met, that it would feel different. That all those Hollywood clichés were clichés for a reason. It was supposed to be unmistakable, that feeling, wasn't it? Like a punch to the stomach.

But here now in this restaurant, he was feeling curiously empty as he approached the table. When she turned around and their eyes met, there were no stars or fireworks or anything else. There was only the two of them, gazing at each other, each a little bit awkward in their nervousness.

"Thanks for coming," he managed to say as he slid into his seat. As soon as he did, he realized he should have kissed her cheek, but the moment had already passed. He unfolded his napkin and looked at her from across the table, trying to match up the girl before him with the one who had written to him about how much she loved poetry.

"Did you have any trouble with the photographers?" she asked, her voice a bit shaky. He could tell she was anxious, but he wasn't sure what to do about it. The first few times he'd gone out with girls from home after his face started appearing in magazines, he'd tried to put them at ease by telling them not to be nervous, but this always seemed to have the opposite effect, and they'd just become more jangly, more pink-cheeked, more self-conscious. He watched now as she twisted a silver bracelet around her wrist, unable to quite sit still.

"They weren't too bad," he said. "Nothing like the ones in L.A."

"I bet," she said, and Graham picked up the menu, trying to think of a way to change the subject. He wasn't sure how to tell her that he was the one she'd been talking to all these months. Should he drop a hint? Ask her about her mom or her dog, mention some random subject they'd already discussed, something more obvious than ice-cream flavors, like her childhood trips to Quebec or her end-of-term paper on Irish poetry?

His hands were growing damp with sweat as his mind raced through the possibilities. He'd imagined that once he sat down, the truth would come spilling right out of him. But now that he was here, there was something holding him back, and he swept his eyes around the restaurant and wiped at his forehead.

"So what's good here?" he joked. "The lobster?"

"Well, yeah," she said, clearing her throat. "It's their specialty."

He glanced up at her and forced a smile. "I was only kidding," he said, and she flushed a deep red. "I think I'll get the surf 'n' turf."

"So have you ever been to Maine before?" she asked. "Or is this your first time?"

"First time," he said. "Before I started acting, I'd never left the West Coast."

"Wow," she said. "I've never been to California."

"Have you lived here all your life?" he asked, though he already knew the answer, that she'd been born in D.C. and moved up when she was little.

"Yes," she said, and he snapped his chin up. "My parents too, and my grandparents. It's sort of a family tradition, this town."

Graham leaned his elbows on the table, frowning. "Really?" he said. "Your whole life?"

"Yeah," she said, giving him an odd look.

Before he could say anything more, the waiter arrived with a shrimp cocktail. "Compliments of the chef," he said, setting it between them and then lingering for a beat too long.

74

"Thanks," Graham said, and to his surprise, the waiter—a lanky guy with curly blond hair and a crooked nose—gave him a menacing look in return.

"Yeah, sure," he said, clearly making an effort to sound tough, though his voice was unsteady. He turned to head back to the bar, but the words that drifted behind him were unmistakable: "It's really for Quinn."

Even after he was gone, Graham found himself staring across the table in confusion, his eyes narrowed as he tried to locate his question.

"Sorry," she was saying. "That's just how it is in small towns. Everyone knows everyone else, and when you grow up with these guys, they can be a little overprotective..." She trailed off when she seemed to notice the look on Graham's face. "What?" she asked. "What's wrong?"

"Are you...?" he began, then shook his head. "I mean..."

"What?" she asked again, staring at him in confusion.

"Quinn?" he managed, and she nodded.

"Yes?"

"Your name is Quinn?"

"Um, yes," she said, then something seemed to click and she threw her head back. "Oh man. Did I never actually introduce myself? I can't believe I did that. I'm so sorry."

Graham's face was still twisted as he tried to work out what was going on. "But the shirt you were wearing earlier..."

Again, he could see a look of understanding pass across her eyes. "Ah," she said. "I get it now."

He waited for her to go on.

"I had a little run-in with a chocolate milkshake right before you came in," she said, miming an explosion. "So I borrowed my friend Ellie's."

The name, when she said it, felt like something physical; it seemed to hit him square in the center of his chest. "So you're *not* Ellie?"

She laughed. "No, I'm Quinn."

"So we *haven't* been writing e-mails to each other?"

Now it was her turn to look baffled. "Uh, no."

Graham was shaking his head in a mechanical motion, and though he was aware of it, he seemed unable to stop. "You're *not* Ellie O'Neill," he repeated, and she nodded again. "And we *haven't* been in touch."

"What?" she said. "No. Why? Wait a minute. Does that mean you've been in touch with..." She let out a sharp laugh. "You've been in touch with *Ellie*?"

"Yes," Graham said, suddenly unable to stop grinning. "Look, I'm sorry for the mix-up. I really am. I know this must seem really odd to you."

Quinn stared at him. "You and Ellie."

He nodded, then thought better of it and shook his head. "Not exactly," he said. "I mean, we've never even met before, obviously."

"I thought you said..."

"We've just been e-mailing, so I don't actually know her," he explained, then added: "But I want to."

"This makes no sense at all," Quinn said, slumping back in her seat. "I have no idea what's going on right now."

The waiter returned to clear their plates, but neither of them had touched the shrimp. He gave Graham another threatening look before turning around again. Once he was gone, Quinn sat forward.

"So you and Ellie have been writing e-mails to each other," she said, her tone matter-of-fact, and Graham nodded.

"I got in touch with her accidentally a few months ago, and we started writing back and forth," he said. "It was one of those things that just sort of...happened."

She was eyeing him carefully. "And now here you are."

"Right," he said. "Here I am."

"In Henley."

"Yup," he said with a feeble grin. "Beautiful Henley, Maine."

It took only a moment for her eyes to widen as she connected the dots. "And is that why?"

"Why what?"

"Why the movie's here this summer?"

Graham tried not to look sheepish as he shrugged. "Sort of."

"You came here to meet her?" she asked, her tone increasingly incredulous, and when he nodded, she shook her head again, as if trying to absorb all of this. "Wow," she said, almost to herself, and then she said it again:

"Wow." She picked up her water glass, but made no move to take a sip. "I can't believe she never told me. This whole time she's been pen pals with Graham-freaking-Larkin, and she doesn't even tell me." She closed her eyes, just briefly, then blinked them open again. "And here she's been going around acting like she couldn't care less that you're in town."

The smile slipped from Graham's face, and he cleared his throat. "Well, in fairness, she doesn't know it's me that she's writing," he said, hearing the defensiveness in his own voice. He reached for his glass and took a swig.

Quinn let out a little breath of air, then raised her eyes to meet his over the rim of the glass. "You probably saw her already. She was right outside Sprinkles when you came in. She's kind of tall. With red hair?"

Graham's heart bounded in his chest, and he lowered the glass, thinking of the girl with the green eyes, the one who had been sizing him up. "Yeah, I think I did see her." His eyes strayed to the door, and he forced them back to the table. "That's great," he said, craning his neck for the waiter, then picking up his menu again. "I'll see if I can go find her tomorrow."

Across the table, Quinn watched him; he could feel her pointed gaze, and after a moment, he lowered the menu and looked up at her.

"Go ahead," she said, and he raised his eyebrows.

"Go ahead where?" he asked, trying to keep his voice

steady. But when the cameras weren't rolling, he was a terrible liar, and he knew she could tell.

"Go find her now," Quinn said with a half smile. "You've come all this way, and I'm not going to make you sit through a whole dinner with me."

"No," Graham said in weak protest. "I'm having a good time."

She rolled her eyes. "Really, it's fine," she said, casting a glance over her shoulder at the waiter, who was still lingering near the kitchen. "I'll make Devon eat with me." She winked at him. "And I'll still let you pay."

Graham laughed. "You're sure?"

"I'm sure," she said, and before either of them could change their minds, Graham fished a handful of bills from his wallet and laid them on the table, then rose from his seat.

"She's probably home right now," Quinn said, pointing to the window behind Graham, where the main street of the town had grown quiet as the dusk settled over it. "It's the little yellow cottage near the corner of Prospect and Sunset."

"Thank you," he said, and this time, he remembered to kiss her on the cheek.

She smiled. "Tell her to have fun on my date."

Just as Graham was about to rush out the front door, Joe appeared at his side. "I sent them away," he said, nodding out across the street, "but I'm sure they're still around here somewhere, so if you're planning an escape, I'd go out through the kitchen."

Graham thanked him and hurried past the pots of whistling lobsters and the chefs in white shirts. Just before slipping out, he paused beside Devon, who had watched with a stunned expression as Graham charged into the kitchen.

"How do I get to the corner of Prospect and Sunset?"

"Just head down Main Street and take a left onto Prospect," he said, looking flustered. "You'll run right into it."

"Thanks, man," Graham said, then gave him a little pat on the shoulder as he pushed open the door. He nodded back at the dining room. "She's all yours."

Outside, he pulled in a deep breath of salty air. The light was fading over the water, and the whole world was steeped in shades of blue. There was a breeze coming from the east that lifted Graham's hair from his forehead, and he felt light on his feet as he set off down the road, propelled by that rarest of things: the promise of a second chance. As he walked past old homes and B&Bs, the lights starting to come on in the windows, he thought of the red-haired girl he'd seen just hours ago, the way her eyes had lingered on him with a strange sort of intensity, and his heart banged in time with his footsteps, a rhythm that carried him up the street with renewed energy.

When he saw the sign for Sunset Drive, he slowed down and began to examine each house. It was hard to tell the white ones from the yellow in the dusk, but as he approached a small clapboard colonial, he saw that the porch light was on. And even before he could register its color, he noticed the girl sitting curled on the swing, and he knew that he had arrived.

As he walked up the path, she looked up from her book. The light above her was small and buzzing with insects, and it reached only so far in its efforts to push back the gathering darkness. When he stopped, she lifted her chin, craning her neck, and Graham could tell from the uncertain look in her eyes that he was only a shadow to her, a mere silhouette.

But from where he was standing, he could see her perfectly: the wavy red hair and the oversize T-shirt with a smiling lobster on the front, the way her legs were tucked up beneath her on the swing, and the freckles across her nose. He could see her, and it was just like he'd thought. It was just like being punched in the stomach.

From: EONeill22@hotmail.com
Sent: Sunday, June 9, 2013 6:08 PM
To: GDL824@yahoo.com
Subject: Re: what happy looks like

Welcome surprises.

5

At first, there was nothing beyond the edge of the porch but darkness. If not for the crunch of gravel, Ellie would never have known someone was there at all. She listened more intently. But there was only the chirping of crickets and the rush of the waves down the street, and behind her, the sound of the dog skittering madly around the wooden floors of the house. She squinted out, but beyond the pool of light where she sat, there was nothing; she could only sense someone out there the way you can feel someone watching you across a crowded room—that prickle of awareness, that shiver up your spine.

"Hello?" she called out, laying her book down on her lap. Her voice sounded strange even to her, wavery and thin. She heard the person take another step forward, and though she was blinking hard, her eyes still hadn't adjusted enough to see who it was. "Quinn?"

This time, there was the sound of a throat being cleared, and Ellie realized it wasn't Quinn at all. She rose from the porch swing, a little bead of worry starting to work its way through her. Henley was as safe as any small town—probably even safer—but the feel of the place changed in the summertime, its very molecules seeming to shift as it made room for an influx of strangers, and any of her friends or neighbors would have called out by now, rather than lurk in the shadows.

"Sorry, I didn't meant to scare you," the person said, a deep male voice that carried across the lawn as the blurry figure approached. "It's just... me."

He took a few steps closer, and like someone emerging from the water, he seemed to appear in pieces; first his eyes, then his mouth, then finally the rest of his features, coming into focus all at once as the light fell across him to reveal the familiar face of Graham Larkin.

He'd been in only two movies so far—the highly antici-pated final installment of the Top Hat series wouldn't be out until later in the summer—and though Ellie hadn't seen either one of them, she was still aware of his usual range of expressions from the many times she'd seen him on talk shows and red carpets. There was always something brood-ing about him, an edge of impatience. But now, standing here on the bottom step of her front porch, he looked noth-ing if not sheepish, and it was all so unexpected, so entirely unlikely, that her first instinct was to laugh.

He said nothing, but his mouth turned down at the cor-ners, and he reached up and rubbed at the back of his neck. He was wearing a blue-and-white-checked shirt with a pair of sunglasses dangling from the pocket, looking oddly uncertain, and it almost felt to Ellie like the whole thing was staged, like she'd fallen into a scene from a movie.

"Sorry, I'm—"

"I know who you are," she said. "Where's Quinn?"

He looked at her blankly for a moment, and then his eyes seemed to snap into focus. "Oh," he said. "She told me where you lived."

Ellie tilted her head at him. "Why? And if it didn't go well, how come *you're* here and not her?"

"There was kind of a mix-up, actually," he said, coming up to the middle step. He smelled of mint and something else, something soapy. It was intoxicating, in a way, being this close to him. He looked like he was waiting for her to ask what he was talking about, but she remained silent, pressing her back against the screen door, and after a moment, he cleared his throat. "She was wearing your shirt."

Ellie frowned. "What?"

"Earlier today," he said. "At the ice-cream place."

"Okay..." she said, unsure where he was going with this.

"So I thought she was you."

"Why?" she asked. "You don't know me."

"That's why I thought she might *be* you."

Ellie gave him a hard look, then turned to scan the darkness behind him. "Are you filming a reality show or something? Is this some kind of joke?"

Graham jerked his head from side to side. "No, why?"

"Because I'm really confused," she said. Behind her, the dog—a little beagle with floppy ears—had appeared at the door, his black nose pressed against the screen, his tail wagging. Ellie ignored him, her eyes trained on Graham, who seemed equally thrown off; he was either a really good actor or he was just as confused as she was. "Did Quinn put you up to this?"

"No," he said as the dog began to whine. "I swear."

"Then what?" she demanded. "What do you want?"

He looked slightly taken aback by this, and Ellie suspected it wasn't often that people spoke to him that way. But it had been a long day, and she was tired, and having a movie star on her front porch was feeling less like some kind of sweepstakes prize and more like an unclassifiable problem.

"You're E. O'Neill," he said. It wasn't a question, but a simple fact, and Ellie eyed him suspiciously.

"Aren't movie stars supposed to *have* stalkers?"

For the first time, his face slipped into a smile. "Yeah, I guess this must seem pretty weird," he said. "I'm just excited to finally meet you."

She let out a short laugh. "Again, isn't that something *I* should be saying?"

The dog began to paw at the screen door, his whimpers turning into full-fledged howls, and Ellie knew that it wouldn't be long before Mom emerged to let him out.

"Shush," she muttered, and he sat back on his haunches and fell abruptly quiet.

Graham leaned to look past her. "Hey, Bagel."

Ellie had been half turned to face the dog, but now she whirled back around again. "How do you know his name?"

"You told me," he said, and then paused before continuing, as if this were a matter of no real importance. "It's a great name for a beagle. Really clever. I was a lot less creative with Wilbur."

Her heart was beating fast now, her thoughts tripping over themselves, but when she spoke, her words were measured. "You have a dog named Wilbur?"

Graham's eyes met hers, and he shook his head. In the dim lighting, his face remained neutral, but there was a smile just below the surface, and his eyes were giving him away.

"Nope," he said, and Ellie's head felt suddenly light. She opened her mouth to speak, but nothing emerged.

Graham was smiling now as he watched her. "Wilbur," he said quietly, "is my pig."

Ellie nodded. "Wilbur is your pig," she mumbled, trying to force her mind to catch up. She drew in a shaky breath and looked at him carefully. It was like the simplest of math problems; the answer was right there in front of her, but even so, a part of her was still having trouble believing it.

All this time, it had been him. All those e-mails, all those late-night conversations. All those silly details about school and her mom and everything else. All that thinly veiled flirting. All this time, she'd been writing to Graham Larkin.

She'd told him about the poems in the frames, and how she liked to pretend to be a tourist sometimes, falling into step behind large families with cameras. She'd written about how she learned to juggle this winter when there were no customers at the shop. She'd babbled on about the location of her locker and the unfairness of her chemistry teacher, the reasons she liked winter better than summer and her failed attempt at planting flowers this spring. She'd confessed that she loathed her freckles and that she hated her toes. She'd even admitted that she didn't really like lobster.

And now here he was, standing on her front porch with his thousand-watt smile and his perfect hair and those eyes of his, which seemed to go right through her, and she knew what she was supposed to do. She'd seen the movies. But to her surprise, Ellie didn't feel ecstatic or lovestruck or even incredulous.

What she felt instead was embarrassed.

"You should've told me you were *you*," she said, her cheeks hot. "Were you trying to make me look stupid?"

Graham stared at her, unable to hide his surprise, and Ellie couldn't help taking a small amount of pride in this. Most girls probably tiptoed around him, but she wasn't one of them. She might have been duped, she might have been made to look like an idiot, but at least she wasn't some kind of groupie.

"No," he said, and then he said it again: "No. Not at all."

"Then what?" Ellie demanded, meeting his gaze with a level stare.

"It was just an accident, and then I didn't say anything because—"

"Well, you should have," she told him. "If you had, I never would have..."

Graham raised his eyebrows. "You never would have told me all that stuff?" he said with a little nod, then lifted his shoulders. "Exactly."

His voice was so hollow then that Ellie could think of nothing more to say. Her heart was still pounding, and she kept a hand on the doorknob to steady herself.

"Look, I'm sorry," he said. "Maybe I should have said something. But believe me, I wasn't trying to make you look stupid." He paused, flashing a little grin. "You could never look stupid."

In spite of herself, Ellie smiled at this. She studied him there in the dim lighting, trying to work out whether he was being genuine or whether he was just a genuinely good actor. She could see a thin moon-shaped scar just above his left eyebrow, and with a jolt, she remembered him telling her about this; it was from when he'd jumped off the roof of a van. At the time, she'd been picturing a sandy-haired boy in a leafy suburb, and then an older version of that same gutsy kid, more self-conscious now, perhaps even a little bit nerdy, but with a hint of his former boyish grin as he parked himself behind a computer to open her e-mails.

Now she closed her eyes and tried to edit this image, placing Graham Larkin there instead, writing about his mother's oatmeal cookies and his obsession with Wii tennis and his complete inability to throw his socks in the laundry basket at the end of the day.

All this time, it had been him.

All this time, she suddenly realized, he'd been writing to her too.

She opened her eyes, and her hand slipped from the doorknob. The screen rattled, and from the other side of it, Bagel scrambled to his feet with a gruff bark, and then another. Ellie turned to placate him, but it was too late. Through the screen, she could see Mom's bare feet on the stairs, and seconds later, she was standing beside the door in a pair of moose boxers and an I ♥ MAINE T-shirt. Bagel danced around her, his tail whisking the air. Ellie turned to look at her through the screen, blocking the door.

"He needs to go out, El," Mom said.

"Give me a minute, okay?" Ellie asked, flashing her a meaningful look that seemed to get lost through the screen.

"What's up?" Mom said, pushing the door, and though it opened only partway, Bagel slipped out and went barreling over to Graham. Ellie gave up with a sigh, and Mom stepped outside too, her mouth forming a small circle of surprise.

Graham was stooped to greet the dog—who had rolled onto his back in sheer joy over the prospect of meeting someone new—but now straightened and extended his hand.

"I'm Graham Larkin, Mrs. O'Neill," he said. "I'm sorry to come by so late."

Ellie was waiting for Mom to make a joke about how nine o'clock is the Henley equivalent of midnight, or how Bagel was always happy to receive guests at this hour. But instead, her eyes strayed out to the yard behind them, raking the darkness for signs of anyone else, and Ellie shifted uncomfortably.

"He just stopped by..." she began, but wasn't sure how to finish that particular sentence.

"I just stopped by to introduce myself," Graham said, looking suddenly boyish, less like a movie star and more like a regular kid caught out after curfew. "But I guess I should get going."

Mom forced a smile, her instinct for customer service kicking in despite her wariness. "Well, it was nice to meet you," she said. "And welcome to Henley."

"Thanks," he said, then nodded at her shirt. "So far, I heart Maine too." His eyes slid across the porch to find Ellie's. "I'm really glad someone told me about this place."

Then, with a little wave, he turned and walked down the porch steps and out into the dark of the yard. Bagel threw his head back, letting out one crisp bark that seemed to echo across the quiet neighborhood for far too long. Mom was staring at Ellie, waiting for some sort of explanation, but it was hard to imagine what she might say. All she could think about was that she was the one who had brought him here.

And suddenly, she was really glad too.

From: GDL824@yahoo.com
Sent: Sunday, June 9, 2013 9:28 PM
To: EONeill22@hotmail.com
Subject: Re: what happy looks like

Meeting new people.

From: EONeill22@hotmail.com
Sent: Sunday, June 9, 2013 9:43 PM
To: GDL824@yahoo.com
Subject: Re: what happy looks like

You already said that one.

Graham was only half listening as his manager strutted around the trailer like some sort of demented rooster, flapping the morning's newspaper with one ink-smudged hand.

"Is *this* why you wanted to come early?" asked Harry, tossing the paper onto the table beside where Graham sat slouched in a folding chair. The trailer was small, with little more than a miniature dining area and a tiny changing room with a costume rack that had been set up by a wardrobe assistant. For the past two years, Graham had worn things like top hats and capes and dark robes with velvet lining. But this film was a contemporary love story, and the clothes hanging nearby weren't a whole lot different from his own: board shorts and solid-colored T-shirts and flip-flops. He wondered if he'd be able to keep some of them at the end. There were few things he hated more than shopping.

He peered over at the picture in Page Six of the *New York Post*, which was taken from a distance, but clearly showed him at the Lobster Pot with Quinn. She was turned to the side, so that all you could see was a curtain of shiny hair, but there was Graham across from her, leaning over intently. If he had to guess, it was probably the moment he learned she wasn't Ellie. There was only a small caption beside the photo, which read "Larkin's New Love?" and a one-paragraph article that Graham didn't bother to read.

"No," he said truthfully, and Harry fell into the other chair with a sigh.

When Graham first signed with him, Fenton Management had been up and running for only a few years. Before that, Harry had been an entertainment lawyer who had grown tired of contracts and fine print and thought he might have a knack for managing the careers of actors instead. His first client was a round-faced, bespectacled kid from a popular sitcom, and after that, he'd somehow scraped together a decent roster of young actors with dubious levels of talent.

Before Graham had signed the contract for the trilogy, back when the casting was still under wraps and nobody could have known how quickly his star would rise, Harry had been the only one willing to take a meeting with him. Graham would always be grateful for that, for his faith in him, a completely untested high school kid whose only credit was a middling performance in *Guys and Dolls*. Now he was by far Harry's biggest client, and in addition to the usual amount of time and attention this position merited, it also seemed to have earned him an often grumpy, middle-aged shadow while on location.

"This is bad," Harry was saying, running his hand through what was left of his hair in a worried manner. "You can't just waltz into a town like this, ask out the first girl you see, and then leave her high and dry."

Graham looked over. "Is that what the story said?"

"No," he said with a shrug. "But word's out."

"I didn't leave her high and dry," Graham explained. "It's just that there was a mix-up..."

"That's not the point," Harry said, scraping his chair around so they were facing each other. "The point is that you're supposed to be with Olivia."

Graham glared at him. "Am I?"

"In a town like this, with no other girls around for the next few weeks, everyone figured you two would just—"

He raised an eyebrow. "Just what?"

"You have to admit, it would be great publicity for the film—and for you," Harry continued, oblivious to the look on Graham's face. "You're at a crossroads here, career-wise. Your next project, your next girlfriend—these are all important considerations. And don't look at me like that. This is why you pay me the big bucks—to tell you these kinds of things. To take you to the next level, we need to step carefully, okay?" He paused and threw up his hands. "Plus, she's *Olivia Brooks*, for Christ's sake. It's not like I'm suggesting that you sleep with a troll."

"You don't get to tell me to sleep with anybody," Graham said, rising from his chair.

"I didn't mean it like that. I just meant—well, you can at least try, can't you?"

Graham walked over to the tiny window at the back of the trailer, which looked out over the set. The cameras were already positioned, and the director—a young guy named Mick, who was coming off an indie darling that had surprised everyone by garnering an Oscar nomination—was pacing with a gaggle of production assistants at his back. Soon, Graham would be called out there to run down the street after Olivia, sweep her up, and kiss her passionately. And not just once, but probably more like eighteen to twenty times.

"There *are* others girls around, you know," he said without turning around. "Just because this isn't New York or L.A. doesn't mean there aren't interesting people."

"Right," Harry said. "I'm sure she was lovely."

Graham smiled, remembering the look on Ellie's face when she first saw him under the lights of the porch, but then he realized Harry was talking about Quinn. Before he could say anything, there was a knock on the door, and they both turned.

"Five minutes, Mr. Larkin," someone called, and Graham took a deep breath. No matter how many times he did this, no matter how prepared he felt, this was the moment when his stomach always dipped. There was an art to being himself now, and it didn't come without effort. In some ways, it took more acting for him to carry himself a certain way on set than it did to lose himself in his character, a teenage boy whose father had just died in a tragic boating accident, and who had complicated feelings for the girl who had witnessed it.

Without another word, Graham brushed past Harry and out the door of the trailer, breathing in the heavy air before hurrying down the steps, where a PA with a headset and a clipboard was waiting to escort him the twelve feet it took to walk to his mark, as if he might get lost along the way. Graham was used to this by now; sometimes you were treated like a god, and other times, like a four-year-old.

They'd already rehearsed earlier, and now the director greeted him with a few last-minute notes. They were shooting out of order, so today's scene was actually one that would come near the end of the film, when his character finally broke out of his haze and realized what had been in front of him all along. Graham looked up as that very someone approached, dressed in an absurdly short jean skirt and a red bikini top.

"Hey," Olivia said with a little smirk. Her long blond hair was pulled back in a messy ponytail that had probably taken the hair people hours to make so perfectly casual, and her makeup was applied in such a way as to make it look like she wore none at all. "I heard you've been enjoying the town."

"Just checking out the local cuisine," he said, trying to keep the edge out of his voice. Olivia was undeniably gorgeous, but something about her grated on Graham. She'd been in the Hollywood machine for years now—she'd started her career as a precocious kid on a popular medical drama—and the truth was, it showed. He first met her a couple of years ago at a party for one of her films, and when they'd been introduced, she'd barely looked at him, only tossed a haughty glance his way as she lit her cigarette before moving on to someone far more famous. That was before the first Top Hat movie had come out, and from the way she acted around him now, he guessed she probably didn't remember that particular night. But then, from what he'd heard about Olivia, she didn't remember a lot of nights.

The main street of town had been completely blocked off for filming. At the opposite end of the road, Graham could make out the ice-cream shop, and he wondered if Ellie was there now. Along the sides of the street, crowded behind metal gates, people leaned in with their cameras ready, taking photos and videos as a few big-shouldered security guards paced in front of them.

Graham wiggled his fingers and cleared his throat. He enjoyed shooting on location—studio lighting being no match for the sun—but he felt edgy today in front of an audience. When he first started acting, he'd been unsettled to discover that the filming so often happened out of order, and this was exactly why: it seemed impossible to work up to the big kiss when none of the preceding moments had been explored yet. It just wasn't the way things worked in real life, and he felt like he could use a bit more of a drumroll.

Still, he knew most guys his age would give anything to kiss Olivia Brooks, and here he was being paid—and nicely—to do it. At the moment, she was discussing something with the assistant director on the other end of the set, and Graham hopped up and down a few times, trying to get his head in the right place as he waited. The wardrobe supervisor ran over and held out a hand, but it took him a second to realize she was waiting for him to take off his shirt. As he peeled it over his head, the crowd let out a high-pitched cheer, and Graham couldn't help laughing, even as someone else trotted over with a comb to tease his hair back into place. He scanned the crowd once again, hoping that Ellie wasn't there watching, though he suspected this would be the last place he'd find her.

When it was finally time to start, Graham took a long breath. He was supposed to go running down the street, hook Olivia around the waist, and then half pick her up as they kissed. It was, to be honest, a bit more acrobatic than Graham thought was realistic, and when they'd practiced it, it hadn't gone particularly well. He wasn't bad at scooping her up, but the momentum of the whole thing and the way that they spun often meant he missed her when he went for the kiss, and twice he'd gotten her neck instead.

"This isn't *Twilight*," she'd snapped.

Now he was poised to run, and the moment the director called "Action," he was moving fast down the street. He'd been a center forward on his soccer team before he stopped going to school, and this part was fun for him, the sea air in his lungs, his muscles straining, his flip-flops slapping at the pavement. A blue car with a stunt driver inside pulled out from the curb and Graham did a little half hop to avoid it, but as he moved sideways, the strap of his flip-flop broke, and he ended up tripping over it.

The director yelled "Cut" and the cameramen poked their heads out from behind the huge black boxes. As the stunt man backed the car into the start spot again and Olivia sighed from down the street, an assistant from the costume department ran out with a spare sandal, which Graham tugged onto his foot. He wondered how many they had back there; it would be interesting to know what the flip-flop budget was for a movie like this.

On the second take, he made it all the way down to Olivia, and he even managed to execute the kiss perfectly, but when he looked up again, the director was frowning.

"That felt like . . . nothing," he said. "At best, that'll get a yawn out of the audience. Let's aim a little higher, shall we?"

Graham glanced over at the crowd, wondering if he should be embarrassed at this affront to his kissing skills. On the next try, he thought he'd done better, but was met with similar criticism.

"Boring," the director said. "Could we create a little more chemistry?"

Graham gritted his teeth. The guy might be brilliant, but he had an annoying habit of constantly saying "we" when he meant "you," and Graham was pretty sure chemistry wasn't something you could just create anyway; it was either there or it wasn't, and with Olivia, it simply wasn't. Yet somehow, even though there were two people involved in this kiss, Graham was the only one getting a lecture. Still, he nodded gamely, and set himself up to try again.

This time was apparently no better.

As he stood there listening to Mick talk to him about passion and beauty and the true meaning of love, his eyes wandered past the cameras and the crowds and the security guards, to where a girl with red hair was cutting across the town green.

"We have to make them believe it," Mick was saying, and he reached out and thumped Graham on the chest. "We have to make them feel it *here*."

"Uh, can you hold on just a minute?" Graham asked, taking a few steps backward. "I just need a short break..."

"Yes," Mick said. "Good. Exactly. Let's give this a bit of a think, and when you come back, I want you to be filled with passion. Got it?"

Graham nodded, his eyes still on Ellie. "Got it."

He started out walking as casually as he could manage, but as soon as he was past the security barrier, he picked up a run. He was aware of the many pairs of eyes on his back as he jogged through the square of green grass at the center of town, but he couldn't make himself care.

She was walking fast now, her eyes deliberately forward. She wore a jean skirt not unlike Olivia's, only longer, with a plain black tank top, and her red hair was tied back in a loose ponytail. As he approached, he could see the sprinkling of freckles on her arms and legs, the skin beneath them pale in the morning light.

"Ellie," he said when he was a few feet away, the word coming out in a puff of air. He paused to catch his breath as she turned around, looking unsurprised to find him there. Her eyes darted over to the film set, about a hundred yards behind them, and she took a few steps to her left, moving around the side of a gazebo. Graham hesitated only a moment before following her.

"Hi," he said, his heart still beating fast. "How are you?"

She smiled. "Did you go for a swim?"

He shook his head, confused, and then realized he was wearing nothing but swim trunks. "No," he said, suddenly self-conscious. "I'm in costume. We're shooting a scene over there."

Ellie nodded. "So what are you doing over here?"

"I wanted to say hello."

She smiled. "Good morning."

"Howdy," he said with a grin. Her eyes were very green, and he felt suddenly and uncharacteristically flustered as they landed on him. "Are you on your way to work?"

She nodded.

"What are you doing later?"

"Why, are you going to ask me to dinner at the Lobster Pot?"

Graham started to answer and then realized she was kidding. "I was just hoping maybe I'd run into you."

She smiled. "Well, that's the nice thing about small towns."

Graham was about to respond when she turned and began to walk away, making her way up the green with surprising speed. He couldn't help but be stunned by the quickness of it all, and there was nothing for him to do but watch her go, hoping she might turn around. But she never did, and it wasn't until she reached the door of a blue storefront that Graham realized what had caused her to take off. Behind him, a group of photographers was rushing over, stumbling a bit on the uneven grass in their efforts to reach him first.

As the frontrunner finally made it up to Graham, he dropped his camera bag, panting. "Who was that?"

Graham only shrugged as the guy snapped a few half-hearted pictures of him standing alone on the lawn.

Afterward, when he arrived back down at the set, Mick looked up from his notes and stubbed out his cigarette, his eyebrows raised.

"Well?" he asked. "Are we feeling more inspired now?"

Graham smiled. "Yes," he said. "We are."

From: GDL824@yahoo.com
Sent: Monday, June 10, 2013 10:22 AM
To: EONeill22@hotmail.com
Subject: this afternoon

Ellie!

(Just giving you a proper Russian salutation, now that I know your name.)

I'm done shooting at 4 pm today. Want to go in search of an authentic whoopie pie?

Yours,

Graham!

7

The reception in the shop was only ever spotty at best, so Ellie spent the morning flitting between the cash register and the ancient desktop computer behind the counter, grateful that her mother wasn't in yet to ask any questions. Last night, she'd explained away Graham's visit by claiming he was looking for Quinn, and this morning, she'd managed to avoid Mom altogether by ducking out early to open the store.

The truth was, Ellie wasn't sure what to say, or even how she felt about any of this yet. All she knew was this: as she logged on to the computer for the sixth time this morning, she was desperate to see that familiar e-mail address show up on the screen.

It didn't matter that she'd only just seen him out on the green. It didn't matter that she now knew who he was. It didn't even matter that it was Graham Larkin, of all people. For more than three months now, this was the thing she'd most looked forward to—that breathless moment as the page unfurled itself on the screen, bringing with it the promise of a new e-mail from him. That small chain of bold letters and numbers—GDL824@yahoo.com—was all it took to set her heart pounding.

Now it was like her brain was split in two. One half understood that the person writing to her was just down the street. But the other half still couldn't let go of the more general idea of him, the comforting and mysterious stranger with whom she could talk about anything. His sudden presence here had thrown her wildly off balance, and even as she noticed—with a little thrill—that a new e-mail from him had indeed arrived, there was something disconcerting about it. It was like talking to someone on the phone from across the room; even though you could see his lips moving, and even though you could hear the words, it was hard to process the fact that the two things were somehow the same.

The e-mail was just like him: clever and sweet and a little bit funny. And he wanted to see her again. She closed her eyes and let her fingers hover over the keyboard for a moment. When she opened them, she hit the reply button and thought about all the reasons there were to say no.

The problem was, she wanted to say yes.

Sorry, she began, typing slowly, one key at a time. Then she erased each of the five letters and sat back with a sigh. Most girls, she knew, would be delighted to find out they'd been corresponding with a movie star. But to Ellie, it just seemed unfair. She wanted nothing more than to spend time with GDL824 this afternoon. It was Graham Larkin she wasn't so sure about.

She was still staring at the screen when the door to the shop was thrown open, and she only just managed to close her e-mail as Quinn arrived breathlessly at the counter. Last night after Graham left, Ellie had discovered a text from Quinn that said simply *!!!*. But Ellie had no way of knowing whether those little exclamation points signaled enthusiasm or anger or something in between.

And so she hadn't written back, even though she wanted nothing more than to sit down with her best friend and marvel over the fact that somehow—unbelievably, ridiculously, impossibly—the random guy from California she'd been trading e-mails with for months had somehow turned out to be Graham Larkin.

Quinn leaned against the counter, breathing hard. "I'm late for work," she said, coughing a little. "But apparently we have a lot to talk about..."

"I know," Ellie said, pouring her a glass of lemonade from the pitcher they offered customers. She swallowed hard, realizing how nervous she was to look up and meet Quinn's eyes. Just yesterday, she'd helped her get ready for her big date, had watched the way her friend lit up at the prospect of the evening. Yet through some strange quirk of chance, Graham had ended up on Ellie's front porch at the end of the night, and she felt awful that—however unknowingly—she might have ruined things for Quinn. "Listen, if I'd known it was him—"

But Quinn only shook her head. "I don't care about that," she said. "I mean, I'm not saying it wouldn't have been fun to have a fling with a celebrity this summer, or that it's not hard to get my head around the idea of you and Graham Larkin, but..."

Ellie braced herself. "But?"

"I can't believe you never told me," she said, looking genuinely hurt. "All this time you've been keeping it a secret? I thought the deal was that we tell each other everything."

"It is," Ellie said, lowering her eyes. "We do. It's just that—"

She was interrupted by the sound of the village clock as it rang out over the town, a series of deep thudding tones, and Quinn swore under her breath.

"I've got to go," she said. "We'll have to finish talking about this later."

"Okay," Ellie said, aware of the guilty blush that was making her cheeks hot. "I promise I can explain..."

"You better," Quinn said, and to Ellie's relief, she offered a small smile. "Otherwise you won't get to hear about what happened to *me* last night."

"What happened?"

"Nothing much," she said, raising her eyebrows. "Just that Devon Alexander kissed me."

Ellie's mouth fell open. "How did *that* happen?"

"After Graham left to find you, Devon ended up having dinner with me, and I think he was feeling bad that my big date left, so he was being really sweet, and afterward he walked me home, and it just sort of happened." Quinn was shaking her head, though it was hard to tell whether it was with amazement or disbelief. Everyone knew that Devon had been in love with her since the second grade, but she'd never been remotely interested in him, and had in fact spent as much energy ignoring him as he'd spent adoring her. "And the thing is, it was kind of not so bad."

"Kind of not so bad?" Ellie said, and Quinn's face broke into a real smile this time.

"Okay, fine," she said. "It was kind of good. Can you believe it?"

Ellie laughed. "No, actually."

"So what about you?"

"What about me?"

"Did you kiss Graham Larkin?"

She laughed. "Weren't you running late?"

"Yeah," Quinn said, glancing at her watch. "I've got to go. But you're not off the hook, okay? I'll call you later." She downed the last of her lemonade before dashing back over to the door. Just before stepping outside, she turned around again. "Hey, El?" she said. "Don't be weird about this thing, okay?"

"What do you mean?" Ellie asked with a frown.

"It's just that he's actually nice. And it's obvious he really likes you. So just try not to get in your own way."

"I don't..." Ellie began to protest, but the door bounced shut before she could finish. She stood there for a moment in the quiet of the shop, thinking about Graham, and about Devon and Quinn and how unlikely that was. Her eyes slid back to the computer screen, and she bit her lip.

This time, her fingers seemed to move on their own.

Yes, she typed, just to see what it felt like.

The door opened again, and once more, Ellie clicked away from her in-box, looking up as a family of tourists wandered in. She flashed her most welcoming smile, but they were immediately distracted by the barrels of beach toys near the door. The two boys each grabbed a foam noodle and began jousting as their mother tried to wrestle them from their hands, but it was the youngest one that Ellie was watching, a small tow-haired girl who couldn't have been older than four.

While the mother dealt with the boys, the father took the girl's hand and led her over to the display of postcards, kneeling beside her and pointing at the various scenes. Her face was serious as she picked out one after another, holding them by the edges, her eyes big as she studied them.

Watching the two of them, Ellie couldn't help the thought that always came to her in these moments, petty and jealous as it was: that there was no way that little girl would remember this. Childhood memories were like airplane luggage; no matter how far you were traveling or how long you needed them to last, you were only ever allowed two bags. And while those bags might hold a few hazy recollections—a diner with a jukebox at the table, being pushed on a swing set, the way it felt to be picked up and

116

spun around—it didn't seem enough to last a whole lifetime.

Still, whether this one would count for her or not, there was no doubt this girl would have more memories of her father than Ellie, who only had a handful to go back to again and again. Now, after so many years, they were fuzzy and well worn, like papers that had been folded and refolded enough times that you might mistake them for cloth.

Her father had been a first-term congressman and a rising star in the Republican Party when he met her mother, a waitress at his favorite diner, who was ready with his pancakes and coffee every morning before he even walked in the door. Over time, ordering turned to talking, which turned to flirting, which turned into something more, and before long, she was pregnant with Ellie.

The only problem was, he was already married.

Secrets never stay secret for very long. But they managed to keep this one hidden for four years. Mom refused his money, and let him visit only sparingly. During those times, she later told Ellie, Paul Whitman would hang up his expensive jacket and sit on the ratty floor of the even rattier apartment to play with his daughter for an hour or two—he and Mom barely exchanging a word—and then, when the time was up, he would rise and kiss Ellie on the forehead, try once more unsuccessfully to hand Mom a check, and then he would be gone again.

It might have continued like that for longer if he wasn't a politician, and if his name wasn't starting to be bandied about as a future presidential candidate. But as it was, the press had taken a keen interest in him, especially once he decided to run for the Senate. Ellie was four when the story broke. And in its wake, everything else broke too.

For three months, Mom tried to stick it out. For three months, she was hounded by the press, followed everywhere with cameras, harassed by reporters and peppered with questions. The pictures Ellie had seen online showed a younger version of her mother hidden behind a pair of dark sunglasses. In every one, she's carrying Ellie on her hip, pressing her daughter's face into her sweater to protect her from the glare of the unwavering spotlight.

There were a million reasons to leave. But even so, Mom hadn't meant for the whole thing to turn into a secret. At first, she just wanted to get away for the summer, and so she rented a cottage in Henley, a place she remembered visiting once as a kid. But when she arrived there, she'd told Ellie, she felt a powerful rush of relief at the quietness of it all. The clouds were scudding across the sky, casting shadows on the water, and there was a man playing guitar on the village green. It all felt so far away from Washington, D.C., with its sleazy scandals and fast-talking politicians, and, mostly, from the father of her child, who had responded to each and every question from each and every journalist since the story came out with two simple words: "No comment."

So when the first person introduced herself in the ice-cream shop that day and then looked expectantly at Mom in return, apparently oblivious to the infamy that had trailed after her back home, the words *Margaret Lawson* got caught in her throat.

Margaret Lawson was a twenty-four-year-old waitress from Vermont who had dreamed of changing the world, of saving the environment, of making a difference in Washington, but who instead ended up serving coffee to men in business suits to make enough to pay the rent. She was a woman without parents, without family, without roots. Someone whose name had been splashed across the glossy covers of a dozen magazines, someone entirely ill suited for any kind of spotlight. She was a woman who had made the very worst kind of mistake, even if she had gotten the very best possible thing out of it.

Margaret Lawson had no place in this new town, this new life. And so what slipped out instead was a childhood name, which had gathered dust for too many years, paired with her mother's maiden name.

"Maggie O'Neill," she said, extending a hand.

And just like that, Margaret Lawson disappeared, taking Eleanor Lawson with her.

They rarely talked about it anymore, she and Mom. But it was there all the same, when they flipped past C-SPAN a bit too quickly while changing channels, when the newspaper arrived on their front step with a thump each morning, carrying with it news of the political world. And especially when they spoke about money and college, all the things that would have been so uncomplicated if she were still Eleanor Lawson or even Eleanor Whitman, rather than just Ellie O'Neill.

Her father was a U.S. senator now, and a serious contender for the Republican nomination in the next presidential race. The scandal had eventually subsided, as scandals always seem to do. And in every article and blog post and news story on the subject, there was usually still some disclaimer about his alleged affair with the waitress, even after all this time. Sometimes they mentioned the potential illegitimate daughter, but most often that seemed to get lost in all the rest of it. Everyone was far more interested in his real family: his very forgiving wife and their two boys—one a year older than Ellie and one a year younger—who were each as blond as their mother and always seemed to be pictured doing some sort of bonding activity with their father, hunting or camping or fishing.

They undoubtedly ate at fancy restaurants instead of fish shacks, went to private schools with uniforms rather than public schools with budget problems. And they probably wouldn't think twice about asking their father to help pay for a summer poetry course. And though most of the time Ellie couldn't imagine trading the life she had for any of that—even if it were an option—it sometimes seemed unfair that she'd never had a chance to see what it was like to be Paul Whitman's daughter.

If he'd ever looked for them, Ellie wasn't aware of it. She tried not to think about the fact that a man like him could probably have found them quite easily if he really wanted to, could have been touch, called to talk to her now and then, sent birthday cards, or otherwise marked the passing of years. Maybe it was Mom's fault, or maybe it was his; maybe he wondered about them, or maybe not; maybe he missed them sometimes, or maybe the articles were true: maybe they were nothing more than a footnote.

Ellie watched as the little girl handed her father a postcard with a picture of the sun rising over the ocean. But the mother had managed to corral the boys out the door and was calling sharply for the other two to join them. The dad shrugged helplessly at his daughter, whose chin trembled as she clutched the postcard to her chest.

"She can just take it," Ellie found herself saying, and the man spun around with a look of surprise. His daughter beamed at him, then skipped off with the card in hand, a memory that might only make it to the corner, or to the end of the trip, but that would—with any luck—be carried with her at least a little bit further than that.

When they were gone, Ellie turned back to the computer. *I don't think I can*, she wrote to Graham. *Sorry.*

Afterward, she sat and she waited.

Nine minutes later, he wrote back: *Then I'll just go by myself and bring one over to you later tonight.*

Ellie couldn't help smiling at the idea of him showing up on her porch again, then bit her lip and stared at the keyboard. *Tonight isn't good for me either*, she wrote, and then thought for a second before adding, *And I still have no idea what a whoopie pie is anyway...*

Not even a minute had passed when there was a little ding, and his name appeared again. *Then let's find out.*

Ellie hesitated. *No cameras?*

A minute passed, then two, but it felt like much longer. Finally, an e-mail arrived: *No cameras.*

This time, she didn't wait. *Okay,* she typed, before she could change her mind.

And so, five hours later, she found herself taking the long way down to the cove, wondering if she was making a mistake. She understood that there were certain turning points to these kinds of things, opportunities to think better, chances to turn around. But as she made her way past the bait shop and the hut where they rented out Jet Skis, as she wandered along the edge of the main beach and into the clusters of trees that marked its border, Ellie had the distinct impression that she was barreling past those very warning signs, and that soon it would be too late to take any of this back.

There were dozens of reasons why she shouldn't go. He would get bored with her and move on. He would be going home in just a few weeks. He was too famous. He would give away their secret, just by the very fact of being him. He would hurt her without even trying.

But there was a sense of momentum that carried her on anyway, pushing back branches as she neared the cove, the dirt giving way to rocks beneath her feet. She barely noticed any of it, though; she was thinking of the look on his face when he'd stood on the porch the night before, and of all those words they'd sent sailing across the country, each e-mail a kind of poem containing the very best versions of themselves.

Maybe seeing him here was nothing more than a simple addendum to a conversation that had been going on for months now. If the time before she'd known him had been a kind of prelude, then maybe this was all just the postscript.

P.S. Hello there.

P.S. Thank you for coming.

P.S. Here I am.

Ahead, the trees were thinner, opening up to a small cove where the water lapped against slate-colored stones. Ellie came to a sudden stop when she realized he was already there waiting for her, and she hung back amid the trees. He was stooped on the ground, idly sifting through the piles of rocks. As she watched, he held one up, tilting his head to the side, and from where she was standing, Ellie could see that it was shaped like a lopsided heart.

She remembered an e-mail he'd written her just a few weeks ago. They'd been talking about grade school memories, and he'd confessed that he always had trouble making valentines as a kid, especially the kind where you had to fold your piece of construction paper and trace out half a heart.

They always came out looking like pink blobs, he'd written. *Isn't that really all a heart is anyway?* Ellie had replied.

Now she took a deep breath and steadied herself. He half turned, and she could see in his profile that he looked different here on the beach, less striking somehow, more familiar. It certainly wasn't what she had imagined GDL824 would look like, but it also wasn't quite like the movie-star version of Graham Larkin either.

At the moment, he was simply Graham.

She thought of the way the Russians would say it— *Graham!*—and she felt her pink blob of a heart pick up speed. It was, she realized, a shout and a surprise and a jolt of happiness all at once, the truest thing there was, and so, without another moment's hesitation, she stepped forward to deliver her greeting in person.

From: GDL824@yahoo.com
Sent: Monday, June 10, 2013 4:24 PM
To: EONeill22@hotmail.com
Subject: birds of a feather

I couldn't find the rock you were talking about, but I think I'm at the right place. It's pretty much just me and the seagulls, so I should be easy to spot...

(I'm the one without feathers.)

Graham was a million miles away when she finally arrived at the beach. He'd been trying to run through his lines for tomorrow's scene, an impassioned monologue his character makes after leaving his father's funeral and heading out to the very place where he'd died, an old lobster boat called the *Go Fish*. But the words were proving slippery today, whipped away by the wind coming in off the ocean.

He was picking through the smooth stones that blanketed the beach—so different from the pale sands of California—when he heard the sound of her footsteps behind him. He pulled in a breath before turning around.

"Hey," he said, glancing up at her and then away again. For some reason, he was having trouble looking at her directly, though it was all he wanted to do at the moment. Everything around them was gray—the trees, the rocks, the sky, even the slate-colored water—and in the midst of it all, there was Ellie, with her red hair and white T-shirt, her jean skirt and rubber flip-flops. It should have been the most ordinary thing in the world—this girl on the beach—but somehow, it felt to Graham like he was staring at the sun.

"Find any treasures?" she asked, nodding at the rock in his hand, and when he held it in his palm to take another look, he realized that he actually had. It was, to his surprise, shaped like a heart. His cheeks went warm, and he slipped it into his pocket with a little shake of his head. If he showed it to her now, she'd think he was some kind of sap. She'd think he was no different from the characters he played in his movies.

"Want to walk?" he asked, his voice unintentionally gruff.

She nodded, and they set off together down the beach, their feet slipping on the rocks. Neither said anything for a while, but the silence was comfortable, and the sound of the waves provided all the soundtrack they needed. Ellie was half a step ahead of him, and he wondered where she was leading them. The stones were loose and uneven, and Graham found himself stumbling every so often. As he lurched forward once again, he saw a hint of a smile on Ellie's face.

"This is crazy," he said. "How can you call this a beach?"

"I guess we're just tougher out here," she said with a grin.

"Are you saying Californians are wimps?"

"No," she said. "I'm just saying *you're* a wimp."

Graham laughed. "Fair enough," he said. "But when do we get to solid ground?"

Ellie pointed, and up ahead he could see the thin ribbon of a trail leading up a small embankment on the opposite side of the beach. They followed it into the woods, ducking beneath the low canopy of leaves, and within minutes, they were spit out onto a quiet road.

"Are you planning to murder me?" Graham asked, looking around at the empty street, the rutted asphalt, and the swaying trees.

"Only if you keep asking so many questions," she said as they set off down the road, keeping to the shoulder, which was strewn with pebbles.

"Seriously, though, where are we going?"

Ellie gave him a sideways glance. "We're on a quest," she said, as if it were obvious.

"A quest," he repeated. "I like that."

"Like Dorothy trying to find her way home again."

"Or Ahab looking for the white whale."

"Exactly," she said. "Only we're on the hunt for whoopie pies."

"Aha," Graham said, looking pleased. "So you're a believer now."

She shook her head. "I'm still skeptical. But if there's anywhere that would have them, it would be this place."

He was about to ask what place she was talking about, but then the road forked, becoming abruptly busier, and he could see a strip of buildings up ahead—a home and garden store, a real estate office, a used car lot, and right in the middle of it all, one of the pinkest buildings he'd ever seen. The yard surrounding it was dotted with picnic tables, each topped by a bright green umbrella, and there was a giant vanilla ice cream cone wearing sunglasses perched on the roof.

"The Ice Cream and Candy Emporium," Ellie said, sweeping her arm grandly in its direction.

"Wouldn't this be the competition?"

"It's summer in Maine," Ellie said. "Trust me, there are enough customers to go around."

"I'm getting a little nervous," Graham joked as they made their way across the parking lot. "What if they don't have them?"

"I doubt they will," she said. "I keep telling you, they're not a thing."

"They are," he said. "They're the official state treat."

"So you keep saying."

Graham paused just outside the door. "Should we put some money on it?" he asked, but her expression changed, the smile slipping away, and he realized he'd said the wrong thing. "Or not money," he said quickly. "But let's make a bet."

Her face relaxed again, much to Graham's relief. He was reminded of an e-mail she'd sent him months ago, not long after they'd first started talking, about how she'd gotten into some kind of summer poetry course and wanted desperately to go.

So why don't you? he'd written, but as soon as he'd hit send, he realized what the answer would be, and his face

130

burned as he sat at his desk in the sprawling house, wishing he could take it back.

It wasn't long before her response reached him.

I can't afford it, she'd written. *Isn't that the worst reason you've ever heard? I've got to figure out a way to make it work, because I'd hate myself for missing it because of something as stupid as money.*

She'd assumed he would understand, he realized, because he was seventeen, and what seventeen-year-old doesn't have money problems? He could no longer remember exactly how he'd responded, and he wondered what had happened, if she'd figured out a way to pay for it. He hoped so.

It was a strange thing, attaching those floating conversations to the girl in front of him now, pinning so many collected details to the person like buttons on a shirt.

Ellie was still watching him with raised eyebrows. "What kind of bet?" she asked, and Graham thought for a moment.

"If they have whoopie pies in there, you have to have dinner with me tonight."

"That's not much of a consequence," she said. "I was kind of thinking of making you do that anyway."

Graham couldn't help grinning. He found himself doing a mental tally of all the girls he'd dated over the past few years, the ones who sat by their phones waiting for him, the ones who pouted when he didn't call. Even the girls who seemed normal when he first met them at the gym or the grocery store always ended up wearing too much makeup or impossibly high heels when they finally went out; they agreed with everything he said and laughed when he wasn't being funny, and not one of them—not a single one—would have ever made so confident a declaration as Ellie just had.

For the first time in a while, he felt like himself again.

"Okay," he said, giving her a stern look. "Then we should probably just pick the restaurant now, since there's no way they won't have whoopie pies in there. Unless, of course, we're no longer in Maine. I wouldn't be surprised if you just made me walk all the way to Canada..."

"We're only one town away," she said, rolling her eyes. "And you haven't won yet." They were standing just outside the entrance now, the sweet smell of chocolate drifting through the screen door. "If they don't have whoopie pies in there..."

"Which they will," he chimed in.

She shook her head as she paused to think; her mouth was twisted in concentration.

"If they don't," she said eventually, "then you have to make me one of your drawings."

He couldn't hide the look of surprise on his face. For a moment, it felt as if she'd seen right through him. Graham was always careful about discussing things like this in public, and though his drawings were hardly anything at all— they were just doodles, really, sketches of skylines—it still was a piece of himself that he kept close.

He'd forgotten that he told her about them: a late-night

e-mail sent after some premiere party, when he'd sat alone in his room in the big, empty house and written to this girl across the country about how his pencil moved as if on its own. He'd told her that it was an escape, this type of art, the best kind of travel. He'd told her it made him happy.

How could he have forgotten that the person he was writing to all those months was the same one standing before him now?

It took him another moment to find his voice. "Deal," he said finally, and her face broke into a smile.

"Great," she said, pushing open the door. "Hope you brought a pencil."

Inside, the place was at least twice the size of the shop back in Henley, lined with colorful bins of candy and giant lollipops. There were buckets of saltwater taffy, bins full of jelly beans, and a glass case with more than a dozen different kinds of fudge. Graham was eyeing a display of vintage candy when he realized Ellie was watching him. When he caught her eye, she jerked her head toward the cashier, and he wandered over obediently.

He'd forgotten his baseball cap—the thinnest of disguises, but still a kind of shield against recognition—and when he stepped up to the counter, the woman reacted as if she were following a script: a bored glance up, a look away, and then a sudden realization. It was all there: the double take, the widened eyes, the open mouth. At this point, it usually went one of two ways: there were those who cried out, who jumped around and screamed and pointed, and there were those who tamped down all of their instincts to make a scene and simply went about their usual business with shaky voices and trembling hands, waiting until after he'd left to pick up their phone and call everyone they know.

To Graham's relief, this woman fell into the second category. She gaped for only a moment before lowering her eyes, as if afraid to look at him.

"I was just wondering," he began as she worked to compose herself, to keep her face carefully neutral, "whether you might have whoopie pies here?"

"Whoopie pies?" she asked, already looking apologetic. "I don't think we do."

She began to glance desperately around the shop, as if they might suddenly materialize on one of the shelves, and Graham could almost feel how badly she wanted to come through for him. He was about to wave it away and buy something else when Ellie stepped up beside him.

"Can I ask you one more question?" she said. "Just for research purposes?"

The woman nodded, chewing her lip.

"Have you ever even *heard* of a whoopie pie?"

"I don't—" she began, then looked at Graham, who raised his chin up and down almost imperceptibly, and the cashier's eyes drifted back to Ellie. "Actually, I think I have. Yep."

Graham beamed at her, just as Ellie gave him a little punch to the ribs. Laughing, he jumped away in surprise.

"Fine," he said. "You win."

The woman blinked a few times, and Ellie smiled at her. "Thanks," she said. "I think we'll just have some ice cream."

Afterward, they took their cones outside to one of the picnic tables, where they ate fast, trying to keep them from dripping. They were the only ones out there, alone except for the cars that rushed by, and the occasional seagull.

"This does feel sort of like cheating," Ellie said, and he looked across at her, his stomach tightening. She'd never mentioned a boyfriend, but then, they'd always avoided anything too specific, and he realized now he'd never even thought to ask. He was still working out how to phrase his question when she held up her ice cream.

"Ah," he said, realizing what she meant. He felt his shoulders relax. "I'm sure the good folks at Sprinkles will forgive you."

"Especially since it was in pursuit of a quest."

"A failed quest," he pointed out.

"Still."

"I think you have to be more of a believer for these things to work," he said, wiping some ice cream from his face. "How are you supposed to find what you're looking for if you're not convinced it's even out there?"

"Yeah, well, if I remember correctly, Ahab caught a few glimpses of Moby-Dick, and Dorothy definitely knew her home was in Kansas," she said with a grin. "At the moment, the whoopie pie is still nothing but a myth."

Graham smiled too, and when their eyes met, they remained there like that for several seconds, stuck in an odd kind of staring contest, before Ellie looked away.

"Okay," she said, tossing the last of her ice-cream cone to the seagulls that were milling about nearby. "Time to pay up."

She fished a pencil out of her bag, then grabbed a menu from the pile stacked beneath a rock in the middle of the table and flipped it over, sliding it across to Graham. He wiped his hands on his shorts and frowned.

"I never said I was good," he told her, taking the pen. "Just that I liked doing it."

"That's the best kind of good."

"Any requests?"

"One of your cities," she said as he bent his head over the paper. He could feel her watching him as he drew, sketching out a series of boxes. He'd been telling the truth; he *wasn't* good. It was really more geometry than art, what he did, but he felt himself settling into the motion, the precision of the lines and the sureness of the corners. There was something methodical about it, something cathartic; when he drew, the rest of the world fell away.

He'd filled nearly half the page before she spoke again, and her words startled him enough that his pencil ripped a tiny hole in the paper. He rubbed at it, trying to smooth it out again, then glanced up.

"Sorry," he said. "What?"

"That woman recognized you."

136

He held the pencil very still and felt his muscles go tense. "Yes."

"That must be..."

He waited for her to say what everyone else always said: That must be cool. Or that must be weird. That must be disconcerting. That must be a dream come true. That must be interesting or awful, crazy or bizarre.

Instead, she shook her head and started again. "That must be hard."

He raised his eyes, but said nothing.

"It would be for me, anyway. All those people recognizing you. All those cameras. All those eyes." She lifted her shoulders. "It must be really, really hard."

"It is," he said, because it was. Because it was like walking around with your skin turned inside out, tender and pink and shockingly exposed.

But at the moment, the only person looking at him was Ellie, and that was different. He didn't want to think about all the rest of it.

"You get used to it," he said, though it wasn't exactly true. It was just a thing to say when the truth was too hard to explain.

She nodded, and he turned back to his drawing, finishing up the last few buildings, putting in the windows and the doors, tending to the stairs and the sidewalks, adding the occasional flowerpot or fire escape. There was a world to be built right there on the page, and Graham didn't look up again until he'd finished.

"Ta-da," he said eventually, sliding it across the rough wood of the picnic table. Ellie propped an elbow on either side of it, and he could see only the top of her red hair as she studied it for what felt like forever.

Finally, she looked up at him. "Seems like a nice place to live."

"Probably not as nice as Maine."

"Except they have whoopie pies there," she said, pointing to a squat building he'd labeled "Whoopie Pie Factory."

"They have them here too," he said. "Don't worry, we'll find them."

"Aren't you gonna sign your work?" she asked, nudging the drawing back over to him, and for a second, he hesitated, all the usual alarm bells going off in his head. But this was different; he knew she wouldn't sell it online, or let it fall into the hands of bloggers or photographers or journalists, all the many wolves that paced the perimeters of his life. He scrawled his name across the bottom of the page, then started to fold it, matching up the corners, but she reached out and grabbed his hand.

"Don't," she said, and he stopped. But even so, she didn't let go. Her hand felt hot against his, and it sent a jolt straight through him. After a moment, her cheeks flushed pink and she pulled away, turning to take a small book from her bag.

"You can't fold it," she said, holding the page between two fingers and slipping it neatly inside the cover of the book. "You'll ruin it."

"Doesn't something have to be valuable first?" he joked. "Before it can be ruined?"

"Anything can be ruined," she said with a little shrug as she rose to her feet.

Graham stood too, and as he did, the stone heart fell out of his pocket, rolling to a stop on the grass near the foot of the bench. Ellie was already making her way back toward the road, but he paused to pick it up, examining it for a moment before slipping it back into his pocket, where he hoped it would remain safe.

From: EONeill22@hotmail.com
Sent: Monday, June 10, 2013 6:32 PM
To: GDL824@yahoo.com
Subject: if you get lost...

I know you said you didn't need directions, but in case you've forgotten, the address is 510 E. Sunset. It's the yellow house on the corner. (Which, coincidentally, looks a little like the whoopie pie factory in your drawing...)

They parted at the top of Sunset Drive, and Ellie followed the road the rest of the way on her own. The sea air was heavy this evening, and a fog was rolling in, making everything look indistinct and slightly unreal. But she barely noticed; she was too busy thinking about the last few hours: the way Graham had looked up from his drawing, the way he'd grinned at her across the candy store, the way his hair curled slightly at the back of his neck as she followed him up the beach.

But mostly, she was trying to figure out why—at the time—she'd thought it would be a good idea to invite him over to her house for dinner tonight, and the fact that he'd actually said yes. Now the list of everything she needed to do before he arrived was running through her head like some sort of unending news ticker, and she was trying hard not to panic.

It seemed impossible that this might turn out well, but if there was even the slightest chance that it could, she'd need to make sure Mom left on time for her book club (for once), that the kitchen was clean (for once), and that Bagel got enough exercise beforehand so that he'd act like a beagle instead of a banshee (for once). And that was just for starters. There were about a thousand ways this could go horribly wrong. Hopefully there would be enough food in the house to make something resembling an actual meal. Hopefully Mom didn't have inventory from the shop all over the living room. Hopefully the air conditioner had miraculously fixed itself while she'd been out.

Hopefully.

The road curved downhill, and she let the momentum carry her faster, her sandals slapping the pavement as she wondered what she could have been thinking. It was just that she couldn't imagine going out to eat with him in town tonight; not with the photographers there, not after what happened with Quinn just the night before, not with everyone she knew keeping an eye on them. And so when he'd suggested the Lobster Pot again—half joking, she knew, but still—Ellie found herself inviting him over instead.

"I can't promise much in the way of gourmet food," she told him, "but I can guarantee there won't be a lobster in sight."

"Wow," he'd said. "You really know how to sell a place."

But he'd accepted. He was coming over. To her house. In one hour.

Ellie was already halfway up the driveway before she realized, with a start, that Quinn was perched on the porch swing, using one foot to rock back and forth as she examined her nails.

"Hey," she said, looking up at the sound of footsteps. "Where've you been?"

"Out for a walk," Ellie said, sitting down beside her. The swing creaked beneath their combined weight, and she remembered the two of them coming out here with blankets when they were little. They'd huddle together, pretending the bench was a boat, closing their eyes and letting the waves down the street complete the illusion that they were out at sea.

"Where to?" Quinn asked.

But Ellie knew that wasn't what she really wanted to know. "With Graham," she said quietly, looking at her sideways.

Quinn shook her head. "It still seems kind of unbelievable, doesn't it?"

Ellie could think of nothing to say to this; it was true. The whole thing was nothing if not unbelievable.

"So I have about a million questions," Quinn said, tucking her legs up beneath her on the swing. "How'd he first start e-mailing you? And really, how could you not tell me you were writing love letters to someone? I mean, even if you take Graham Larkin out of the equation, that's still something I should know. I'm your best friend." When she paused to consider this, her face darkened slightly. "Seriously, El. When did you become the kind of person who keeps secrets?"

Ellie looked away, unsure how to respond. Quinn had no idea that she'd gotten right to the heart of the truth about her. She didn't realize that for the whole twelve years they'd been friends, Ellie had been doing just that: keeping secrets; at first, out of a promise to her mother, and then later, when they were older, out of habit or instinct or maybe both, a muffling of something too big to say out loud.

"I'm not..." she began, but trailed off. "I was going to tell you."

"Yeah?" Quinn asked. "When?" There was a sudden hardness behind her eyes now. It was as if she'd known she was upset about something, but hadn't until this moment been able to pinpoint just what it was.

"Soon," Ellie said, swiveling to face her more fully. "I swear. I just didn't know what exactly this was, or if it would turn out to be anything at all. I thought it was just some random kid on the other side of the country who I'd probably never meet." She sighed. "I guess I didn't know if it was real."

"And now?"

She glanced down at her hands. Her thumb was smudged with gray from where she'd picked up the pencil Graham used for his drawing earlier. She fought the urge to take the piece of paper out of her bag and examine it again.

"I don't know," she admitted. "Maybe."

Quinn raised her eyebrows, and Ellie shook her head.

"Or maybe not. I mean, he's Graham Larkin," she said,

but even as she did, she was thinking the opposite. That he hadn't seemed like Graham Larkin today. He'd seemed like that random kid on the other side of the country.

Behind them, the screen door opened, and Mom stuck her head out, using her foot to keep Bagel—who was constantly attempting a jailbreak—inside the house. "I *thought* I heard someone," she said. "What're you guys up to?"

"Ellie was just telling me about—" Quinn began, but stopped abruptly when she noticed Ellie's widened eyes.

"I was just seeing if she wanted to stay for dinner," Ellie said a bit too quickly.

Mom shrugged. "I've got book club tonight, but you two are welcome to whatever's in the fridge."

"Thanks," Ellie said. "What time are you leaving? You probably have to go pretty soon, huh?"

Mom glanced at her watch. "In a little bit," she said, then ducked back through the door along with the dog.

When she was gone, Quinn turned back to Ellie. "What the hell was that?"

"Sorry, it's just that Graham's actually coming over soon, but I haven't had a chance to talk to her about it, and she wouldn't be happy that—"

"So you're lying to your mom now too?" Quinn asked, her eyebrows raised. "Seriously, what's with all the secrets?"

"This is different," Ellie told her. "It's complicated."

"How?"

She lowered her eyes. "I can't tell you."

"Let me guess," Quinn said. "Another secret."

147

"I'm sorry," she said. "Really. There's more to it than..."
She stopped and shook her head. "I wish I could explain."

"Don't bother," Quinn said, standing up. "I have to go.
I've got plans tonight too."

"Really?"

Quinn's eyes were cold. "Is that so hard to believe?"

"Of course not," Ellie said quickly. "What are you
up to?"

"I'm hanging out with Devon."

"You are?" she said before she could think better of it.
But it was too late. Quinn had whirled around and was
watching her with narrowed eyes.

Ellie couldn't help it. For the last four years, all she'd
heard about was how ridiculous Devon was. He was too
tall and too skinny; his hair was too curly and his glasses
were always lopsided. She and Quinn had spent countless
hours laughing about the way he followed her like a shadow,
and everyone at school remembered the time freshman
year that Quinn's locker had gotten jammed on Valentine's
Day. When the janitor finally managed to open it for her, a
whole pile of pink envelopes came tumbling out, and for
months after that, poor Devon was teased about his crush
on the janitor, a stooped man in his seventies.

But clearly something had changed last night, and Devon
was no longer a punch line. Just like that, Ellie felt like
some sort of invisible boundary had shifted, and she found
herself on the opposite side from Quinn, who was now
glaring at her.

"Yes, *really*."

"I'm sorry," Ellie said. "Really. I guess I'm just still getting used to the idea of you and Devon."

Quinn stood there on the steps for another moment, frowning at Ellie across the porch. "Well, I guess not everyone's cut out to date a celebrity," she said, and then, without another word, she walked off toward the road.

"Quinn," Ellie said, but Quinn didn't turn around, and there was nothing to do but watch her go. As she sat there on the porch, her heart sank. Even if she were to run after her, she knew there wasn't much she could say right now. Because the problem had nothing to do with Devon and it had nothing to do with Graham; the problem was that Quinn was absolutely right, more than she even knew. Ellie *had* been keeping secrets from her, and the only way to make things right was to tell the truth. But that wasn't an option.

She'd been in enough fights with Quinn over the years to know that it didn't matter how or when you apologized. If she wasn't ready to hear it, then it wouldn't change anything. Quinn would come around in her own time—she always did—but Ellie had never been very good at the waiting, and even now, her stomach was already churning at the thought.

Tomorrow, she'd call. Tomorrow, she'd start her apology campaign. But for now, there was no time to worry about it. Graham would be here in less than an hour, and she still hadn't been inside to survey the damage.

When she pushed open the screen door, Bagel came barreling down the front hallway, pinballing off the walls and scattering the collection of rain boots and umbrellas that lined them. Ellie stood on the ratty welcome mat and watched the dog kick up a dust bunny from underneath the table in the foyer. With a sigh, she dropped her bag beside the door and ventured into the kitchen.

Mom was eating a cup of yogurt at the sink, absently watching the news on the ancient TV beside the toaster. One whole counter was covered in newspapers, the dates ranging from yesterday to two weeks ago, and the sink was brimming with dishes.

"What time is book club?" Ellie asked, eyeing Mom's outfit, which consisted of sweatpants and a plaid button-down with slippers.

Her eyes drifted over to the microwave clock. "Oh," she said, looking genuinely surprised. "It's right now."

"You better go then," Ellie said, hustling her out of the kitchen and then lingering in the hallway to make sure she made it all the way up the stairs. Then she turned to the sink, grabbed a sponge, and began to attack the dishes.

"I thought Quinn was staying for dinner," Mom said when she appeared again a few minutes later, wearing the same plaid shirt but now with a pair of jeans and loafers.

"She had to run some errands in town first," Ellie said, ducking her head so Mom wouldn't notice how red her face was; she'd never been much of a liar. "We'll be fine, though. Take your time."

150

"Okay," Mom said, grabbing her keys from on top of a pile of coupons. "Will you be sure to feed Bagel too?"

Ellie nodded and waved a soapy hand, letting out a breath when she heard the door slam shut again. She leaned against the sink with a sigh, daunted by the state of the house. When she turned her head, Bagel was sitting by her foot, tail wagging furiously.

"This is going to be a disaster," she told the dog, who only smiled a big doggie smile and continued to wave his white-tipped tail.

By the time she finished the dishes, cleared some of the debris from the counters, tossed the ball for Bagel, and fed him a meal only marginally less appetizing than the dinner options in the fridge, there were just a few more minutes to shower and change and inspect the place before Graham was meant to arrive.

Upstairs, Ellie was about to throw on her usual jeans, but instead chose a green sundress her mom had recently bought for her, ripping off the tags with her teeth. She usually hated to wear green; with her red hair, she worried it made her look like a Christmas ornament, but as she stood in front of the mirror, she realized it looked better than she would have thought. Not exactly up to Hollywood standards, but it would have to do.

With two minutes to spare, she headed back downstairs, running through her checklist again. She wasn't really expecting him to be on time; boys were always late, and her limited knowledge of movie stars suggested they would probably be even worse. There would still be time to tidy up, hide any embarrassing childhood photos, take down a few of the lobster knickknacks that littered the house.

But as she walked back into the kitchen, her heart fell.

There were no more newspapers on the counters, no more silly magnets on the fridge; she'd hidden Bagel's squeaky toys in a cabinet and the dishes were all put away. The house looked nice, maybe as nice as it ever would. But standing there, seeing it as if through Graham's eyes, Ellie understood that it would never look nice *enough*.

It was small and cluttered and shabby. The twelve years they'd lived there showed in the scuffed walls and the scarred wooden floor, the thin film of dust that coated every framed photo. The knob on the kitchen sink had been broken for so long they almost forgot there was something wrong with it, and it was hard to know when the white refrigerator had turned beige.

Her eyes darted around the room, and she pushed down a wave of alarm. How could she have thought this would be a good idea? He wasn't just some guy; he was a movie star. His bathroom was probably bigger than their kitchen, his bedroom bigger than their whole house. Ellie had never been to California, but she imagined everything there as sleek and new, about a million miles away from this ramshackle place, the paint worn by the salt from the ocean, the porch sagging from years of wear.

She reached for her phone, thinking she'd e-mail him and change their plans. The idea of going into town and facing all those photographers was intimidating, but could it be worse than this? Having Graham Larkin stand on the cracked linoleum floor of their kitchen, eating leftovers out of their chipped bowls?

She knew there would be consequences if her picture ended up in the papers. Her mom would be furious, but it was more than that too: it was the possibility that someone might put two and two together. Their whole existence here was built upon a secret, and it would take only one mistake to ruin everything.

But behind her, the dog was drinking out of the bathroom toilet, and on the windowsill, the air conditioner groaned loudly before chugging to a stop.

Ellie bit her lip and stared at the phone in her hand.

But it was too late.

With a sharp bark, Bagel went crashing down the hallway, and a split second later, the sound of the doorbell rang out through the tiny house.

From: GDL824@yahoo.com
Sent: Monday, June 10, 2013 7:24 PM
To: EONeill22@hotmail.com
Subject: Re: if you get lost...

I'm on my way. (And trust me, I'm not lost.)

10

For the past hour, Graham had been wandering the streets of Henley. When he told Ellie he needed to run back to his hotel and check on a few things, he'd been lying. He just wanted to give her some time to get ready. The moment the dinner invitation had slipped out of her mouth, he could see that a part of her had wanted to take it back.

He should have told her not to worry, right then and there, as they stood at the top of Sunset Drive, the late-afternoon light coming through the leaves in a way that made the freckles on her nose stand out. He wished he'd told her that he'd grown up in a house not much bigger than hers, where the bathroom tiles were crumbling, and the basement smelled funny, and the stairs conducted a chorus of creaks and groans each time someone had the nerve to climb them.

He should have told her that his parents still lived there, only now, when he came to visit, his mother prepared the house as if for a stranger, some visiting dignitary or long-lost relative who might be impressed by flowers on the windowsill or neatly folded towels, all meant to disguise the true nature of the place, to make it unrecognizable when all Graham really wanted—all he was ever there for in the first place—was the exact opposite: to find his way home again.

But the words had failed him. He'd become so accustomed to keeping those sorts of thoughts to himself that he no longer seemed capable of sharing them at all.

In town, he walked with his head down, moving past small groups of tourists examining the menus outside of local restaurants. At the end of the street, the movie set was silent, the hulking trailers dark and empty. They'd long since wrapped for the day, but even so, Graham knew Mick would still be buzzing around somewhere, going over the script or checking on the equipment before tomorrow's scene, which would be their first filming out on the water.

As he passed a hardware store with one of those old-fashioned mechanical horses out front, he noticed a sign in the window announcing the annual Fourth of July festival, and he paused to examine it more closely. Every year, it seemed, there was an all-day party in the town square, a concert and cookout followed by dancing and a fireworks display, and even now, Graham could almost picture it: the streets filled with people, kids running around with sparklers, the distant pop of firecrackers, and the swell of music in the air. It reminded him of the celebrations in his own hometown, and he was struck by the memory of all the parades he'd watched with his parents when he was younger, the three of them waving flags as the marching bands boomed past.

He was halfway down the block, heading in the direction of Ellie's house, when it occurred to him that he'd still be in Henley then. The production wouldn't be moving back to L.A. until a couple of days after the Fourth, and though Graham couldn't remember the exact schedule at the moment—had, in fact, hardly even looked at it yet—he was sure they must have at least a little bit of time off during the holiday weekend.

Before he had a chance to think it through, he pulled his phone from his pocket and dialed his parents. As it rang, the possibilities of the weekend expanded in his mind, and he found himself smiling at the idea of it. His parents had only ever visited him once on set, and that was right at the beginning, during one of his first scenes, which had been shot in a studio in L.A. They'd been hopelessly out of place, the two of them standing off to the side in their cable-knit sweaters and glasses, his mom shivering from the low temperatures in the studio, his dad squinting against the glare of the lights. During a break, his mother had given him a kiss on the cheek and explained that she wasn't feeling well, and Graham watched them walk out the door with a leaden feeling in his stomach, a sense that something had already been lost between them.

But this would be different. He could show them around,

impress them with his knowledge of the production, let them see him in action in a place where they'd be more comfortable. He'd take them on a tour of the town, buy them dinner at the Lobster Pot, bring them to the festival so that they could watch the fireworks together, just like they had when he was younger. Maybe he'd go fishing with his dad. Maybe they could even meet Ellie.

When the answering machine picked up—the same recorded message that had been on there for years—he snapped back, clearing his throat. "Hey, guys," he said, then hesitated. "It's me. Just wanted to see if you had plans for the Fourth. If not, I was thinking maybe you could come out and visit the set. You'd love it here. It sort of reminds me of home. And it could be fun for you to spend the weekend. I'm in Maine, by the way. Can't remember if you knew that. Anyway, let me know what you think..."

He trailed off, then hung up fast, already feeling less certain of his plan. His parents hardly ever traveled. When Graham was a kid, they took exactly one family vacation a year, driving two hours to an oceanside motel, where they'd stay exactly three days before returning home again, pink-cheeked and sun-drunk from their hours on the beach. It wasn't that they weren't curious about the world; it was just that it was all they could afford on two teachers' salaries.

"We live in California," they'd always say cheerily. "Our whole life is like a vacation."

But the California that Graham had grown up in was

160

very different from the one he lived in now. It was even different from the one where he'd gone to school, a twenty-minute drive from home that might as well have been twenty hours. Just before his freshman year, he'd managed to win a partial academic scholarship to a private school a few towns over, and his parents used the money his grandparents left him to make up for the rest. It was an amount that had seemed vast to Graham at the time, and he'd felt guilty about taking it when there were so many other things they could have done with it: make repairs on the house, replace their puttering car, pay off the bills that seemed to .collect on his dad's desk with alarming frequency.

Now, of course, Graham had enough money to do all of those things: he could buy his parents a brand-new home or a whole fleet of cars, send them on a trip around the world or pay down all their debt without even blinking. But the only thing they really wanted—the only thing they'd *ever* really wanted—was for him to go to college.

It wasn't that they weren't supportive of his acting, but they seemed to regard it as something to be tolerated, a stopover on the way to higher education rather than something that might shape the rest of his life. The only movies his dad ever watched were old black-and-white classics, and he didn't consider anything made in the last few decades to count as art. When Graham took them to the premiere of his first movie, they clapped and smiled in all the right places, but he'd been acutely aware of how it all must have looked to them: the fight sequences strewn with high-octane special effects, the over-the-top dialogue, and, worst of all, the scene where he'd finally kissed the heroine, which had not until that moment struck him as unbearably cheesy.

Graham knew that even as they tiptoed around him, strangers in the foreign terrain of his new life, they were hoping he might come to his senses, get this whole acting thing out of his system. They had a habit of talking about his career as if it were a gap year of sorts, as if he were putting off college to run away for a season with the circus or spend a few months studying the mating habits of monkeys in Bali. But the truth was that Graham had no intention of going to college next year. Once he finished his high school equivalency with the help of his on-set tutor, that would be it for him.

Part of it was that he truly enjoyed acting, and he couldn't imagine walking away from the ever-expanding opportunities in his future, all the actors he still wanted to work with and the roles he still wanted to play. And part of it was that he just didn't see the point. The idea of college was to study hard in order to get a good job, in order to make a lot of money. But he already had plenty of money, enough to last him his whole life. And he could learn anywhere, couldn't he?

But if he was being really honest, it was about more than just that. The way he'd always pictured college—hurrying to classes in ivy-leafed buildings and trudging up snow-covered pathways in the winter, sitting perched on the bleachers during football games and debating philosophy in rooms full of bright-eyed students—seemed hopelessly distant from his new life, where he'd completely lost the ability to blend in. And the last thing he wanted was to be one of those celebrities who fancied themselves a scholar, making a halfhearted effort at being a normal college kid while being trailed by cameras and gawked at by classmates, missing finals to jet off and shoot an indie film in Vancouver. Graham had no interest in being any more of a spectacle than he already was.

He knew his parents were quietly hoping he'd change his mind, and he hated to disappoint them. But he felt sure about his decision. And that had become just one more reason that they no longer seemed to understand one another, that they'd become less like a family and more like three people who had once lived together for a time.

What they needed, Graham was thinking now as he neared Ellie's house, was an old-fashioned family vacation. What they needed was food and flags and fireworks in a place that was about as far from California as you could get. In just a few short days here, he already felt like a different person. Maybe Henley would work its magic on his parents as well.

But when the door opened and Ellie appeared—her long hair still damp from the shower, looking beautiful in a bright green sundress—he realized it wasn't Henley at all.

It was her.

He leaned forward to kiss her—a movement so automatic it felt like tying his shoe or climbing the stairs, something you do without even thinking about it—and he was still several inches away when he wrenched himself back unsteadily, everything coming into focus with an abrupt-ness that startled him.

They hadn't even had their first kiss yet, and here he was, leaning in like it was something that happened every day, a motion like a ritual, like they'd kissed a thousand times before. It took a moment to right himself, and he pulled his shoulders back as he regained his equilibrium. He didn't want to be half asleep the first time he kissed Ellie. For that, he wanted to be wide awake.

She was eyeing him with a look of confusion, and Graham couldn't tell what she was thinking. Hopefully she didn't realize that's what he'd been about to do.

Hopefully she just thought he had terrible balance.

"Hi," he said with a sheepish grin.

"Come on in," she said, looking somewhat flustered herself.

She ushered him into a hallway that smelled of lemon cleaning solution, and Graham stooped to pet Bagel, who was sniffing his shoes with a businesslike air. They both followed Ellie into the kitchen, where the table was set for two. The room was dimly lit and there was still a hint of dish soap in the air. But Graham hardly noticed anything beyond that; his eyes were pinned to Ellie's green dress as she moved between the cabinets and the refrigerator and back again, her face apologetic.

"It's not like we ever have a lot of good stuff here," she was saying, "but I figured there'd at least be a frozen pizza or something."

"So what you're saying is," Graham teased, "there's no lobster?"

She narrowed her eyes at him. "Very funny."

"It's fine," he said, moving beside her to examine the contents of the pantry. He pulled out a nearly empty box of crackers and a can of tuna. "We'll have a smorgasbord. A little of this and a little of that."

"I'm sorry," she said, leaning against the sink. "We probably should've gone into town. I can't believe I'm feeding you stale crackers."

"Are you kidding?" he said, sweeping an arm around the room. "Not just anyone gets to eat at Chez O'Neill. I've heard this is one of the most exclusive establishments in Maine."

"That's true," she said with a grin. "We only cater to A-list celebrities."

They rummaged through the refrigerator, spilling everything out onto the counter and then standing side by side as they assembled the meal, a random assortment ranging from microwave popcorn to apple slices, two leftover pieces of pizza, and some frozen peas. What looked less than appetizing went right to Bagel, and the rest made it to the kitchen table, where they arranged the dishes in front of them as if it were a buffet.

"So," Graham said as he pulled out a chair. "Did you ever figure out if you're doing that poetry course?"

Ellie looked surprised at the question, and he smiled, because it was the same way he'd felt when she mentioned his drawings earlier, like she'd plucked the thought straight out of his head. She stood on tiptoe to grab a bowl from a high shelf, and when she turned around again, she nodded.

"I'm going in August," she said, but there was a catch in her voice. "I'm pretty excited about it. They have this one professor there that—"

"So you figured out how to pay for it?" he asked, and Ellie went stiff. She turned her back to him again, dumping a partially empty bag of tortilla chips into the bowl. Already, Graham was regretting the question. When they'd talked about this over e-mail, it had been so easy for her to tell him these things, but something had shifted now, and the question no longer felt quite right in person.

"Not exactly," she said lightly. "But I've got another month or so to figure it out."

"How much more do you need?" he asked, and she looked embarrassed.

"Enough," she told him, her face coloring. There was an awkward silence, and Graham realized his mistake. Part of him had wanted to rescue her, to swoop in with the money she needed, but he could see now that this would only make it worse. And by bringing up the issue of money so casually, he'd managed to remind her again of who he was: not the boy on the other end of the e-mails, but the movie star who was sitting in her kitchen. He could feel the easy rapport between them turning brittle, and he cleared his throat as she set down the bowl of chips, desperate to change the subject.

"This looks good," he said, and he could see her shoulders relax. "I've never had fortune cookies with chips and salsa before."

"Well," she said with a slow-blooming grin, "we're on the cutting edge of the Chinese-Mexican fusion movement here at Chez O'Neill."

"I like it," he said. "Three stars."

"What?" she said, sitting down across the table from him. "Only three?"

"That's the most you can get, I think."

"That doesn't seem like a lot," she said. "I'd prefer ten."

"How about two thumbs up?"

"Now you're confusing this with the movies," she said, licking some peanut butter off her finger. "Speaking of which, how's it going?"

"The movie?"

She nodded.

"Okay," he said.

"You don't sound very excited about it."

"No, I am," he told her, reaching for an apple slice and popping it into his mouth. "It's nice to be doing something different. And the director's really...interesting."

"Think you'll work with him again?" she asked. "I mean, you must get your pick, right?"

"I guess," he said. "But I haven't figured out what I'm doing next."

"Well, what do you want to do?"

"Something that matters."

She tilted her head to one side, considering this. "You mean something that matters to *you*?"

He nodded. "Hopefully."

"You'll know it when it comes along," she said. "But it must be kind of fun to be playing a new character. I saw the trailer for the first movie, and there was that part where—"

Graham sat forward. "Wait," he said, laughing. "You only saw the trailer?"

Ellie reached for her water and took a sip, hiding behind a blue plastic mug that was emblazoned with a smiling whale.

"You never saw the movies?"

"Well, the third one isn't even out yet," she said, setting her mug back on the table and picking up a fortune cookie.

"Yeah, but the first two?"

She shrugged. "Quinn tried to drag me to the first one, but it's not really my kind of movie."

"I thought every teen girl in America was obsessed with them," Graham said, amazed. It had been an embarrassingly long time since he'd met someone who hadn't seen those films, or at least pretended they had.

"You're thinking of you," Ellie corrected. "Every teen girl in America is obsessed with *you*."

He laughed. "So I take it you're not a big Graham Larkin fan?"

"I am now," she said, cracking open the fortune cookie.

She drew out the little strip of white paper with a frown, then laughed. "It says: *You will receive a fortune cookie.*"

"No way," Graham said, and she passed it over so that he could look for himself. "That's the best fortune ever."

Ellie took a bite of the cookie. "Well, it's the most obvious, anyway."

"Most fortunes don't ever come true," he said, shaking his head at the tiny scroll. "But this one already did. I mean, would you rather have a fortune that promised you a delicious cookie and came true instantly, or one that promised a million dollars and never came true at all?"

"At the moment, I think I'd take a million dollars," she said, brushing the crumbs off the table so that the dog, who was beside her in a flash, could finish it off. "The cookie wasn't nearly as delicious as advertised."

"Bagel seems to disagree."

"His palate is similar to that of a vacuum cleaner," she said, looking down at him fondly. "So are you ready for your scene tomorrow?"

He shrugged, but it wasn't very convincing.

"I bet you were supposed to be learning your lines instead of hanging out with me all afternoon," she said, leaning forward on her elbows. "Do you know them?"

"More or less," he said, folding a piece of pizza in half. Bagel, who had taken up a new post beside him, thumped his tail a few times, and Graham tossed him the crust. "I've been carrying them around in my pocket all day, so I'm hoping there's been some osmosis action."

"I'm sure all the great actors rely on osmosis," she said, then reached a hand across the table. "Can I see? We could practice."

Graham sat back in his chair. "It's okay," he said, suddenly embarrassed. Acting on set was one thing; acting in front of the girl you liked was another. He wasn't about to get into character in front of Ellie. "I'll be fine.

"Come on," she said, bobbing her outstretched hand. "It'll be fun."

"Fine," he said, sitting up to pull the folded papers from his back pocket. "But I'm not doing it for real, okay? Just running the lines."

"I don't get to see the full Graham Larkin effect?" she teased, taking the section of script from him. "I guess I'll just have to stop by the set tomorrow."

"You'll have to be a pretty good swimmer then," he told her. "We're gonna be filming out on a boat."

"Okay, Ahab," she said, studying the lines on the page. When she looked up again, her face seemed somehow different; her lips were pouty, and she was looking at him from underneath her eyelashes. She tossed her hair in an exaggerated way, and it took Graham a moment to realize where he'd seen the gesture before: she was mimicking Olivia.

"Not bad," he said, but he was also relieved when she dropped the act and examined the script one more time with a more familiar expression.

"Okay, here we go," she said, clearing her throat. " 'Where

are you going, Jasper?'" She stopped and looked up with raised eyebrows. "Your name is Jasper?"

He shrugged, and she continued.

"'Come back!'" she shouted with a melodramatic flourish, loud enough to cause Bagel to lurch up, his collar jangling, his head cocked to one side.

Graham reached down and gave him a little pat. "That was great," he told Ellie. "Not at all over the top."

"I never said *I* wasn't doing it for real," she pointed out. "Your line."

"'I need to be alone right now,'" Graham said in a flat voice to underscore the fact that he wasn't really playing along. "'I just need some time to think.'"

Ellie tilted her head to one side. "I know I'm not an expert, but I'm betting you could do it with a little more feeling."

"Everyone's a critic, Bagel," he told the little dog, who whined at him in sympathy as Ellie turned back to the script.

"'You have no idea what you need right now. You have no idea—'" She paused there, her eyes still on the page.

Graham honestly couldn't remember what came next. He'd planned to study his lines later in the hotel room, and his call time wasn't until noon tomorrow, so he'd have the morning too. He'd memorized whole scenes before with less time than that to spare.

"You're supposed to kiss me," Ellie said, looking up at him with an unreadable expression. Graham's stomach

171

dipped, and he stared across the table at her, unable to formulate a response. The room was quiet except for the ticking of the clock above the stove and the soft breathing of the dog, and it took a moment for Ellie to shake her head. When she spoke, her voice sounded very bright. "It's in the script," she said, pointing at the page without taking her eyes off Graham.

He nodded quickly. "Right," he said, blinking fast.

"You're supposed to kiss me," she said again, then blushed and held up the crumpled papers. "I mean, Olivia. Or—" She glanced at the words. "Zoe. Really? Jasper and Zoe? Who writes this stuff?"

She was back to examining the script now, but Graham wasn't really listening. Her words were still rolling around in his head: *You're supposed to kiss me.*

She was right, of course. He was supposed to kiss her. He was supposed to kiss her just a little while ago, when he arrived at the house. He was supposed to kiss her earlier today on the beach. And that day in town. And that first night, right outside on her porch.

Suddenly, it seemed there were about a million times he was supposed to have kissed her, even without the benefit of a script, even without any sort of direction. Almost without thinking about it, he placed his hands on the table and scraped back his chair. It wasn't until she smiled at him that he realized he was smiling too.

"I think it's important," he said as he stood up, "to follow the script."

"Yeah?" she said, her smile widening.

But a light swept across the darkened windows above the sink then, disappearing briefly before landing squarely in Graham's eyes again. He stepped aside, blinking, and when he turned back to Ellie, she was up and out of her chair.

"Shoot," she muttered. "She's home early."

"Who?" Graham asked, feeling disoriented. A moment ago, everything had been in slow motion, and now it was as if someone had yelled "Cut!" and the spell was broken. *I was supposed to kiss her*, he thought, and the whole evening felt suddenly like a song that had been switched off before the last bars had played, leaving only a wrenching sense of incompleteness.

"My mom," Ellie was saying as she cleared the table. "She must not have been a fan of the book."

Outside, the headlights went out, and Graham could hear a car door slam. Bagel went trotting over to the back door, and a minute later, Ellie's mom appeared, her face tightening when she noticed Graham standing there in the middle of her kitchen, his hands in his pockets.

It had been a long time since he'd met someone who looked at him with such open suspicion. In his old life, he'd been great with parents; he was a nice kid, charming enough to win over most anyone. And in his new life, he'd gotten used to people falling all over themselves in an effort to please him. But the way Ellie's mom was eyeing him now, with a peculiar kind of mistrust, was something entirely new.

Graham shifted from one foot to the other and attempted a winning smile, which seemed to have no effect whatsoever.

"I thought Quinn was coming over," Mrs. O'Neill said to Ellie, her eyebrows raised as she dropped her purse on the kitchen counter.

"There was a change of plans," Ellie mumbled. "You remember Graham, right?"

Mrs. O'Neill nodded, but didn't offer a smile. "Nice to see you," she said, though she managed not to make it sound that way. "Enjoying Henley?"

"Yes," Graham said, biting back the "ma'am." "It's lovely here." He cleared his throat and dropped his eyes to the floor. He'd never used the word *lovely* before in his life.

"And how long are you all in town?"

"Another few weeks," he told her. "But I wish it was longer. It's really a lovely place." He coughed, his face hot. It seemed impossible that he'd just said the word *lovely* twice in under a minute. "Actually, I just invited my parents out for the Fourth," he said quickly, feeling himself begin to ramble, but unable to stop. "I thought they'd like it here too."

From across the room, Ellie gave him an encouraging smile. "That'll be fun," she said. "How long will they be here? We could give you some ideas of stuff to do while they're in town."

"Probably four or five days," Graham said, thinking even as he did just how unlikely that was. But he felt suddenly desperate for it to be true. "My dad and I are pretty into fishing, so we'll probably do that for some of the time."

"Sounds like fun," Ellie said, casting a glance at her mom. "Well, it's late..."

"Yeah," Graham said, taking a step toward the door. "Yeah, it is." He gave Mrs. O'Neill an awkward little wave. "Thanks so much for having me." Then he turned to Ellie, smiling at her from what felt like a great distance, even as he wanted nothing more than to cross the room and finish what they'd started. "I'll see you"—he was about to say "tomorrow," but thought better of it—"around."

And with that, he was sidestepping the dog on the way to the front hallway. Even as he made his way out the door and onto the porch, he was surprised to hear them begin to argue, their whispers drifting through the screen, harsh and raspy and much too loud.

Outside, the night had cooled off, and he stood there for a moment, trying to make sense of what had just happened. Maybe she was one of those mothers who didn't want her daughter spending time with boys. Or maybe it was just that they'd been alone in the house after dark. Or that she'd had a bad day. But whatever the reason, Graham knew it was best to make a quick exit, and he took a deep breath before stepping quietly off the porch.

He was almost to the end of the driveway when he heard the screen door bounce shut behind him, and then the sound of Ellie's bare feet on the pavement as she ran to meet him, shaking her head as she approached.

"I'm sorry—" she began, but that was as far as she got, because Graham couldn't wait any longer. He leaned in, his lips meeting hers, which tasted faintly of peanut butter, and he closed his eyes, and he held her by the shoulders, and he kissed her.

It was exactly as he'd thought it would be, like the first time and the millionth time all at once, like being wide awake, like losing his balance. Only this time, it wasn't just him; this time, they were losing their balance together.

From: EONeill22@hotmail.com
Sent: Monday, June 10, 2013 10:43 PM
To: GDL824@yahoo.com
Subject: Re: if you get lost...

I'm glad you didn't get lost.

11

Ellie woke to the smell of pancakes: a peace offering. Ever since she was little, this was all it took to signal the end of a fight. She and Mom had never argued very often, but when they did, it was a strictly nocturnal affair. The unspoken rule was that the next morning was a clean slate, and all of it—the dirty looks and the sharp words—would be left behind, leaving only heart-shaped pancakes in its place. The best kind of truce.

This morning, however, was different. Mom stood at the stove in her flannel pajama pants as usual, a cup of coffee in one hand and a spatula in the other. But when Ellie slid into her seat at the table, Mom only tossed her a thin smile before turning back around again.

It was Ellie's fault for cutting short their argument last night. By the time Graham left, she'd been vibrating like a tuning fork, shaking with anger over her mother's behavior.

"You can't just be rude," she'd whispered, once she was

certain he was out of earshot. "It's not his fault. I was the one who invited him over."

"Without telling me," Mom said, glaring at her. "I have no idea what you're doing hanging around with some teen heartthrob in the first place—"

"*Mom*," Ellie said, flushing.

"You know what's at stake here, and yet you deliberately go behind my back—"

"We were just eating dinner," she said, raising her hands in exasperation. "And the reason I made him come here is so we wouldn't get caught by any photographers in town. So it's not like I'm—"

"If you don't think they'll find out anyway, if you don't think everyone will know in about two seconds, then you're even more out of your league than I thought." Mom put two fingers to her temple like she had a terrible headache, and then let out a slow breath. "I mean, do you even know this guy, Ellie?"

"*Yes*," Ellie said, her voice low and fierce. "I know him. I do."

Mom shook her head as if she hadn't heard. "He's a movie star, for god's sake. He lives in California. He's going to be out of here in just a few weeks. How can you *possibly* think this is worth it?"

Ellie just stood there, letting the words wash over her. The air seemed to have gone out of the room, and even Bagel held perfectly still. But the question wasn't a difficult one; what her mother didn't understand was that

Graham wasn't some summer adventure, and he wasn't a fling. The reasons he was worth it had nothing to do with the reasons that so many girls pored over his pictures in the magazines.

It was much simpler than that. It was that he'd been happy to eat stale tortilla chips at her house tonight. And that he'd sketched her an entire city when she'd asked. It was the way he joked around, and the look behind his eyes when they met hers. It was all the hundreds of e-mails he'd sent her, the words they'd traded back and forth like precious currency for so many months.

It was that he already seemed to know her better than almost anyone, and it had been just a single day since they'd finally met in person. And if that was the case, then imagine what a few *more* days might bring.

Mom was still looking at her, waiting for an answer, but Ellie didn't bother. Instead, she spun around and headed for the door.

"Ellie," Mom called, but she didn't sound angry, just weary and confused. And it wouldn't have mattered anyway, because Ellie was already picking up speed, hurrying out the door and down the driveway, where the back of Graham's white shirt was still glowing in the surrounding darkness.

When he kissed her, it was like the answer to the question.

It was the only thing she needed to know.

"I'm sorry," she'd whispered again, once they broke

181

apart. He still had his hands on her shoulders, and he was gripping them like he wasn't sure he wanted to let go.

"It's okay," Graham said, glancing over at the lit windows of the kitchen. "But I should probably . . ."

Ellie nodded, and he leaned down to kiss her once more. She imagined there were thousands of girls who wanted to kiss Graham Larkin, who had imagined this very moment, but standing here in the darkened driveway, it wasn't like something out of a movie. It was better.

"Come find me tomorrow, okay?" he said, starting to walk away.

"Good luck with your scene," she said, and when he smiled, her heart lurched.

Afterward, when she'd stepped back inside the house, edging into the kitchen with a sheepish look, it was to discover that Mom had already gone upstairs. And so the argument simply dangled there, unfinished until this morning, when they were now forced to deal with it over their typically peaceful pancake breakfast.

"Look," Mom began, sliding a plate onto the table in front of Ellie, and then sitting down in the chair beside her. She leaned forward, and a strand of auburn hair slipped out of her ponytail. "Maybe it's unfair of me to judge without knowing the whole story."

Ellie reached for the bottle of syrup. "We've been e-mailing," she said without looking up. "For months now."

"How?" Mom asked. "I mean, how did you—"

"It was a mistake," she explained. "A mistyped e-mail

address. He was trying to write someone else, but it came to me instead, and we just started talking. I didn't know it was him. Graham Larkin, I mean. I thought it was just some guy."

"Well, that's comforting," Mom said. "I suppose we'll save the lecture on Internet safety for another day..."

"Mom," Ellie said with a groan.

She held up her hands. "I'm only saying that there are a lot of crazy people out there..."

"*Mom*," Ellie said again. "That's not the point."

"Okay, okay. Then what's the point?"

Ellie lifted her eyes. "The point is..." she said, then trailed off, taking a deep breath. "The point is that I'm glad I didn't know who it was, you know? Otherwise I never would've gotten to know him. Not really. Not like I do now."

Mom nodded. "And you like him."

"I do," Ellie said, her voice suddenly thick. "A lot."

On the griddle, the second batch of pancakes began to burn, and Mom rose from the table, then stood there long after she'd flipped them, her back to Ellie, her head tipped to the window above the sink.

"I don't know what to say," she said eventually, turning around. "I don't want you to get hurt."

"He wouldn't—"

"Ellie, come on," she said, and something in her face stopped Ellie cold. All of a sudden, she realized they weren't just talking about Graham. They were talking about her father too. "You know there are about a million ways this could go wrong," she continued, her voice strained. "Not just because of who he is, and not just because he's leaving soon." She pressed her lips together, considering her words. "You saw the way he gets followed around."

"You can't tell me not to date someone because he gets his picture taken a lot," Ellie said. "Do you even realize how crazy that sounds?"

"Everything about this is *already* crazy," Mom said, sliding the last two pancakes off the stove and onto a plate before returning to the table. "Things like this," she said, shaking her head. "They don't end well."

"You mean because it didn't end well for *you*," Ellie said with a frown. "This isn't the same thing. He's not some sleazy senator. I'm not some—"

"What?" Mom said, looking at her levelly. "Some cheap waitress?"

"I didn't say that," Ellie said, shaking her head. "You know I didn't mean that."

"Your father..." she began, then paused, looking far away. "It was complicated."

"Right," Ellie said. "But this is different. Graham is different."

"That's not the point," Mom said, glancing down at her plate. Neither of them had touched their food, and the pancakes were growing cold on the table. "He's someone in the public eye. And you don't want to get dragged into it."

"But what does it matter?" Ellie asked. "What happened with you and him—with my father—it's not like it's a secret. It's already been out there. So I don't understand why it's such a big deal if people find out. I don't get why we still have to hide."

"We're not hiding," Mom said, stabbing a piece of pancake with her fork. "We're just living our lives like normal people. That's not the same thing."

"But you don't want my picture in the papers."

"It's not just that," she said with a sigh. "It's that I don't want you under the microscope. Your picture would just be the start of that. You get that, right? All it takes is one photo of you and Graham Larkin for the photographers to start following you around. Then people start digging for information. And they think they have the right to share anything they might find. You were too little to remember the last time." She shook her head, wincing a little. "It's awful, what they do. There are no boundaries at all."

Ellie took a bite and chewed slowly, thinking this over. "But if that's the only reason, then wouldn't it be my decision?" she asked. "My risk to take?"

"It's not that simple," Mom said. "It affects me too. And your father."

Ellie snorted. "We're trying to protect *him* now?" she asked, sitting back in her chair and folding her arms. "He's never done one single thing for us, never even tried to find us—"

"You know that's because I told him not to."

"—and yet you still worry about him? If he ends up running for president, they'll probably find us anyway. So what's the difference?"

"They might," she said. "But they also might not. That was three campaigns ago now. There are new scandals all the time. They'll bring it up like they always do, but it doesn't mean they'll necessarily seek us out."

"I thought you just said there were no boundaries."

"As far as politics goes, it's old news," she said. "But as far as celebrity gossip? It's a big story. Anything involving that kid seems to be a big story." Mom pushed the last pancake around on her plate. "Don't you get it? We have a life here. I worked hard to make that happen. And once something like this is out there, you can't take it back."

Ellie's voice, when she spoke, was very small. "But I really like him."

"I know," Mom said, reaching out to put a hand on top of hers. "But even if your father wasn't an issue, you don't want this. Trust me. Nobody wants to wake up to photographers camped out on their front lawn. I'm sure Graham Larkin would say the same thing."

As she walked to work later, Ellie wondered if that was true. When she'd asked Graham about being recognized, he hadn't wanted to talk about it, though when it came to the photographers in town, he seemed oddly resigned, treating them with no more ill will than a pesky stray dog that refuses to take a hint. She'd seen so many photos of him in Quinn's magazines, leaving the gym or trying to have a quiet dinner at a restaurant, and it didn't seem possible that someone could ever get entirely used to that sort of thing.

As she passed the trailers, she noticed the crowds were thinner than usual, and she remembered Graham saying they'd be filming out on the water. Even so, she spotted one of the photographers smoking a cigarette off to the side, and she quickened her pace, still unsettled by the morning's conversation. She was grateful her first shift was at Sprinkles; even if Quinn was still mad at her, it would be better than being stuck in a small space with Mom all day as she tried to figure out what she was going to do about Graham.

But when she pushed open the door of the shop, she was surprised to see Devon's curly head pop up from behind the counter.

"Hey," she said, walking over and dropping her bag. "Where's Quinn?"

He slid his eyes away. "She asked me to cover her shift."

"How come?" Ellie asked. "Is she feeling okay?"

Devon nodded, but he still wouldn't look at her.

"Is she avoiding me?"

After a moment, he lifted his gaze. "I don't think so," he said. "I bet she just had something else she needed to do."

Ellie nodded. She'd known Devon since he was four years old; he was nice to a fault and unfailingly earnest. If he was lying, it was only to spare her feelings. With a sigh, she reached for the metal tub they used for dirty ice-cream scoops, taking it over to the sink in back, where she could be alone.

They spent much of the morning in silence. In between customers, Devon sat perched on a bar stool reading a worn copy of *The Great Gatsby*, and Ellie fought back the urge to pepper him with questions.

When her shift was up, she began to gather her things, and Devon lowered his book. "That's exciting about the movie guy."

Ellie smiled. "I guess."

"Want me to tell Quinn you said hi?"

"That'd be great," she said. "Thanks."

He nodded and resumed reading, but when she was nearly to the door, Ellie stopped and turned around again.

"Hey, Devon?" she said, and he looked up, his glasses slipping on his nose. "That's exciting about you and Quinn too."

His smile broadened. "Thanks."

Outside, the wind had picked up, and Ellie stood blinking away the dust and grit that were flying around. Down the street, she could see an unfamiliar boat coming into the harbor, two men in dark Windbreakers leaning off the bow, and even before she spotted Graham and Olivia, she guessed it was the one they were using for the movie. Someone cut the engine as it neared the buoys that marked the far edge of the harbor, and the boat slowed, a few seagulls making lazy circles above it.

Ellie was far enough away that she couldn't make out

anyone's face, but she could see that Olivia was standing very close to Graham, even as he looked out at the wake of the boat. She wondered if she should be feeling jealous. She realized most girls probably would. But from everything she knew about Olivia, it seemed like a guy would have to be schizophrenic in order to be interested in both her and Ellie at the same time. And from the way Graham had kissed her last night, she knew that wasn't the case. She knew he was only interested in her.

It was this that propelled her down the hill: the memory of that kiss. She was supposed to be at her mom's shop right now; her shift was just beginning, and there was plenty she needed to do. But as the boat came closer to the dock, Ellie found herself walking toward the water, as if drawn by some kind of magnetic force.

She still didn't know what she was going to do. Deep down, she understood that her mother was right. And not just about the cameras, but about all of it. The same thoughts kept tumbling around in her head, like clothes left too long in a dryer. He was too big a star. His life was too different. He'd be leaving soon. He'd hurt her.

But at the moment, none of that seemed to matter.

She simply wanted to be closer to him.

By the time she made it down to the bait shop that was perched at the edge of the marina, the boat had drawn up alongside the dock and she could read the name painted on the stern: *Go Fish*. Graham climbed out onto the gray wooden dock. He was dressed in a suit and tie, which struck Ellie as an odd choice of sailing apparel until she remembered that the scene took place just after his character's father's funeral, when Jasper flees the church in order to take the boat out on his own, only to be followed by Zoe.

A gust of wind skipped over the water, and Olivia used one hand to pin down the bottom of her dress as someone took the other to help her off the boat. When she was safely on solid ground, she and Graham made their way together up the long walkway, flanked by the director and a few assistants, all of them with headsets and clipboards and grim expressions. Two members of the crew stayed behind to secure the equipment; Graham had mentioned yesterday that they wouldn't be done until late in the afternoon, but Ellie suspected they had to break early because of the weather.

A crowd had gathered along the harbor wall, and the screams reached a fever pitch as the two stars approached. A few oversize security guards patrolled the edges, but this didn't prevent the tourists from recording it all on their phones or the tween girls from leaning over the rail with wide-eyed glee as Graham approached. Olivia paused to whisper something in his ear before stopping to sign a few autographs, and the rest of the paparazzi appeared as if from nowhere, moving in to bear witness to the moment with their heavy cameras.

Ellie had come to a stop near the harbormaster's office, still a safe distance away from the crowds, but as he headed back toward his trailer, Graham looked over. His eyes found hers quickly, so quickly it was almost like he'd known she would be there. She smiled reflexively at him, but before she had a chance to do anything else—shake her head or give him some sort of sign—he changed direction, walking toward her without seeming to notice that the attention of the entire dockside had shifted his way.

From where she was standing, Ellie's knees went weak, her legs suddenly wobbly, and for a brief, panicked moment, she remained frozen there like that, unsure what to do. Graham was completely oblivious, waving as he drew closer, his smile widening. Over his shoulder, the photographers had abandoned Olivia's autograph session and were tracking Graham with their lenses. The words that Mom had spoken earlier now flashed through Ellie's mind—*Once something like this is out there, you can't take it back*—and she found herself moving away.

I can't, she thought, hoping he would understand.

But of course he didn't. She caught his eye only for a moment, just long enough to see the confusion in his face, and she felt a quick stab of guilt. But it was too late. Already, she was cutting around the side of the bait shop, the shortcut down to the beach. And then, like the best of magicians, she made herself disappear, leaving the rest of the three-ring circus behind her.

From: GDL824@yahoo.com
Sent: Tuesday, June 11, 2013 12:18 PM
To: EONeill22@hotmail.com
Subject: weather report

E,

We came in early because of the wind. I'm gonna go ahead and assume that's what carried you off too. We're working late tonight, but I'll try to stop by afterward . . .

G

12

All afternoon, Graham was tailed by a kind of low-grade panic, making it impossible to concentrate. As they waited for the weather to improve, he pretended to study the script, but his mind was elsewhere. Outside, the wind buffeted the sides of the trailer, and he rubbed his eyes and willed himself to focus.

It took two hours for the weather to shift, the world going quiet again, and there was a new urgency to the production as they headed back out on the water, trying to make up for lost time in the last of the good light. Graham could feel everyone's impatience with him as he stumbled through his lines, tripping over the words, missing his positioning, fumbling with the gears even as an expert called out instructions from off camera. The water was choppy, biting at the sides of the wooden boat, and even though the wind had weakened, the hair people were still fighting a losing battle in their efforts to keep Olivia's ponytail in check.

Graham kept his feet planted wide near the bow as Mick conferred with two of the cameramen, deciding whether to pack it in once again or press on and see what they could get. The *Go Fish* rose and fell on the blue-gray waves, the deck canting from side to side. If Graham's performance was being taken into consideration, he was pretty sure they'd be heading to shore. The scene called for raw emotion and hard-earned declarations of love. It required anguished looks and choking voices, but Graham was simply unable to muster that kind of passion at the moment. Not today. Not for Olivia. Not after watching Ellie walk away from him.

He should have still been flying after last night. When he'd kissed her, it had felt like the striking of a match, something hard and bright in his chest, a part of him he hadn't even realized was waiting to be lit.

But this morning, he'd seen the look on her face across the harbor path, just before she turned away, and it had pushed the breath right out of him. He couldn't blame her. He shouldn't have waved in the first place. As soon as he had, he'd felt the surge of attention at his back, and anyone in her position would have done the same thing when faced with such a mob. But even from a distance, he could read her expression so plainly it was like she was speaking the words aloud: *I'm sorry*, she'd managed to say, without saying anything at all.

And then she was gone.

It was probably just a moment of panic. He was probably overreacting. But still, Graham couldn't shake the feeling that she'd been walking away from more than just the crowds and the cameras.

The sun had already set behind the steeple of the church when they docked for the second time, but the day was far from over. They were scheduled to shoot another scene outside one of the local bars this evening, and as he crossed the road toward his trailer, Graham could already see the enormous lamps being set up, a small oasis of artificial twilight on the otherwise darkening street.

A production assistant was calling to him from across the lot, but he wasn't needed on set for another twenty minutes, so he kept his head down, pulling his phone from his pocket as he walked. He scrolled past e-mails from his agent and publicist, his business manager and a girl he'd met at the gym before leaving L.A. But there was still no word from Ellie, and as he bounded up the steps of his trailer, he hit the call button, listening to it ring. He was already assembling the message he would leave if she didn't pick up—something casual and upbeat to hide his growing worry that she hadn't responded to his e-mail—but when he opened the door, he was pulled up short by the sight of Harry, who was sitting at the small table inside. He lowered the phone again, fumbling to switch it off.

"Who was that?" Harry asked, setting aside a sheaf of papers.

Graham didn't answer. He reached into the mini fridge for a bottle of water, then sat down opposite his manager.

Harry smiled, but it was a smile with a warning inside it. "The redhead?"

Graham tipped his head back and took a swig of water, his eyes on the ceiling. When he'd finished, he wiped his mouth with the back of his hand and said, in a voice that didn't entirely sound like his own, "What redhead?"

"C'mon," Harry said. "Everyone saw you chasing her earlier."

"I wasn't—"

"You've got to cool it with these locals." He leaned back in his chair and scratched the back of his head. "You think I haven't seen this happen before? You get out of L.A., and suddenly there are a thousand girls screaming your name—"

"It's not like that."

"I'm sure it's not," Harry said, though he didn't sound convinced. "But the point is, this isn't the right moment for you to suddenly turn into some kind of skirt chaser."

Graham snorted. "When *is* the right moment for that kind of thing?"

"I'm serious. We're at a crucial juncture here, and your image is important. I don't need you out with a different girl every night." He pulled a tabloid from beneath the stack of papers on the table in front of him, sliding it over to the edge. "Just one."

Graham regarded it warily, surprised to see a glossy photo from yesterday's shoot. It had been taken during the moment when he first lifted Olivia for the big kiss, the two of them still in motion, eyes shut, arms entangled, a moment that could easily be construed as more than just acting when taken out of context. The caption below read: "On-screen chemistry or real-life romance?"

"Nice work," Graham said, letting it drop.

Harry beamed. "It's why you pay me the big bucks, remember? Though you'd make my life a whole lot easier if you'd stop chasing the redhead and just take Olivia out to dinner one night."

"I'm pretty sure it's your job to make *my* life easier," Graham said, standing up from the table. He reached over to toss his water bottle into the overflowing garbage can beside the fridge, and then, for good measure, sent the magazine flying in there as well. "And she has a name, you know."

"What is it?"

But Graham was already out the door.

In the street, the set had come to life again. After a disappointing day out on the water, there was now an undercurrent of energy to the place, everyone moving with purpose, animated by the idea of a clean slate and a fresh scene.

It was almost fully dark, with only a pale smudge of pink along the edge of the water. A block away, enormous lights flooded the sidewalk in front of the bar, the site of Jasper's unraveling, and Graham knew he should be turning his mind to the scene ahead. But he paused to slip his phone out of his pocket one more time, anxious to see whether there was any word from Ellie. Instead, he was surprised to find a message from his mom.

Up ahead, a wardrobe assistant was waving him over. But Graham made no motion to follow her, pausing to cup a hand around the glowing screen of his phone as he read. His eyes skipped over the words: a string of excuses, a list of previous plans for the holiday weekend, worries about air travel and the cost of the trip, suggestions that they might be out of place with his "movie friends" anyway, apologies and promises to make it up to him when he returned to California.

In spite of all this, it still took a moment for the full weight of the message to become clear to him.

They weren't coming.

He should have expected it. There'd been no reason for him to think their answer would be anything but no. Still, it wasn't until he lowered the phone that Graham realized— against all logic—he'd actually been counting on seeing them.

The wardrobe assistant was now standing before him, and she cleared her throat loudly. He glanced up, feeling a bit dazed. She was short and round-shouldered and at least ten years older than Graham, but she was still look- ing at him with a kind of awe, as if he were doing her a great favor by finally acknowledging her.

"They're ready for you," she said, and he nodded, tucking the phone back in his pocket, his face carefully neutral.

Even later, once his costume was on and his hair was gelled and he'd been deemed camera-ready, he wore a similar expression, a well-maintained blankness, a way of making room for someone else entirely: Jasper and his problems, Jasper and his thoughts, Jasper and his complicated feelings for Zoe.

But the rest of it was still there too, just below the surface: Graham and his problems, Graham and his thoughts, Graham and his complicated feelings for Ellie. And so much more: his reluctance to see Olivia, his annoyance with Harry, his disappointment with his parents, his impatience to get this whole damn scene over and done with so that he could find Ellie, the one sure antidote to everything else that was crowding his head.

They finished shooting early. But this time, it wasn't because of the weather, or the lighting, and it definitely wasn't because Graham couldn't conjure up the right combination of emotions. In fact, as soon as they'd wrapped for the day, as an army of workers emerged as if from nowhere to begin breaking down the set, Mick walked over and clapped him on the shoulder.

"That was some pretty intense stuff," he said. "Think we could see that kind of thing again tomorrow?"

Graham's laugh was rough. "I'll see what I can do."

But what he was really thinking was this: He wanted just the opposite. He wanted calm. He wanted Ellie.

On the way to her house, he tipped his head back to gaze at the wash of stars above, which had been wiped out by the klieg lights on the set. Now they were thick as static across the navy sky, and Graham was reminded of the box in their basement at home where his father kept an antique telescope. The wood was intricately carved with little suns and moons, and as a kid, Graham had wanted nothing more than to haul it upstairs and point it out the window, to capture the stars in those curved panes of glass. But he saw it only once a year, when Dad laid a cloth across the dining room table and lifted the telescope as carefully as he might a dying person.

"Can't we try it?" Graham always asked, leaning in close to watch as his father polished the wood and cleaned the lenses with the same velvety cloth.

"It's too valuable," Dad would say. "You don't want anything to happen to it."

But that's exactly what happened to it: nothing. As far as Graham knew, it was still sitting down there in the cobwebby basement, and what he had always accepted as practical now struck him as a colossal waste.

By the time he reached the hill that sloped down to meet Ellie's driveway, he was half jogging. The lights were on in the kitchen, and he forced himself to slow down as he reached the steps, taking a deep breath. At the door, he raised a hand, but found he couldn't knock.

He paced from one end of the porch to the other, then

back again, not quite sure what was wrong with him. Suddenly, he felt paralyzed. He paused in front of the doorbell, then turned away, slumping onto the wooden swing, where he sat with his elbows on his knees, his face in his hands. What was wrong with him? He'd never been this unsure of himself when it came to a girl, not even in his old life.

He was still sitting there like that—hunched and miserable, unable to bring himself to knock—when he heard footsteps from inside, and his stomach churned. But when the door cracked open, it was Ellie's mom who stepped outside. She raised her eyebrows, but said nothing, and Graham rose from the swing.

"I'm sorry to bother you," he said. "I was just about to knock."

One side of her mouth inched up into the beginning of a smile, a look he'd seen echoed on her daughter's face. "That's what I thought about ten minutes ago," she said. "I figured I might as well kick-start the process."

He cleared his throat. "Is Ellie home?"

"Yes," she said. "But it's late."

Graham knew this was his cue to leave, and he felt a flash of annoyance. He straightened his shoulders, digging in. He refused to walk away. Not yet. "Would it be possible to see her for just a minute?"

"I don't think so," she said, and he was surprised to see a look of genuine pity cross her face. It took him a moment to understand what it meant, that look, to feel the full impact of it square across his chest.

It wasn't Mrs. O'Neill that was blocking his way. And it wasn't her who was saying no.

It was Ellie.

The realization threw him into a stupefied silence, and he found himself completely unable to ask the next logical question: *Why not?* or *What happened?* or, worst of all, *What did I do wrong?* Instead, he simply directed his gaze to the uneven boards of the porch.

"It's just not a great night," Mrs. O'Neill said, putting a hand on his shoulder.

The next question came easily, though he suspected that the answer to this, too, would probably be unwelcome. "How about tomorrow?"

She hesitated, opening and then closing her mouth. After a moment, she gave her head a little shake. "Good night, Graham," she said, and then she stepped back into the house, leaving him alone on the porch.

From somewhere inside, Bagel let out a bark at the sound of the door. As he backed off the steps, Graham looked up. There was only one lit window on the second floor, and in the wedge of visible space, he could see a bookshelf. For a moment, he let himself imagine it—Ellie curled up on her bed, the dog at her side—and the thought seemed to crack at something inside him.

He'd read the scripts. He knew how the story was supposed to go. Boy meets girl. Girl likes boy. Boy kisses girl.

And then? The possibilities were endless. But the one thing Graham knew was that it wasn't supposed to involve *this*: standing alone on the wrong side of a door with absolutely no idea what had happened.

He'd thought this was the start of something. But clearly she'd changed her mind, and he felt stunned by how quickly the whole thing had unraveled, the end coming before the beginning really even had a chance to begin. His poor telescope heart—that fragile, precious thing— would have probably been better left in the box.

PART II

SAVED DRAFTS

From: EONeill22@hotmail.com
Saved: Thursday, June 13 2013 11:27 PM
To: GDL824@yahoo.com
Subject: (no subject)

Dear Graham,

I'm really sorry.

From: EONeill22@hotmail.com
Saved: Sunday, June 16 2013 3:02 PM
To: GDL824@yahoo.com
Subject: (no subject)

Dear Graham,

From: EONeill22@hotmail.com
Saved: Sunday, June 16 2013 3:05 PM
To: thisisquinn@gmail.com
Subject: (no subject)

Quinn,

I'm so sorry. I wish I could explain.

From: EONeill22@hotmail.com
Saved: Tuesday, June 18 2013 5:15 PM
To: GDL824@yahoo.com
Subject: (no subject)

G—

From: EONeill22@hotmail.com
Saved: Wednesday, June 19 2013 8:07 AM
To: thisisquinn@gmail.com
Subject: (no subject)

Q—can we please talk?

From: EONeill22@hotmail.com
Saved: Thursday, June 20 2013 9:29 PM
To: cbodine@harvard.edu
Subject: (no subject)

Dear Ms. Bodine,

I wanted to let you know that I will no longer be able to attend the poetry course in August. Unfortunately, I don't have the funds necessary to

---

From: EONeill22@hotmail.com
Saved: Thursday, June 20 2013 9:38 PM
To: paul_whitman@whitman.senate.gov
Subject: (no subject)

From: EONeill22@hotmail.com
Saved: Friday, June 21, 2013 7:18 PM
To: GDL824@yahoo.com
Subject: (no subject)

Hey Graham,

From: EONeill22@hotmail.com
Saved: Sunday, June 23, 2013 10:10 AM
To: cbodine@harvard.edu
Subject: (no subject)

Dear Ms. Bodine,

I'm so sorry that I won't be able to come to Harvard for the poetry course after all. Unfortunately, my plans have changed, and my parents and I will be on a family vacation then.

From: EONeill22@hotmail.com
Saved: Monday, June 24, 2013 4:51 PM
To: thisisquinn@gmail.com
Subject: (no subject)

Quinn,

This is crazy. We really need to talk. Can we meet up sometime?

Love,

Ellie

From: EONeill22@hotmail.com
Saved: Wednesday, June 26, 2013 10:34 PM
To: GDL824@yahoo.com
Subject: (no subject)

Dear Graham,

I hope everything is going well with the movie...

From: EONeill22@hotmail.com
Saved: Thursday, June 27, 2013 3:40 PM
To: GDL824@yahoo.com
Subject: (no subject)

Hi.

From: EONeill22@hotmail.com
Saved: Friday, June 28, 2013 11:11 PM
To: GDL824@yahoo.com
Subject: (no subject)

Hello.

From: EONeill22@hotmail.com
Saved: Sunday, June 30, 2013 7:31 AM
To: GDL824@yahoo.com
Subject: (no subject)

Good morning.

From: EONeill22@hotmail.com
Saved: Monday, July 1, 2013 8:24 AM
To: GDL824@yahoo.com
Subject: (no subject)

I miss you.

13

It was nearly impossible to avoid someone in a town like Henley. There were only so many places to go, so many intersections and stoplights and restaurants. There were only so many trees with trunks big enough to duck behind.

So after nearly three successful weeks of dodging Graham, Ellie was feeling pretty proud of herself. She'd seen him just twice from afar, and he was always flanked by enough of an entourage—paparazzi, film crew, and fans— to act as a warning signal.

Quinn, on the other hand, seemed to be everywhere. Although that didn't mean they'd spoken—they hadn't. In fact, they'd hardly said a word to each other in weeks.

"How's Quinn?" Mom would ask, completely oblivious, whenever Ellie returned after a shift at Sprinkles, and there was nothing to do but plaster a smile on her face.

"She's great," she'd say, fighting back the words underneath those, which were too depressing to admit: *I have absolutely no idea.*

It wasn't entirely her fault, this thing between them, and if Quinn weren't so stubborn, it would have blown over weeks ago. Still, Ellie was the one who'd started it, and she wished desperately she could find a way to apologize. But she'd drafted e-mails without managing to send them and prepared speeches without managing to say them.

At work, Quinn had taken to bringing Devon as a kind of shield against any real discussion, and the two of them would sit at one end of the counter, talking and joking, while Ellie stood awkwardly at the other end, as far away as was possible in such a small space. Every now and then, Quinn would ask Ellie for a cup or a spoon using the kind of polite but icy tone you might adopt when speaking to a complete stranger you'd heard nothing but awful things about—but that was it. Even on the hottest days, when the sun bore down on the town with a spiteful intensity, she never bothered to ask whether Ellie had put on sunscreen anymore.

About a week ago, just as Ellie started to wonder if she'd actually managed to become invisible, she overheard them talking about a party at the beach.

"Big plans tonight?" she asked as casually as she could manage, but this was only met with a lengthy silence. When it became obvious that Quinn wasn't going to respond, Devon cleared his throat.

"Just a barbeque," he said. "Should be pretty low-key."

"Which means no celebrities," Quinn said without looking up.

214

Ellie swallowed hard. There was no way for Quinn to know what had happened between her and Graham. And it would have been so easy, right then, to let the whole story come spilling out, to watch it register across Quinn's face: first as guilt for ignoring her at a time like this, then as regret for not being there, then as sympathy for what she was going through.

But Ellie wasn't looking for pity. She was looking for her friend.

Besides, telling her would mean having to answer that most difficult of questions—why had she walked away from him in the first place?—which would only bring them back to the place where this had all started: a secret that couldn't be told.

"Which beach is it?" Ellie asked, and Quinn glanced over at her for the first time, her eyes flashing.

"It's a secret," she said pointedly.

After that, Ellie decided it wasn't even worth trying. Instead, she set about ignoring Quinn in the same way that Quinn was ignoring her, which only served to create a wall between them so much thicker than if it had been built by only one of them.

Still, it was worse with Graham. It might take time with Quinn, but Ellie knew she would come around eventually. This wasn't the first time they'd fought, and it wouldn't be the last.

With Graham, however, Ellie suspected she'd broken something that might never be fixed. That night when he

215

showed up at her house, she'd sat huddled at the top of the stairs, listening to the voices drifting through the front door, and wishing she had the courage to walk downstairs and tell her mom to let him in, to say that none of the rest of it mattered: not the past, not their secrets, and especially not her father.

But she'd made her decision. She'd walked away from him at the harbor that day, and now she was left playing a desperate game of espionage as she skulked around town, trying her hardest not to run into him again.

Because the truth was, she wasn't sure she'd be able to walk away a second time.

And so today, like every day, Ellie stood in the doorway of Happy Thoughts, looking left and then right before stepping outside. It had been only three weeks since they'd forked over enough money to get the air conditioner at home fixed, and now, on the hottest day of the summer, the one at the shop had broken down too, sputtering to a halt with one last dying groan. After a morning spent alternately fanning themselves and banging on the rusted hunk of metal, Mom finally sent Ellie out for some iced tea.

On the village green, someone had set up a sprinkler, and there were a few kids in saggy bathing suits running through the water. Most everyone else was inside today, waiting for the shimmering heat to break. But even so, Ellie scanned the area with the nervous air of a criminal as she crossed the green, casting furtive glances at the shops on the other side.

The town's only deli had replaced a Henley institution the year before, a little general store called Marv's that had been there as long as anyone could remember, and as a nod to tradition, it was now called the Sandwich Shop Where Marv's Once Was, which was still inevitably shortened to Marv's. As soon as she pushed open the door, Ellie sighed with relief at the cool air, which lifted the heavy coat of heat right off her. Her cheeks were still flushed and her tank top was still sticking to her, but she felt immediately better. It was like walking into a refrigerator.

There was a line at the counter, so she lingered near the door, more than happy to take her time as she stood under the air vent. A small table beneath the window held the day's newspapers, and she picked up the local one, leafing through it idly.

"What can I get you, kiddo?" asked Meg, the owner, who had walked down to the far end of the counter, a notepad in one hand and a pencil in the other.

"It's okay," Ellie said, waving a section of the newspaper. It was an unspoken rule that locals were served first here, but she was in no hurry to get back to Happy Thoughts, which felt like a furnace today. "I can wait."

Meg shrugged. "You look hot," she said. "Can I at least get you some lemonade or an iced tea or anything?"

"That's actually what I'm here for," Ellie admitted. "I'll take two iced teas."

Meg gave a little salute and then elbowed her way toward the back, while Ellie returned to the paper. She'd randomly grabbed the real estate section and was skimming a piece about how the disappearing shoreline on one of the barrier islands was affecting the price of the enormous homes there when she noticed a familiar name in a narrow column at the bottom:

As he prepares for a much-needed vacation over the coming holiday weekend, Senator Paul T. Whitman told reporters that he plans to leave work behind for a few days.

"We'll be celebrating America's birthday," he said. "I can't think of a better reason to knock off and relax with my family."

The presidential hopeful will spend four days in scenic Kennebunkport, Maine, a town famous for being the summer home of former president George H. W. Bush.

So is Whitman, the senior senator from Delaware, trying to follow in the elder Bush's footsteps?

"We'll see," he said, laughing. "But no politics this weekend. I'm just planning to take my boys out on the boat, catch some fish, and relax."

Ellie lowered the paper, blinking fast.

Kennebunkport was less than an hour away, and it was this—the proximity of the thing—that made her hands tremble where she gripped the paper. She knew he was always out there somewhere, her father, but she was only ever aware of him in the way you're aware of a distant planet, always moving, always orbiting around you but never getting close enough to really matter. All her life, she'd heard about him on the news, followed his speeches and campaigns, his family vacations, his dinner parties and fund-raisers, but she was no better informed than anyone else in the country.

He was, in a way, the very opposite of Graham. He was someone who, by all logic, Ellie should know better than anyone, someone who should be so much more to her than just a name in the paper, whereas there was no worldly reason she should ever have gotten to know Graham Larkin any better than the dozens of people lining up along the fringes of the set each day in the hope of getting his autograph.

The bell above the door jangled then, and when Ellie looked over, she drew in a sharp breath. It was as if he'd marched straight out of the thought in her head, materializing on the other side of the glass in a faded blue T-shirt that matched his eyes, which were hidden by a pair of dark sunglasses.

She was so startled to see him there that she found herself moving backward, and it took only two steps before she managed to bump into the display of gum and candy. The whole thing teetered for one horrible, endless moment before crashing to the floor, the packets falling heavily and one of the containers splitting wide open, sending pale green mints skittering in all directions like runaway marbles.

The entire back half of the shop turned to look. Graham pulled open the door the rest of the way, nudging his sunglasses down on his nose to peer over the lenses at the mess. But Ellie remained frozen in place, even as Meg dashed out from behind the counter with a broom. "Don't worry, don't worry," she was saying, her words loud in the suddenly quiet shop. "I'd been meaning to move that display anyway."

She brushed past Graham without any sort of acknowledgment and began sweeping up the mess as Ellie stood helplessly in the middle of the now-colorful floor. She was acutely aware of her dirty tank top, her messy ponytail, the fact that she'd spent the morning sweating in a corner of the shop occupied by a giant stuffed lobster. She realized she was still gripping the newspaper hard in one hand, and she rolled it into a tube, unable to think of anything to say. All she could do was stare uselessly at the floor.

Graham had let the door fall shut behind him, and without a word, he stooped down beside Meg, using both hands to gather the mints into piles while the rest of the customers looked on, apparently as dumbfounded as Ellie. She stared down at his broad back, the same back she'd followed up the beach that day, and her heart thumped hard against her chest. Even standing right below the vent, she was suddenly too warm again, her eyes prickly, her face tingling. She wondered if this is what heatstroke felt like.

"Disaster averted," Graham said, straightening up again as Meg headed into the back with the broom. The other customers had started to remember why they were there in the first place, turning back to the counter to order their sandwiches, and to Ellie's relief, the unnatural quiet that had settled over the shop dissolved again, giving way to the clink of silverware and the sound of laughter.

"Thanks," she said quietly, unable to look at him, though she could feel his gaze like a kind of heat. He cleared his throat and pushed his sunglasses to the top of his head, and when he raised an eyebrow, the moon-shaped scar above his left eye shot up as well. Ellie felt her heart jump in her chest, as if that too were connected by the same fragile string. She wanted to say something, but her tongue was thick in her mouth, and before she had a chance to even try, the door opened again, and once more, there was a collective hush as Olivia walked in, looking fresh-faced and unbearably cool.

"Sorry," she said, walking right up to Graham. She held up her phone, the jeweled case flashing. "My agent." She crinkled her nose at him, her eyes falling to a single green mint that was stuck to his knee. "Was that you on the floor?"

"We had a little situation," he said, brushing it off. "Cleanup on aisle four."

Olivia looked around distractedly. "Don't they have someone else to do that sort of thing?"

"Yes, they do," Meg said, suddenly beside them again, a sweating cup of iced tea in each hand. "You two looking for a sandwich or a table or both?"

"Both, I suppose," Olivia said, sounding less than convinced as she surveyed the tiny seating area, where families of tourists ate their lunches out of wicker baskets.

Ellie tucked the newspaper under her arm, avoiding a searching look from Graham, and took the cups from Meg. "Thanks so much," she told her. "I've got to get back."

"Good to see you," Graham said, and Ellie nodded stiffly. As she pushed open the door, she heard Olivia ask, "Do you know her?"

She didn't wait to hear his response.

Outside, she forced herself to hurry back across the green on wobbly legs. The door to the shop was propped open with an old lobster trap, and though she was greeted by a wall of hot air, heavy and stifling, Ellie still felt a swell of relief at having returned.

Mom was leaning on the counter, propped up on one elbow, mopping at her forehead with a bandanna. When she saw Ellie, she straightened up.

"You look like you just ran a marathon."

"It sort of feels that way," Ellie said, setting the dripping cups on the counter. She hadn't realized her hands were shaking, and she tried to steady them as she slipped the newspaper from underneath her arm and hid it behind one of the bins of toys lined up at her feet so that she could come back for it later.

"You okay?" Mom asked, and Ellie nodded.

"I'm fine," she said, but that wasn't quite true. She was dazed by what had just happened. She was shaken by the article about her father. She was tired of running away from Graham. She was miserable. She was heartbroken. She was anything but fine.

"Good," said Mom. "'Cause I thought we could finish up the windows."

Ellie sighed wearily. Mom had an exhausting habit of changing out the two window displays every few weeks. "Today?" she asked, though what she really meant was, *In this heat?*

Mom chose to ignore her. "It's as good a day as any," she said. "I'm thinking the crustacean chess board should go on one side, maybe with some seashells around it, and then we could put some of your frames on the other."

"Fine," Ellie said, walking over to the window boxes to begin clearing out the beach balls that had been there since school let out.

"I'll do that," Mom said. "Can you add some more poems to the new frames? We're a couple short now."

Ellie reached down for the small volume of poetry she kept tucked in her bag. They'd sold two frames last week, both housing poems by Elizabeth Bishop, and Mom was sure that was why. The woman had apparently spent nearly fifteen minutes reading through them before deciding which to buy.

Now, as she settled on the stool behind the counter, Ellie was already debating between Auden and Yeats. But when she opened the book, a loose page slipped out, and she was surprised to find herself holding Graham's drawing.

Her eyes followed the lines on the page, the whole thing a study of geometry, with arrow-straight edges and precise corners. It was like falling into a dream, and she felt herself getting lost inside the lines, the simplicity of the page a safety net against the memory of the day it was made.

She ran a thumb across the tiny hole where the pencil had gone through the paper when she interrupted him. Behind the drawing, she could see the faint imprints of certain words, and she flipped it over and examined the menu, suddenly back in that shop with Graham, the air filled with the sweet smell of chocolate.

She sat there for a long time, holding the drawing by its edges, her mind drifting. And then she stood and carried it to the back of the shop, where she selected one of the new frames—a sturdy-looking black one—and removed the back. As she slid the drawing inside, she was careful to hide the signature along the bottom, the uneven gray line that might give away the artist.

When she brought it out to the front of the shop, Mom frowned.

"That's not a poem," she said, but Ellie didn't listen.

She set down a pink index card that read "Drawing not for sale" and then placed the frame on top of it, propped in the window alongside the others so that it was angled south, where it would face the water and harbor. Where it would face Graham.

"Yeah," she said, "it is."

From: GDL824@yahoo.com
Sent: Wednesday, July 3, 2013 11:44 AM
To: EONeill222@hotmail.com
Subject: (no subject)

Hey Evan,

Looks like I'll be home this weekend after all. Hard to believe it, but we're on schedule with the shoot, and I'm ready to get out of here. If you could just feed Wilbur around lunchtime on Saturday, he should be fine till I get back later that night.

Thanks again, man. Give the hog a hug for me.

GL

The moment he saw her in the deli, Graham understood his mistake.

He hadn't forgotten about her. But he *had* given up.

And now, sitting across the table from Olivia, he felt a quick flash of certainty, a desperate flailing knowledge that he'd done the wrong thing. He should have tried harder. He should have shown up at her house every night, called her every day, e-mailed her every hour. He shouldn't have taken no for an answer.

He shouldn't have walked away.

And now it was too late.

She hadn't even looked at him. Not once.

Across from him, Olivia was squinting at the menu, which was scrawled on a chalkboard above the deli counter. "How can there be *no* salads," she said, a whiny note to her voice that she managed to drop only when she was in character.

"I'm sure they can throw some lettuce in a bowl for

you," he said distractedly, and she looked at him as if he'd suggested she eat off the floor.

For almost three weeks now, he'd been imagining what would happen if he ran into Ellie again. But none of those scenarios involved being out with Olivia.

"Excuse me," she was saying, waving down the woman who'd helped sweep up the candy earlier. "Would it be possible to get some sort of arugula salad? Do you have any pear? Or goat cheese?" She turned to Graham with a dazzling smile. "I could really go for some goat cheese."

It was clear the woman was trying not to laugh. "We only have what's on the menu," she said, gesturing to a board filled with options like roast beef, turkey, and ham. "And you order up at the counter."

Graham rose to his feet. "I'll get it."

"I guess I'll have a turkey sandwich, then," Olivia said, pulling out her phone with a sigh. "No bread."

"Not much of a sandwich," the woman muttered, moving around the table and back to the counter.

A few people tried to let Graham cut ahead of them in line, but he politely declined. He glanced out the window, where he could see the O'Neills' shop on the other side of the green, then looked back over at the table, where Olivia was fanning herself with one manicured hand.

Harry had been unrelenting in his efforts to convince Graham that dating Olivia would be the second best thing he could do for his career. The first, of course, would be to pick his next project from the long lineup of scripts that were fanned out across the coffee table in his hotel room, each synopsis worse than the one before it, movies about aliens and robots and vampires. There was a musical version of an old sitcom, one where Graham would play his own identical twin, and a buddy comedy about two high school freshmen who pretend to be in college for a night.

"I know, I know," Harry would say each time he dropped off another script. "But we need to figure out what's next."

Graham realized that too, but he wanted to choose carefully.

For the past couple of weeks, he'd thrown himself into the shoot, approaching each scene with new energy, hitting all his marks, nailing each and every one of his lines. At night, he fell asleep on the uneven hotel bed with a marked-up copy of the script on his chest, and in the mornings, he ran lines in his head while he showered and brushed his teeth.

There wasn't much else for him to do. Without Ellie, the town had started to feel small, and he was getting tired of eating every lunch in his trailer and every dinner in his hotel room. Harry was wearing on him, and Mick only wanted to talk about work. Occasionally, he played cards with some of the other cast members, but most of them were older, so he usually ended up passing the time on his own. And there were few things lonelier than a blinking TV screen and a half-eaten plate of room-service food on an unmade hotel bed.

Last night, when he turned on the TV, he'd been surprised to discover that *To Kill a Mockingbird* was on. He hadn't seen it since he was little, curled on the couch with his parents, all three of them sharing a bowl of popcorn, and he was captivated now as he watched, entranced by the classic feel of it. All of his peers could have their dance movies and raunchy comedies and action flicks. Graham realized that what he wanted was to do something like this. Something that mattered.

On their way back to the set this morning, Olivia had fallen into step beside him. Graham knew that she already had her next two pictures lined up: a Disney movie about a modern-day princess and a comedy about two college roommates. And while he might be skeptical about her choices, he envied her in some ways. She knew exactly what she wanted, and she knew exactly where she was going. It was more than he could say for himself.

"What are you doing for the Fourth?" she asked, adjusting her sunglasses as they walked toward the cluster of cameras, each of them perched on a dolly, ready to chase them down the street later this morning.

There'd been a mutiny among the cast and crew when Mick had suggested working through the holiday. There were only three days of shooting left—even less for Graham, who was slated to be finished after the second morning—and the director had wanted to push straight through and get back to the studio in L.A. But after a month of working nearly every single day, everyone was in desperate need of a break, and so he'd finally relented. They'd have the holiday off before returning to finish up, and everyone now seemed to be making plans. Graham had overheard some of the crew talking about going drinking out on a rented boat, while others would be joining in the town's celebration.

"I'm thinking of flying down to Manhattan for the day," Olivia said without waiting for his response. "I'm starting to forget what civilization feels like."

"That'll be fun," he offered, and she gave him a sideways glance.

"Want to come?"

He raised his eyebrows. "To New York?"

"To Manhattan," she said, as if they were two different things entirely. "You have to admit it would be nice to get out of here."

To his surprise, the idea was not entirely unappealing, especially after so many days alone, and he wondered if she really meant it. He searched her face, trying to decide whether this was a real invite and whether she was genuinely hopeful that he might come. Was it possible that she actually liked him, that it wasn't all about the publicity?

But before he could respond, Olivia smiled. "It's not L.A., of course, but I'm sure we wouldn't be completely under the radar," she said, slowing as they approached her trailer. "You don't have plans yet, do you?"

Graham thought again of the Fourth of July weekend he'd imagined: a parade and fireworks, sparklers and symphonies, a small-town celebration, and the chance to spend some time with his parents. He'd never responded to his mom's e-mail, and there'd been no more word from them until she called last week to say hello. For ten minutes, they'd talked about the weather in California and what she was reading for her book club. When she asked about the movie, Graham steered the subject away as he always did when his parents brought it up, acutely aware that they were only being polite. But when she mentioned their neighbor's Fourth of July barbeque, Graham went silent altogether.

"Honey?" his mom said, her voice thin across the line.

"Sounds like fun," he'd said shortly, and she sighed.

"I'm sorry we're not coming," she said after a moment. "You know how your father is about traveling, and—"

"It's fine, Mom."

"What are you going to do?"

"It turns out I've got to work anyway," he lied, knowing he'd probably be doing the same thing he did every other day here: taking long walks around town, looking out for the fishing boats coming into the harbor, watching movies and sketching pictures and checking in with the guy who was taking care of Wilbur, which he'd done so many times that he'd started getting only the very most sarcastic updates in return ("Pig at large" or "The pig has left the building").

When he'd first arrived here, he'd been so excited to get out of L.A., and he couldn't imagine four weeks would possibly be enough time. But now he realized that the promise of the place had been wholly and inextricably tied to Ellie, and with her absent from the equation, he was suddenly ready to go home.

But they still had a few more days to go, and today, he realized he couldn't face another meal with Harry in his trailer.

"I can't," he told Olivia, who was still waiting for his answer about New York. "But what are you doing for lunch?"

While they ate—or while Graham ate; Olivia just picked at the pile of turkey and lettuce with a fork—he did his best to keep up the conversation, but it wasn't easy. Olivia kept looking around as if they were at a club in Hollywood and someone fabulous might walk through the door at any moment. He attempted to ask what he liked to think of as real questions—where she grew up and what her parents were like, as opposed to standard industry fodder like what her next project was and how she got her start in the business—but he was conscious of the people sitting around them, the tables pressed too close for it to be comfortable to talk about anything meaningful. Besides, Olivia was only halfway there anyhow, dividing her time between Graham and her phone.

In fairness, he wasn't entirely present either; he was still too rattled to concentrate after seeing Ellie.

They signed a few autographs on the way out, and Graham left a tip in the jar. Outside, the cameras had finally caught on, and as usual, Graham slid on his sunglasses, lowered his head, and began to walk quickly back toward the set. But Olivia snaked her arm through his, forcing him to slow down, and he realized she was enjoying this.

He wondered if she was taking advantage of the fact that they were together, or if she really didn't mind the attention. He strolled for as long as he could, his teeth gritted, before whispering, "We need to get back."

"It's not like they can start without us," she said under her breath. "That's the advantage of being the stars."

"Are you two together now?" one of the photographers asked with a wink, and Olivia raised her eyebrows and flashed him a cryptic smile.

The short walk felt endless. As they neared the end of the street, Graham was surprisingly relieved to see Harry, and he disentangled his arm from Olivia's as the older man approached, beaming at the sight of them together.

"Come on," he said, shepherding them back behind the metal barriers that separated the set from the rest of the street, leaving the snapping of the cameras behind. As they walked over to the trailers, he turned to them with a grin. "Have a good lunch?"

"It was practically gourmet," Olivia said, rolling her eyes.

"I thought it was good," said Graham, not sure why he was feeling defensive about the place.

"I'm sure you did," she said, then turned to Harry. "By the time I got there, he was practically eating off the floor."

"Someone knocked over a display of candy," Graham explained. "I was just helping them clean up."

"Probably didn't hurt that she was hot," Olivia said idly, then laughed. "I never realized you had a thing for gingers."

Graham's jaw was tight, and when he glanced over at Harry, he was surprised to see a dark look on his face. But it wasn't directed at Olivia. It was directed at him.

"I better go," he said abruptly, and Olivia glanced up from her phone. "Thanks for lunch."

Harry followed him wordlessly to the trailer, a vein jumping near his temple. Inside, he let the door slam shut behind him, then folded his arms across his chest. "The same redhead?"

"What's the big deal?" Graham asked, pulling out a chair. "I thought you'd be happy about my big date with Olivia. Trust me, she made sure there were plenty of pictures."

"Look," Harry said, grabbing his briefcase from the couch and rifling through it. "You know I just want you to be happy—"

Graham snorted.

"But you can't be getting mixed up with that girl."

"With Olivia?" he asked, playing dumb, and Harry threw him a look.

"With Ellie O'Neill."

A jolt of surprise went through Graham at the sound of her name. "How do you know—"

"I did a little research," he said, then held up both hands in defense. "It's my job, okay?" He pulled a thick brown envelope from the suitcase. "I wasn't going to bother you with this, since we're only here a few more days anyway. But I can see you're still hung up on her—"

"I'm not," Graham said, much too quickly.

"—and clearly you're not over whatever this thing was between you—"

"It wasn't—"

"—but I wanted to make sure you at least had all the information," Harry said, holding out the envelope, which Graham made no move to take. "It's just not a good time to be getting involved with anything that might prove to be... messy. Not right now."

"This is none of your business," Graham said, glaring at him.

"It wouldn't look good for you," Harry said, as if he hadn't heard him. "The papers would be all over it. This could be the kind of hit to your image that we really can't afford."

The envelope was still dangling there in his outstretched hand. When he realized Graham wasn't going to take it, he finally let it drop on the table with a thud, then stood up.

"Trust me, it's for your own good," he said before crossing the trailer. A wedge of sunlight fell on the carpet when he opened the door, and then it was gone again, and Graham was alone.

He stared at the envelope, torn between ripping it open and throwing it away. He couldn't imagine what Harry had discovered, had no idea what made him search in the first place. And he wasn't sure he wanted to know.

He found himself thinking back to his very first e-mail exchange with Ellie, the easy swapping of words, all those messages between them that had been about nothing, when it came right down to it, but that had still managed to feel like something. Like everything.

Until today, it had been weeks since they'd seen each other. And though Graham missed her, though he'd like nothing more than to knock on her door and take her in his arms again, it was more than that too. He was surprised to find how much he missed *writing* to her. For so many months, she'd been the person on the other end of all his musings, and now she was gone and his thoughts were left buzzing around inside his head like frantic fireflies in a jar. He hadn't realized how much it could mean, having someone to talk to like that; he hadn't realized that it could be a kind of lifeline, and that without it, there would be nobody to save you if you started to drown.

Graham touched the corner of the packet, sliding it closer. He suddenly understood how desperate he was for whatever was inside it, whatever scrap of knowledge about Ellie O'Neill was available to him, no matter what it was, or what it might mean.

The envelope stared back at him, enigmatic and official.

It looked like a secret.

It was probably a mistake.

But after a moment, he reached out and took it anyway.

From: EONeill22@hotmail.com
Sent: Wednesday, July 3, 2013 1:21 PM
To: thisisquinn@gmail.com
Subject: white flag

Any chance we can call a truce? I know you're still upset with me, but I could really use a friend right now. (And not just any friend...)

15

It was too hot to do much of anything. Once they'd finished rearranging the window displays, Ellie pulled a stool over near the fan and sat there with her face pointed at the blades, but it did little more than move the warm air around the shop. The only customers who were brave enough to venture inside all day had left before making it too far past the doorway, the stuffiness of the place proving even less tolerable than the sun-baked streets outside.

Finally, around two o'clock, Mom stood up. "I feel like I'm sitting inside a furnace," she said. "Let's close up and get out of here."

Ellie spoke into the fan, her words vibrating. "Where should we go?"

But she already knew the answer. They would go where they always went.

Half an hour later, they were on their way to the beach. Not the one in town where all the tourists went to sun themselves on the rocks like seals, or the kiddie beach with the lifeguards and the roped-off swimming areas, or even the sandy one by the fishing pier.

They went to the cove.

After hanging a sign on the door of the shop—FULLY COOKED; BACK TOMORROW—they'd stopped home to change into swimsuits, grab some towels, and pick up the dog, and now they were headed to the little spit of water not far from their house, a beach so private they'd come to think of it as their own. Ever since Ellie was little, this is where they'd escaped together, bringing sunblock and towels in the summer or cider and blankets in the winter. They'd spent countless afternoons wading in the surf, collecting rocks, and spying on the birds. It was their place, and until she'd met Graham here a couple of weeks ago, Ellie had never before invited anyone else. Not even Quinn.

Now, as they made their way down toward the water, she found herself scanning the layer of stones that cobbled the beach, wondering if it was possible to find more than one heart in a place like this. Mom was laying out the towels in their usual spot, and Bagel had gone crashing into the water, bold and brave and full of bravado, only to be chased right back out again by the most pathetic of waves.

Ellie kicked off her flip-flops and waded in, shivering happily at the chill of the water, which lapped around her knees. Her feet were frozen and her shoulders were warm, and she tipped her head back and closed her eyes, the events of the morning melting right off her.

244

"Three whole weeks," Mom said as she joined her. "I'm going to miss this."

Ellie didn't need to ask what she meant. In her whole life, she'd never been away for longer than a few days, and Mom still assumed she'd be leaving soon for the poetry course on a scholarship that didn't exist. But it wasn't just that. This was her way of preparing herself for something much bigger. When she drove down to Boston and dropped Ellie off in that empty dorm room, it would be a preview of the next summer, when she would go off to college for real. This trip, this August: it was like the beginning of the end. It marked the start of their last year together.

And so she knew what it meant when Mom said *three whole weeks*, and she knew she should reach out across the surf and take her salty hand and say *I know* or *I'll miss this too*. But some small and hardened piece of her heart kept her staring straight ahead at the invisible seam where the water met the sky.

"Three weeks isn't that long," she said finally, her words crisp and unforgiving.

Mom nodded, her eyes far away. She couldn't have known what Ellie was really thinking: that three weeks was everything, and that she might not get that chance. She'd saved up $624.08 so far, and if she kept working at this pace, she'd have just under a thousand by August. But it wasn't nearly enough, and the thought of saying no—of giving up this opportunity, or possibly even worse, asking for help—twisted at something inside her, made her feel miserable and hopeless and mean.

On the shore, Bagel was dashing back and forth, distraught at being left behind. When Ellie whistled, he plunged into the water with a little whine, keeping his nose high as he paddled toward them.

"Listen," Mom said. "I know—"

But Ellie didn't want to hear it; she took a deep lungful of air, then dove into the water, the slap of cold making her whole body vibrate, right down to her teeth. Through slitted eyes, she could see Bagel's churning paws as he circled her in alarm, and she used her arms to push away the water, propelling herself forward several strokes before bursting back through to the surface.

To her surprise, Mom was at her side, shaking water out of her ear. "You can't get rid of me that easily," she said, and Ellie used one hand to wipe her eyes. The ground beneath them had sloped sharply away, and both of them were treading water, their feet busy beneath the surface.

"I wasn't trying to," she said, leaning back so that she was floating, the waves loud in her ears, the taste of salt on her lips.

"I know you're still mad at me about Graham," Mom said, and Ellie looked over at her. There were beads of water on her eyelashes, and her face looked very pale against the water. "You've been so quiet the last couple of weeks, and I know you must be upset, so I just wanted to say that I'm sorry."

A wave lifted them gently, then lowered them again, and a few seagulls wheeled overhead. The sun off the water was uncomfortably bright, and Ellie squinted against the glare, unsure what to say. It was true that she was upset about Graham. She thought she'd been managing just fine from a distance. But seeing him today, being near him—it was like the pull of a magnet, powerful and inevitable. Even now, treading water under the high globe of the sun, she felt her equilibrium had disappeared. She'd walked out of the deli hours ago, but some essential part of her—something too important to lose—had been left behind.

"It's okay," Ellie told her eventually, her voice very small. "It's not your fault."

Mom let out a breath. Her arms were moving fast beneath the water, ghostly and pale. "He'll be gone soon anyway," she said. "It'll get easier."

Ellie opened her mouth to answer, but found she couldn't speak. It was meant to make her feel better, she knew, but suddenly all she wanted to do was cry.

Mom's words echoed in her head again: *Three whole weeks*. That was how much time had been wasted. That was how long it had been since she'd kissed Graham.

Three whole weeks.

Farther out on the water, an enormous yacht glided by, moving slowly against the blinding blue of the horizon, and Ellie thought of the newspaper clipping about her father, and the fact that he'd be in Kennebunkport this weekend with his family, probably on a yacht not unlike that one. She imagined he'd be staying in some sort of oceanfront mansion, flitting between elegant cocktail parties at night. He'd be spending the days out fishing with his two blue-eyed sons, who looked like catalog models but—given what Ellie had read about them—probably couldn't get into the Harvard poetry program if they tried.

She swallowed hard, stung by the unfairness of it. It wasn't just that she was working all these hours to scrape together money for a course she probably wouldn't be able to go to anyway. It was that this was just the start of it. Next would be college: all those applications for loans, and Mom up late at night with a calculator, crunching the numbers. There were the ever-present worries about the house and the shop, the endless conversations about budgets and the drawers full of coupons, all things that wouldn't be an issue if Paul Whitman were still in their lives.

When Graham had asked her how much money she still needed that night, the question had felt like a bullet. For him, a thousand dollars was probably what you tipped the hotel staff after a week at a resort. He probably earned that much in interest every single day. To him, it was pennies. It was peanuts. It was chump change.

But to her, it still seemed an impossible amount. It may as well have been ten thousand dollars. It may as well have been a million.

There was a lump in her throat as Ellie tore her eyes from the yacht. Bagel had started to paddle for the shore, and they both watched him go, the diamond of white on the back of his head bobbing as he swam.

"I think he's got the right idea," Mom said, giving a little kick in that direction. "I'm getting fried. Want to head in?"

Ellie dipped her chin in the water, shaking her head, then leaned back so that she was floating again, her hair fanning out all around her.

"Not yet," she said. "I think I'll meet you back later."

"Okay," Mom said, starting to swim in. "Don't float away."

The water lapped in Ellie's ears as she bobbed there. Overhead, the seagulls were talking to one another across the great expanse of the sky, and the sun lowered itself toward the beach. She wasn't sure how long she stayed out there, letting the waves carry her, her body light despite the heaviness of everything inside her.

After a while, she flipped herself over and began to swim back to shore, where she wrapped herself in a towel and sat down on her favorite rock—a flat slab that rose above the inlet like a miniature cliff—feeling the salt from the water dry on her face, the sun warm across her eyelids. She curled her toes around the edge of the rock and hugged her knees. Peering down, she was surprised to see a small round disk wedged between the stones, and when she reached for it, she felt a laugh bubble up in her throat.

It was a sand dollar. Not exactly the kind of dollar she needed.

She held it flat against her palm, examining the rounded

edges, and the light tracings of a star in the middle. Out on the water, another expensive boat slid into view, and Ellie squinted out at it, the first, faintest pattern of an idea taking shape in her head. She sat up straighter, her waterlogged mind waking up again, working through the possibilities as she spun the sand dollar absently in her hands.

Starting tomorrow, her father would be only an hour away.

The whole thing seemed suddenly simple, like the most obvious idea in the world. There on the rock, a sense of certainty—of inevitability—was hardening inside her like cement, and she was so busy untangling the thread of a plan that she didn't hear someone coming through the trees. But at the sound of footsteps on the rocks, she whirled around, and her heart lifted at the sight of Graham.

From across the beach, he smiled. He was wearing khaki shorts and a blue polo that made his eyes look bright against all the gray, and there was something in his hand that she was certain must be a rock shaped like a heart.

"You look deep in thought," he said, still standing at the edge of the beach.

Ellie was unable to keep from smiling. "Hi," she said, and he tilted his head, looking at her with amusement.

"Are you daydreaming or plotting?"

"Plotting," she told him, and he seemed to consider this for a moment before taking a few steps toward her.

"Well, whatever it is," he said. "I'm in."

From: GDL824@yahoo.com
Sent. Wednesday, July 3, 2013 4:48 PM
To: harry@fentonmanagement.com
Subject: (no subject)

Harry,

Thanks for the info. I found it enormously helpful.

Graham

16

He'd come back to her, it was true. He was the one to walk out of the woods and onto the beach, to cross the space between them. But he wasn't the only one. It was there in her eyes: she was coming back to him too.

The moment he'd opened the envelope, all of his doubts had fallen away. Harry had clearly meant it to be a warning of sorts, but it had the exact opposite effect. Sitting in the trailer, he'd spilled the pile of papers onto the table—a jumble of Internet searches and archived articles—and he'd read all about her past. But it didn't make him want to stay away from her. He didn't care that she may or may not be the illegitimate daughter of that stiff-looking senator. He didn't care about the potential for negative publicity, or the fact that being attached to someone like that could be bad for his career.

What he cared about was that it explained what had happened between them, all of it: the look on her face when she walked away from him at the harbor that day, the unreturned e-mail, the distance she'd been keeping for the last few weeks.

It wasn't about not wanting him. She was only protecting herself.

But it didn't matter now. They sat facing each other on the enormous sloping rock that jutted out above the surf. The sun was falling lower in the sky, and though she was now wearing shorts and a T-shirt, Ellie still hugged the towel around her like a blanket, shivering in spite of the late-day heat. Her long hair was still damp from the water, and her nose was pink from the sun.

She'd tried to talk first, and so had he, their words tumbling into one another like bumper cars until she made him sit down across from her, and they each took a deep breath, laughing without any good reason except that there was a rare kind of joy in this, being here together again. Even without any explanations or apologies, it felt like a redo, a second chance, a new beginning. It was a gift, and Graham didn't want to be the one to spoil it. But there were things to be said, and so he cleared his throat and leaned forward.

"Me first," he said, and Ellie nodded, her face growing sober. It was hard to figure out where to begin, and Graham hesitated. "I know what happened," he said eventually. "I know that it wasn't about you and me. It was about your dad."

She flinched. "How do you—"

"Harry found out," he said. "My manager. He won't tell anyone. It's just that he knew I liked you, and he was only trying to protect me—"

"Protect *you*?" she said, her green eyes flashing.

"That's just his job," he said. "But it's not the point. It wasn't ever about us, right? Which means it doesn't matter anymore. Now that I know."

Ellie frowned. "Of course it matters," she said. "It doesn't change anything."

"It changes *everything*," Graham said. "I don't care about your past, or who your dad is. It was just about the publicity, right? The cameras?" He lifted his shoulders. "So we'll stay away from them."

"Graham," she said, her voice stern, though the corner of her mouth was twitching in an effort not to smile. "Just think about it for a second. It's not that easy to stay away from them. It's part of who you are."

"It's not who I am," he said, feeling a small flicker of annoyance, and her face softened.

"That's not what I meant," she said, and then, to Graham's surprise, she reached out and touched the side of his face. He felt the heat of her hand on his skin, impossibly soft, but before he could react, she pulled away again, looking embarrassed. "I only meant that it's too big a risk to take. I'm glad you know the story. I've never been able to tell anyone. But being with you—it's too public. I just

255

can't do that to my mom." She paused and looked out across the water. "And Harry's probably right. It can't be the best publicity for you either."

"I don't care," he said. "It's not important."

"It is," she said, looking at him a bit sadly. "And it's just not worth the risk. You're only here for a few more days anyway."

"Exactly," he said, inching closer. "We've wasted three whole weeks."

She lowered her eyes. "I know."

"That's a long time," he said. "I haven't even gone three *hours* without knowing what you've been doing since we first started talking."

She smiled, but it fell away again almost immediately. "We can't do this."

"Because of the cameras?"

Ellie nodded. "You know that the minute we go back into town—"

"Okay," Graham said, looking around the beach. The sun had finally dipped behind the trees, and the waves were tinged with gold. "Then we'll just stay here."

She laughed. "Forever?"

"Sure," he said. "Seems as good a place to live as any."

"Nice waterfront view."

"Plenty of light."

"A beachfront property. And no cameras."

He nodded. "No cameras."

She reached for his hand, and her fingers were warm

against his. "I don't want to lose any more time," she said quietly, and when he leaned forward to kiss her, he could taste the salt on her lips. It was like gravity, this thing between them, a pull as strong as the tides and unlike anything he'd ever felt before. He'd meant it as a joke when he said he could stay here forever, but he suddenly felt it to be true.

When she pulled back, he was unprepared to let her go just yet, so he looped an arm around her shoulders, and she fell back onto his chest, curled up against him. They stayed there like that for a long time, looking out over the water without speaking, the setting sun at their backs.

"Is this where you watch the sunrise?" he asked. "I bet it's the perfect spot."

Ellie twisted to face him with a sheepish expression. "Actually, I've never seen it."

"What? How is that even possible?"

"I always sleep through them," she admitted. "I know, it's terrible."

"But that was on your list."

"What list?"

"Of the things that make you happy."

"Oh," she said. "Right. I guess that was more wishful thinking. Anyway, you lied too."

He raised his eyebrows. "How?"

"You said you liked meeting new people..."

She didn't have to finish the thought. He knew what she

257

meant. And it was true—or at least it had been, before he met Ellie. But now everything had changed.

"I wasn't lying," he said, resting his chin on top of her head. "I was talking about you."

"Good," she said, and he could hear the smile in her voice. "Because I liked meeting you too."

"Hopefully better than you like sunrises."

"Having never seen them," she supplied, and he nodded.

"Exactly. How can you know it makes you happy if you've never experienced it?"

"There are different kinds of happy," she said. "Some kinds don't need any proof."

"Like sunrises?"

"Exactly," she said. "I know enough to know that they're happy things. There's just nothing sad about a sunrise."

"As opposed to a sunset."

"I don't think they're particularly sad either."

"I do," Graham told her. "They're endings, and endings are always sad."

"They're the beginning of the night," she said. "That's something."

"Yeah, but everyone knows that nights are scarier than days."

Ellie laughed. "Maybe we should turn around then."

"How come?"

"Nothing's all that scary if you can see it coming."

Still, they didn't move. The sun continued to set at their

backs, slipping toward the trees and the houses and the whole town of Henley, while before them, the water was busy with boats returning to the harbor. They watched as an enormous sailboat approached, the wind whipping its great white banners. Graham closed his eyes.

"My parents aren't coming," he said, and Ellie stirred in his arms.

"For the Fourth?"

"I thought they would," he said, then shook his head. "That's not really true, I guess. They never go anywhere. But I've also never asked before."

"Are you close?"

"We used to be," he said. "Before."

"Before all this?" she said, and he nodded, knowing what she meant. They both fell silent, charting the progress of the boat, and then Ellie took his hand again. "They're missing out."

"They don't understand it," he said. "All this movie stuff."

"Can you blame them?"

"I guess not," he said quietly. "I don't even understand it myself half the time."

"At least you've got Wilbur," she said, and he laughed.

"That's true."

"And me."

He leaned forward and kissed the top of her head. "That too."

The boat had started to darken into a silhouette against the gold of the water, and a warm breeze lifted the hair from Graham's forehead.

"I'm sorry about your dad," he said, though he was still thinking of his own.

It took her a moment to respond. "I never used to mind," she said. "I got really lucky with my mom. But it's been tougher than usual this summer."

"Because of me?" he asked, but she didn't answer. Instead she pulled away, swiveling around to face him fully, her eyes shiny and determined.

"He's in Kennebunkport for the long weekend."

Graham gave her a mystified look, wondering what this had to do with anything. "Where's that?"

"Just north of here," she said, her jaw set. "He's there with his family, and I'm gonna go up and see him tomorrow."

"That's what you were planning before?" he asked. "Does he know you're coming?"

She shook her head.

"And you haven't seen him since you were little?"

"Right," she said with a nod.

"And does your mom know?"

Ellie bit her lip. "No."

Graham sighed and rubbed at the back of his head. "Do you think this is a good idea?"

"Aren't movie stars supposed to be reckless and irresponsible?" she said, attempting a grin, but it was quick to falter.

"I just don't think—"

"I don't care," she said, her voice infused with a flinty resolve. "I've already decided."

Graham hesitated for a moment, and then he nodded. "Okay," he said. "Then I'm coming too."

She looked surprised. "No, you're not."

"We've got the day off shooting, and I've got nothing to do on the Fourth anyway," he said. "We'll make a road trip out of it."

"You're way too conspicuous."

"I'll blend in."

In spite of herself, she laughed. "Not possible."

"I promise," he said. "I'll wear a cowboy hat. And a fake mustache."

"That's not the slightest bit melodramatic."

"Occupational hazard," he said with a grin.

"How about this?" Ellie said, rising to her feet, the towel still slung around her shoulders. "I'll sleep on it."

"Fine," he said, standing up too. "But I'll start getting my costume ready just in case."

As they began to walk up the beach, he reached for her hand. They were quiet, the rocks crunching beneath their feet, the waves rushing up to the shore behind them.

Three more days, Graham was thinking.

He didn't want to miss a single one of them.

"So are you done for the day?" Ellie asked without looking at him, her head bent as she picked her way over the uneven terrain.

"I am," he told her. "You free tonight?"

"Oh yeah," she said, and he could almost hear the laughter in her voice. "I figure we could take a stroll through town, go to the Lobster Pot, maybe make out a little on the village green..."

"Very funny," he said as they reached the little bank that separated the beach from the trees, and together, they scrambled up the slope. "How about a picnic? We can meet right back here later."

She nodded. "That sounds perfect."

It was darker in the grove, where a bluish dusk had settled into every pocket of space, and Graham allowed himself to be led by Ellie, stumbling a bit as they felt their way toward the street. There was something dreamlike about it, with only the grumble of their footsteps and the sound of their breathing, her smaller hand in his, guiding him along. The beach was only a few yards behind them and the road only a few yards ahead, but right here amid the trees, it felt like they were a million miles away from anything. So when the first flash went off up ahead, it took a moment for him to realize what it was.

If he'd been in Los Angeles or New York, or even just up the road in the middle of Henley, his mind would have moved faster, but here in the gathering dusk, emerging from the solitude of the beach, he was slow to understand the implications. In front of him, Ellie had come to an abrupt stop, dropping his hand. But even as the second light went off and the scene took on a fumbling clarity—

the glint of a motorcycle, the flurry of footsteps, another flash—all he could do was stand there, blinking.

"Graham," came the first shout, and beside him, he could feel Ellie stiffen. "Graham, can you give us a smile? How about a kiss?" There were only three of them, but it felt like more; it felt like they were surrounded.

"What's your name, sweetheart?" one of them asked Ellie, an enormous bald guy who'd been lurking around town since the film crew first arrived. He took a step forward, pacing the edge of the road. They were still mostly hidden in the trees, but there was nowhere else to go from here. "Can we just get one shot?"

It took a moment for Graham to regain himself. He turned to Ellie, grabbing the towel that was slung over her shoulder and whipping it in front of her. When she realized what he was doing, she took it from him, burying her face behind the pattern of seahorses. He put an arm around her shoulders, and though he could feel her resistance, he urged her forward anyway, the two of them tripping over roots and rocks as they made their way up toward the street.

All three of the photographers were snapping pictures now, and it felt different, seeing them here on a quiet stretch of road with no one else around, ominous and just a little bit threatening. They backed up a few steps as Graham's feet hit the pavement, and he tucked Ellie closer to him, hurrying them in the opposite direction without a word.

"C'mon, Graham," the bald guy said, jogging out in front of him, then backpedaling, his camera bumping against his chest. The other two were flanking them, trotting along the shoulder of the road, and Graham glared at the guy to his left.

"Just one shot," he was saying. "One good shot, and we'll leave you alone."

"Get lost," he said through gritted teeth. The photographer lowered his camera, and for a moment, Graham thought that would be it. But then he darted at Ellie, grabbing the end of her towel to yank it away. She let out a little yelp of surprise just as the flash went off, and before he could think better of it, Graham lunged at him, knocking the camera away. It hit the pavement with a splintering sound, and there was the sharp clatter of metal on asphalt, and then a low string of curses as the photographer scrambled to collect his equipment.

The rest of them paused, just for a second. Ellie's towel had fallen to the ground, and seeing an opportunity, one of the other photographers—the bald one—stepped out in front of them. But before he could even raise the camera, Graham was in his face.

"Put it away," he said, his voice low, the words gravelly.

The guy hesitated, but only for a moment, looking around Graham to the third photographer, who held his camera tentatively, the lens pointed at Ellie as she bent to grab the towel.

There was a beat of stillness, then two, as they all stood there, the cameras raised like weapons in a standoff. But just as Ellie straightened up again, a flash cut through the darkness—bright enough to leave them all blinking—and as if the two things were connected, as if one triggered the other, Graham's hand became a fist, and he pulled back his arm, and he punched him.

From. EONeill22@hotmail.com .
Sent: Wednesday, July 3 2013 10:24 PM
To: GDL824@yahoo.com
Subject: (no subject)

You were right. We should've just stayed on the beach forever.

17

Light couldn't possibly have moved faster. Running water. A high-speed train. Nothing, it seemed to Ellie, could have beaten the pixilated photo and accompanying story that spilled out across the fathomless pages of the Internet late that same night.

Sitting on her bed the next morning, the computer propped in her lap, she watched numbly as the articles unspooled across the screen. But she wasn't thinking about the media's version of the story, which seemed to hardly resemble what had happened at all. Instead, she was thinking about the moment itself, the way the photographer had reeled after being hit, tipping sideways like a marionette.

His head had struck the ground with a sound that seemed too heavy to have come from a person, and Ellie had looked on in horror, frozen with shock for a few frightening seconds before he blinked and pushed himself up again. It was Graham who moved first, already shaking his head in apology as he reached out a hand to help him up. But he was stopped cold by a flash, and he turned on one of the other photographers with a menacing glare.

"You asshole," the bald man had said, ignoring Graham's outstretched hand and struggling to his feet on his own. Already, his eye was nothing more than a slit, the skin beneath it puffed up, a crescent of pink that would undoubtedly be turning an angry purple before too long. He pressed two fingers there, wincing, then explored the side of his head where it had hit the pavement. When his eyes focused on Graham again, there was a spark of something so unexpected—smugness, perhaps, or even glee—that Ellie found herself taking a step back.

"You better get ready," the man said to Graham. "I'm gonna take you for all you're worth."

But Graham had already grabbed Ellie by the arm, spinning her around and urging her away from the huddle of black-clad men. She'd hurried to follow him, the urgent *snap-snap-snap* of the cameras trailing after them. But to her relief, she heard no footsteps, and before long, even the flashes had blinked out in their wake.

"You okay?" he asked when they were a safe distance away.

Ellie nodded, though her wrist still tingled from where the towel had been yanked so abruptly from her hands, and she realized she'd left it behind. Somehow, in spite of all that had just happened, it was this—the thought of that seahorse towel, which she'd had since she was a kid, lying wilted on the ground in the middle of an empty road—that caused a lump to rise in her throat.

It was almost fully dark by then, and they'd walked quickly, heads bent and shoulders hunched, propelled by an unsettling mix of anger and fear. Ellie's teeth were chattering, though she wasn't cold. Her mind buzzed with questions both big and small, but she stopped herself from giving voice to them. The way those men had circled them like hyenas, the steady chirp of their cameras—she'd never felt so exposed. Even now, she still couldn't shake the feeling that they were being followed, and she kept whipping around to make sure nobody was there.

As they neared her house, Graham slowed and turned to her. Their eyes met briefly in the darkness, and she could see that his were full of worry. He opened his mouth as if to say something, then closed it again, looking pained.

Already, Ellie was doing an inventory of what tomorrow would bring and she knew that he must have been too, cataloging the phone calls to publicists and lawyers, preparing for the conversation with his manager, thinking through the inevitable fallout. There was nothing more interesting to the world than a self-destructive celebrity, nothing more exciting than a public meltdown. It wouldn't matter that the photographers had been staking them out, or that they'd been overly aggressive. All that would matter was that Graham had punched one of them.

Ellie glanced toward her house. Even through the trees at the end of the driveway, she could see the lights were on in the kitchen. It felt like it had been days since Mom left her bobbing in the water at the beach, and she was probably wondering where she'd gone. It made Ellie queasy to think of explaining to her what had happened tonight.

When she turned back to Graham, he was still watching her. "I'm sorry," he said after a moment, and she watched his lips as he formed the words, reminded of their kiss on the beach. They were supposed to be on a picnic right now, she realized, and the idea of it seemed impossibly distant, like it had been planned by two other people entirely.

Ellie shook her head. "It's not your fault."

"But I made it worse," Graham said, his voice flat. "It'll be so much bigger now. The story."

"It's okay," she said, although she knew it might not be. She'd made the decision to stay away from him in an effort to sidestep this very situation, but then she'd fallen under his spell again, wholeheartedly and perhaps inevitably. And now it didn't seem fair to have gathered so much momentum only to be pulled up short again, yanked back and forth like the worst kind of yo-yo.

Their hearts simply weren't built for this sort of thing.

"I should probably go," she said, her eyes drifting to the house. The air between them felt charged, and Graham forced a smile. But it was an actor's smile—feeble and strained—and it faltered when she took his hand.

"Hey," he said, holding on to her for a moment, his face grim. "I'm gonna do everything I can to fix this, okay?"

She nodded, trying to look convinced, then turned to walk up the driveway, leaving him there on the street. It wasn't until she reached the porch that she slumped against the door, taking a few deep breaths before turning the knob. Inside, she could hear Mom in the kitchen, and she knew somehow that to talk to her would be to break down and cry, and she didn't feel prepared for that just yet—for the explanations and confessions, the weighty implications of the night—and so she called out a hello, her voice thick, and then hurried up the stairs.

In her room, she grabbed her computer and sat cross-legged on the bed, searching for Graham's name. The most recent hits were a picture of him with Olivia in front of the deli from earlier that day and a few articles that speculated about his potential involvement in another movie, but nothing yet about a photographer with a black eye, or a broken camera, or a mysterious girl with red hair whose estranged father may or may not be running for president one day.

She spent the rest of the night there, telling Mom through the door that she wasn't hungry, hitting the refresh button on her computer so many times that the words started to swim and blur, just meaningless chains of letters.

She had no idea what time she fell asleep; she knew only that when she woke up it was still dark out, and it took her a moment to fumble with her phone and see that it was just after five o'clock. The memory of the previous night came back to her in a rush, and she reached for her computer, her head fuzzy with worry.

This time, it was there. All of it. Her heart sank as she read through the headlines: *Graham's Slam; Larkin Doesn't Pull Any Punches; Larkin's Barkin' Mad.* She scrolled through article after article, her stomach churning, wondering if Graham had seen them yet. The first ones had been posted as early as eleven o'clock last night, probably just after Ellie had fallen asleep, and several were accompanied by a photo of Graham just before he struck out, his elbow pulled back like an archer with a bow, his face dark. In the background, Ellie could see the seahorse towel bunched on the street, and behind that, just a sliver of herself: a pale arm and a few strands of reddish hair.

They hadn't gotten anything worth using on her, she realized, though every article mentioned an "unidentified female companion." That seemed to be it, at least for now, but Ellie knew better than to be relieved. She understood the bigness of this, the sheer scope of it, and a worry for Graham pulsed through her like a heartbeat. Some of the articles mentioned a potential lawsuit, while others simply framed him as a sudden and previously unknown menace, as if he were some kind of slumbering beast that had finally awakened. Even if he wasn't sued, she knew how damaging this could be for his image, his career, his movie, and she wished there were a way to defend him, to explain what had happened, how anyone might have done the same.

But she knew she couldn't. And she also knew it wouldn't

be long before someone connected the dots and identified her, some tourist who had seen them together, some local looking to make a buck, some reporter who asked the right questions. It was only a matter of time before the rest would unravel.

She thought about checking her e-mail to see if there was anything from Graham, but she wasn't sure she could bear to read what he might have written or, worse, to find out that he hadn't. Instead, she lifted her hands from the keyboard and looked out the window, where a scrim of light had appeared on the horizon, spliced by the darker shadows of the tree branches.

It was the Fourth of July, she realized, the day she'd meant to go see her father. But now she wasn't sure it was such a good idea. What if they found her name between now and then, those anonymous bloggers and journalists? What if she were to show up on his doorstep only to discover that he'd heard the news? And that he was furious with her for reviving a story that had long been put to bed, one that would distract from his message and have a negative impact on his next campaign?

With a sigh, she hit the refresh button on the computer, and six new stories about Graham Larkin appeared on the list. She swallowed hard and looked out the window again, the sky growing paler at the edges. In the distance, a few seagulls cried out, and down the hall, she heard the groan of the water heater as Mom switched on the shower.

It would be crazy to do this. She'd have to find a way to

borrow the car without telling Mom. She'd have to make sure she wasn't missed at the town festival. She'd have to figure out exactly where her father was staying and pluck up the courage to ask him for money. She'd have to hope the story didn't beat her there, and that nothing would fail her when she arrived—not her legs or her voice or her nerve.

And if she was really going to do this—set out on this ill-advised trip, this one desperate attempt to make things right—then she was going to have to do it now.

From: GDL824@yahoo.com
Sent: Thursday, July 3 2013 11:01 PM
To: EONeill22@hotmail.com
Subject: Re: (no subject)

It's not too late. You bring the crackers. I'll bring my fake mustache.

18

Graham knew he shouldn't have been surprised. But when he opened the door to his hotel room to find Harry in the armchair beneath the window, his hand still flew to his chest, as if to stop his wildly beating heart.

"Jeez," he said, the word coming out in an exhale. Harry only raised a finger to indicate that he was on the phone, throwing him a dark look, and Graham sank down on the end of the bed, rubbing his eyes with the heels of his hands.

There wasn't much to be gleaned from Harry's side of the conversation, and when he finally lowered the phone, they were both quiet. Graham tilted his head to look out across the sea of dirty socks and strewn clothing, pizza boxes and room-service trays, to where his manager was slumped in the chair. His thinning hair was mussed, and he was wearing glasses instead of his usual contacts. There was a laptop perched on the table beside him, and Graham didn't have to see the screen to know what he'd been searching for, though it was hard to believe the information might have traveled that fast.

But here was Harry, clearly aware of the situation, which had occurred not even an hour before. And if he already knew, Graham supposed it was possible the rest of the world did too.

"How'd you even get in here?"

Harry pinched the bridge of his nose. "I told the front desk you were probably passed out drunk."

Graham frowned. "Why would you say that?"

"Because I couldn't possibly think of another explanation for why you might be out punching photographers," he said, and though it was clear he was kidding, when his eyes slid over to meet Graham's across the room, there was a hint of annoyance at what was no doubt coming: a full-blown media storm.

"Obviously I'm not drunk," Graham said, then nodded at the computer. "Is it up yet?"

"Not yet," Harry said.

"Then how do you—"

"I got a call from Mitchell."

Graham looked at him blankly.

"That PA who's always hanging around with the photographers," he explained. "It's gonna move fast."

The phone in Harry's hand rang, and he glanced at the number, then set it aside. In the hallway, they could hear the family next door returning to their room. They'd checked in a few nights ago, and when Graham had passed them in the hall for the first time, they'd all stopped without exactly meaning to. The father was the first to come to his senses, hurrying them along as one of his young daughters cupped a hand over her mouth, the words escaping between her fingers, giddy and disbelieving: "Oh my god, oh my god, oh my god." Even after they'd piled onto the elevator at the end of the hall and the doors had closed behind them, Graham could still hear high-pitched squeals of the two girls, and he hadn't been able to keep from smiling.

Now he tried not to imagine what they might think when they saw his picture on the front page of one of the local papers that were always scattered around the lobby. If it didn't happen tomorrow, it would undoubtedly happen the next day, the photo sure to be dark and grainy, set beneath some kind of silly and melodramatic headline like *Lights Out, Thanks to Larkin.*

"It wasn't bad enough that you broke his camera?" Harry was saying, and Graham tipped his head back with a groan. "You had to punch the guy too?"

"I know," he said. "But he was in my face. They all were. They were basically stalking us."

Harry glanced up at the last word. "Us?" he said, raising an eyebrow. "Let me guess..."

"You don't need to," Graham said, meeting his gaze.

Harry's face was grim, and he reached up to ruffle the back of his hair. Graham could almost see him trying to swallow the words he so desperately wanted to say: *I told you so.* But it was there anyway, in his eyes, and Graham knew he was right. He should have stayed away from Ellie. But he wasn't sorry for the same reasons. He didn't care about bad publicity. He couldn't even muster up any worry over Mick's reaction to all this. All he could think about was Ellie. All he wanted was to make this okay for her.

"So what do we do now?" he asked, sitting forward. "Can we keep this under wraps? Or spin it somehow?"

"I'm trying," Harry said. "If it were only the photos..."

Graham didn't have to ask what that meant. "You mean if I hadn't punched him."

Harry's phone began to ring again, and this time, he brought it to his ear. "Yeah," he said, and then fell silent as he listened. Graham rose to his feet and walked into the bathroom, where he turned on the faucet, splashing cold water on his face, trying to shock away the events of the evening.

He placed a hand on each side of the sink and rocked forward, angry at himself for going down to the beach at all. But when he'd noticed his drawing framed in the window of her mother's shop, there amid all the poems, something about the sight of it had seemed to carry him right down to the cove. And he couldn't for a second regret what had happened there, could still feel it like a stamp across his chest, the place where Ellie had been curled against him.

Under the lights of the bathroom, he examined his hand where his knuckles had come into contact with the photographer's cheekbone as he listened to Harry's voice grow increasingly angry in the next room.

"It's already out," he said a moment later, appearing in the doorway of the bathroom. "Everyone's running with it."

Graham looked up from the stream of water as it coursed over his sore hand. "What about her?" he asked, trying to keep his voice level. "Did they get a clear shot? A name?"

"Unidentified female," he said. "For now, anyway."

He breathed out. "Good," he said. "Can we keep it that way?"

"I'll try my best."

"I know you will," Graham said, turning off the faucet and grabbing a towel. "And I know I shouldn't have done that. It's completely my fault."

"That's true," Harry said, but there was an uncharacteristic softness in his eyes as he leaned against the doorway. He should have been furious. Graham had seen him lose his temper over so much less: a parking ticket, an unhelpful publicist, a greedy producer, and even once, a child actor with a fondness for practical jokes.

Until tonight, Graham had managed to avoid any significant scandals, and Harry had every reason to be livid right now. He would be the one to have to deal with the lawyers, to try to plead with the photographer not to sue. For the next few days, he'd be coordinating with publicists and sweet-talking reporters. He'd be convincing Mick that Graham was still focused on the movie. He'd be trying to keep Ellie's secrets from spilling out, trying to tamp down every bit of information he could, as if it weren't as slippery as water.

And some of it was there, in the set of his jaw and the twitch of his eyelid, an anger that was simmering just below the surface. But there was also an unfamiliar sense of restraint in him too, and for this, Graham was grateful.

"Just tell me what you need me to do," he said, feeling for the first time in a while that this wasn't just business, that they were a team.

"Go get some ice on that," Harry said, nodding at Graham's already bruised knuckles. "And let me do my job."

In his hand, the phone began to ring again, and he winked before bringing it to his ear, already listening intently as he walked back into the other room. With nothing else to do, Graham grabbed the ice bucket from a table near the closet and stepped out into the hallway, standing for a moment with his back against the door.

He knew there were actors who did this kind of thing all the time, and it would never occur to them to feel bad about the mess they'd made or the manager who would have to clean it up, much less worry about the guy they hit. But even though there was no other way the scene could have played out, Graham had never punched anyone before, and the sound of it—an audible crunch of bone on bone— rang in his head even now.

He held the empty ice bucket under his arm like a football as he lumbered down the hall. At the bank of machines, he watched the cubes of ice tumble down in a rush of noise and frozen air, and then he shoved his entire fist inside, wincing at the cold.

When he stepped back into the room, Harry was hunched over the computer. The phone at his side was on speaker, and Graham could hear the familiar voice of Rachel, his publicist, rattling off a list of news sources.

"All of them?" Harry asked, his voice strained.

"Within the hour," Rachel said. "The broken camera didn't help things either."

"Sorry," Graham said, slumping down on one of the beds, and he could almost hear her whole demeanor change, a shift like a tuning fork, sudden and vibrating.

"Hi, hon," she said. "Didn't know you were there."

"Yeah," Graham said. "I'm here."

"What happened?" she asked with forced lightness. "You're usually my easiest client."

Graham must have looked ill equipped to answer this, because Harry stepped in before he could speak. "We'll call you back, Rach, okay?" he said. "Just keep us posted."

"Okay," she said, just before hanging up. "But try to stay out of trouble."

When she was gone, Harry glanced over at Graham. "You look awful," he said. "Why don't you grab a shower? It's gonna be a long night."

Afterward, Graham pulled on the same sandy shorts from the beach and the same striped polo, which still smelled of salt from the ocean. When he emerged from the bathroom, Harry was on another call, and Graham fell back on the bed, his eyes heavy as he listened to one half of the conversation. In spite of all the noise—the rise and fall of Harry's voice, the intermittent buzzing of the phone on the table, the relentless churning hum of the computer—it didn't take long for him to fall into a dreamless sleep.

When he woke, it was still dark out, and across the room, Harry had the computer balanced on his lap, his face lit by the white glow of the screen. There was no part of Graham that wanted to see what was on there, to discover what had been dredged up during the night. He didn't care what they said about him; his only worry was for Ellie.

"Anything?" he asked, sitting up and rubbing his eyes, and Harry startled, looking over at him blearily.

"About you?" he said. "Loads. You want to see?"

Graham shook his head. "And her?"

"Still nothing," Harry said with a tired smile.

He felt a rush of relief. "You're amazing."

"It's why you pay me the big bucks."

"It certainly is," Graham said. Then he slipped into the bathroom, where he stood at the sink. In the mirror, his eyes were rimmed with red, and there was a shadow of a beard across his jaw that made him look vaguely threatening, like he actually was the kind of guy who went around knocking out photographers. He felt a sudden clawing need for air.

"Do you mind if I take a quick walk?" he asked, stepping back into the room, and Harry nodded without looking up from the computer.

"Sure," he said. "I've got this under control for now."

286

"Great," said Graham, reaching for his sweatshirt. "I won't be long."

He closed the door behind him with a quiet click, hurrying down the hallway and into the elevator, then rushing blindly through the lobby and out into the still-waking world, the orange-streaked sky and the coolness of morning, where he stood on the sidewalk and took a great gulp of a breath to calm his thudding heart.

The hotel sat at the far end of the village green, where it presided over the shops and the harbor from a high perch, and when Graham lifted his eyes, he was surprised to see that the town was already busy. He'd expected to see a few fishermen and maybe a jogger or two at this hour, but there were people everywhere, setting up tables near the gazebo and unloading boxes from their cars. A few bleary-eyed children twirled on the grass, and a dog howled from where it was tied to one of the lampposts. It took Graham a moment to realize it was Bagel.

He looked around for Ellie, feeling an inexplicable bolt of panic. If he'd read the news before leaving the room, maybe he wouldn't feel quite so exposed. But now it seemed like the whole world must know something he didn't, whatever details of the previous night the blogs and newspapers had chosen to splash across their pages.

On the other side of the green, a woman was struggling to wrangle a billowing tablecloth in the wind, and the colors— a brilliant red, white, and blue—were a sudden reminder.

It was the Fourth of July.

A group of women with trays of cookies and cupcakes brushed past, too busy to notice him as he stood there, paralyzed with indecision. He knew he should go back up to the room, check in with Harry and find out exactly what parts of the story had leaked and just how much trouble he'd landed in. He should examine the photos, call his parents so they wouldn't be surprised—a thought that filled him with a wobbly kind of dread—and get the game plan from his publicist. He should explain to Mick what had happened, apologize to the photographer, take responsibility for his actions.

But all he wanted was to run in the other direction.

When he saw Mrs. O'Neill—standing on a chair to pin the end of a banner to the gazebo—the memory of Ellie's plans for the day scissored through him, and before he could think better of it, he took off down the street. He tugged up the hood of his sweatshirt to hide his face, moving past the people setting up with his hands shoved in his pockets. At the end of the street, he turned off along the harbor road, past the boats swaying gently in the quiet waters. All of the lobster for today's celebration had been caught already, and where the docks would usually be busy at this hour, there was only silence. Later, people would undoubtedly be out on the water to watch the fireworks, but at this early hour, even the *Go Fish* listed sleepily, excused from a day of filming, just like Graham.

By the time he reached Ellie's house, the chill was gone

from the air. He'd expected she would be asleep, or on the road already, or else busy inside, so when he rounded the corner of the driveway, he was surprised to see her framed by the open mouth of the garage. She was holding a small backpack, her hand on the door of the car, a salt-rusted sedan that had surely been around for years.

"Hi," he called out, and she whirled around, her eyes wide and a guilty blush spreading across her cheeks. But when she saw it was only him, she relaxed again, letting out a shaky laugh.

"I thought you were my mom," she said, opening the car door and tossing the backpack inside. She was wearing jeans and a purple tank top with a pair of sunglasses perched on her head, and she had about a thousand new freckles spread across her cheeks after spending yesterday at the beach.

"I get that a lot," Graham said, walking over to lean against the trunk. "Typecasting."

She smiled at this, but it was quick to fall flat again. "Did you see?"

He didn't have to ask what she was talking about. "No," he said, shaking his head. "I couldn't bring myself to look. But Harry said they didn't get your name."

Ellie lowered her eyes. "Not yet, anyway."

They were both quiet for a moment, and then she cleared her throat.

"I have to get going," she told him.

Graham nodded. "I'm coming too."

She looked at him sharply. "No, you're not."

"What time are we leaving?" he asked, as if he hadn't heard her, but she only frowned up at him, her eyes narrowed.

"I get it," she said. "I get that you want to get out of here today. But last night changed things. This is important, and you're way too conspicuous."

"I told you," he said, attempting a smile, "I'll wear a disguise."

Ellie shook her head again. "Sorry."

When she turned to head back into the house, Graham followed her without an invitation. "What do you think will happen?"

She spun to face him, her green eyes measuring him. "There are a million different possibilities," she said. "We could stop for gas and someone might recognize you. Some twelve-year-old girl in the next car could look over and start texting all her friends. We could have photographers following us on motorcycles." She paused and shook her head. "*You*," she said. "We could have photographers following *you* on motorcycles. This is going to be tricky enough without having Graham Larkin as a wingman."

He was stung by the way she said his name, like he was someone she didn't even know, but he refused to back down. They were in the kitchen now, and Ellie opened the door to the fridge, peering at the shelves like she'd forgotten why she was there in the first place. He walked up beside her, feeling the cool of the artificial air on his bare legs.

"I have to do this alone," she said, her voice soft.

From where he was standing, he could see the freckles sprinkled across her pale shoulder, and he could smell her shampoo—something sweet, like lavender. He swallowed hard, but didn't say anything.

After a moment, Ellie shook her head. "You're too conspicuous," she said again, but this time, the words were wavery and Graham took a step closer.

"Then let's not take a car," he said, an idea taking shape in his mind.

She turned, just slightly, but enough to find herself angled between Graham and the door. "What, then?" she asked, and he smiled.

"We'll go by boat."

From: EONeill22@hotmail.com
Sent: Thursday, July 4, 2013 7:18 AM
To: GDL824@yahoo.com
Subject: (no subject)

I'm running a few minutes late, but I'll see you down there. I can only assume you'll be the one with the mustache...

19

They agreed to meet at the harbor in an hour.

Graham went to get a few things in town, including the keys for the *Go Fish* from the prop trailer, while Ellie fumbled around on her computer, trying to plot the course from Henley to Kennebunkport. From what she could tell, if they made good time, they could be there in just over two hours. It wasn't yet seven o'clock, so even if the news broke early, they should still be able to beat it there.

Outside, the sky already had the makings of a perfect summer day, and the water stretched out as wide and still as a great blue carpet. As Ellie walked into town, her backpack heavy on her shoulders, she counted the merits of their plan in the same way she might count the benefits of an extra ice-cream cone (calcium) or a few extra minutes of sleep (energy). There were a dozen ways she could try to justify taking the boat, but mainly, they were avoiding the biggest snag in Ellie's previous scheme: the fact that she'd have to somehow borrow Mom's car. She'd still been working out how to handle that particular issue when Graham had shown up, all confidence and conviction, and she'd let herself get carried away with him.

The truth was, it didn't matter how she got there: by car or by boat or by high-flying hot-air balloon. No matter how she arrived, the ending would be the same: she'd have to face her father. And the idea of standing before him as he tried to register just who exactly she was—a look of confusion in his eyes, or worse, something even more dismissive, a look of annoyance—was almost too painful to contemplate.

Her reason for going was simple: she was planning to ask him for money. But she also knew it was a lot more complicated than that.

Closer to town, the road dipped away from the trees, curving toward the water, and where the air would normally be filled with the sounds of boats—the deep pealing bells and the blaring of the horns—there was now only the discordant notes of the band as they cued up on the green. From a distance, Ellie could see a blur of red, white, and blue, the usual chaos of food and music and games that colored the festivities, and she was counting on all of that to distract Mom later on, when it would no doubt occur to her that she hadn't seen her daughter all day.

As she stepped onto the long boardwalk, hurrying past the shuttered bait shop, she craned her neck to see if Graham was already out on the boat. The film crew had been given a prime slip for the duration of their shoot, and Ellie knew the trickiest part would be getting out of the harbor unnoticed.

The whole town would be up in the village, but it wouldn't be long now before some of them would begin to load up their own boats. Today was a day for sailing and drinking, for bobbing out under the blazing sun until the sky flipped over into dark and the fireworks were sent scribbling out over all of it. For now, she took comfort in the fact that even if someone saw them, they would never guess their plan; it was only her mom she had to worry about.

Near the gated entrance to the harbor, Ellie was startled to see Quinn up ahead on the road. It was disorienting to run into her here, in this of all moments, and she couldn't help feeling unprepared. They were far enough apart that she could have pretended not to notice her. But when their eyes met, she saw the slightest hitch in Quinn's step, the smallest pause in her momentum. Ellie offered her a smile, and she came to a reluctant stop just a few feet away, the two of them regarding each other across the bed of yellow flowers that separated the boardwalk from the road that ran parallel to it.

"Hi," Ellie said, and Quinn yielded a polite smile. She was wearing a blue shirt from Sprinkles, and it took only a moment for Ellie to realize which one it was.

"You got the stain out," she said with a grin, and something flickered to life behind Quinn's eyes where before there had been only a carefully maintained coolness.

"It's not great," she said, holding out the hem to examine it. "But my other ones were dirty." When she looked up again, she seemed to be considering something. "I still have to give yours back."

297

"Keep it," Ellie told her, and she smiled—this time, for real. "It's the least I can do as your wardrobe specialist."

"That day was sort of a mess," she said, and Ellie knew she was talking about more than just the milkshake. She was talking about all of it, everything that had happened since the movie trailers had arrived in town.

"Listen..." Ellie began, but Quinn interrupted her.

"You'll be at the party later, right?" she asked, her voice light. They'd gone together ever since they were little, year after year spent running through the green with a cupcake in one hand and a sparkler in the other. When they were ten, they stole a whole box of firecrackers and slipped down to the beach at the end of the night, setting them off one by one, and it had since become a tradition. Because of all that had happened this summer, Ellie had assumed this would be the year it would end. But now, the way Quinn was looking at her, she wasn't so sure.

She glanced off toward the boats. "I don't know," she said quietly, surprised to discover that her throat was tight. She wished she could tell Quinn where she was going. It had always been the two of them through everything— every adventure and every expedition—and now there was this awful distance between them, and she tried not to think about all the stories they were missing out on, all the little moments and bigger milestones that had happened over the past few weeks without the other knowing.

Quinn furrowed her brow. "You don't know?"

"I have to run an errand," she said, which was as close to

the truth as she could manage. "But hopefully I'll make it back in time."

Out of the corner of her eye, Ellie could see Graham approaching from the opposite direction, and she was relieved when he turned toward the boat. Her eyes slid back to Quinn. "You'll be there?"

She nodded.

"With Devon?"

"Of course," she said, her tone abrupt, but then she caught herself, hesitating for a beat before inclining her head. "And Graham?"

"I don't know," Ellie said honestly.

Quinn looked thoughtful, her features void of the sharpness that had lately become so routine when they were together. "Well, maybe we'll meet up."

"I hope so," Ellie said, trying not to sound too eager. But she was overcome by a sudden and powerful wish for things to go back to how they used to be. She wanted to stand on the beach and watch the firecrackers go twirling out into the darkness. And she wanted Quinn to be at her side. Not this Quinn, exactly, but the old one. She wanted her best friend.

"I'm late," Quinn said, and to Ellie, this felt like the worst kind of dismissal. "I should go."

"Okay," she said. "It was really good to see you."

The expression on Quinn's face was difficult to read, and it took a long time for her to respond, so long that Ellie was certain she wasn't going to say anything at all. "Your e-mail," she said finally. "I didn't get a chance to write back..."

"It's okay," Ellie said quickly, and Quinn hesitated for another long moment before nodding, her eyes soft.

"It's gonna be hot today," she said. "Don't forget to put on some sunscreen."

Ellie smiled. "I won't," she said, but what she was thinking was, *Welcome back.*

As she made her way over to the harbor entrance, she felt a peculiar buoyancy, a lightness that carried her toward the boat. The sound of the seagulls was bright against the dull rush of the waves, and everything seemed to glint beneath the sun. The morning felt like a mixing bowl just waiting for its ingredients; there was a sense of possibility to it, a promise of something more to come.

When she pushed open the gate that led to the docks, it was to find Graham waiting by the boat, looking unnervingly handsome even in yesterday's wrinkled clothes. She searched his face for any signs that he'd checked in with Harry during the time they were apart, trying to gauge whether anything had changed, but there was nothing but his usual smile, a smile that seemed to be just for her.

"Ahoy," he said, lifting a hand as she approached. "Ready to set sail?"

"They were okay with you borrowing it?" she asked as he held out a hand to help her climb aboard. She hopped over the gap between the starboard side of the boat and the dock, landing unsteadily on the wooden baseboards of the interior. It was much bigger than it looked from afar, and older too—not made up to look old, as she'd suspected, but properly old. She'd half expected it to seem fake, more like a movie prop than a real working lobster boat, but other than a few metal cinches attached to the sides to fasten the cameras and hold them steady while filming, it bore no signs of the production.

"Totally fine," Graham said lightly as he stepped in after her.

The water looked calm, but already Ellie felt the deck swaying beneath her feet, and she held on to Graham's shoulder as she dropped her backpack onto a wooden bench along the port side. There was a small cabin in front with a glass windshield and an old-fashioned-looking wheel for the captain. In the back, several empty lobster traps knocked against one another, and a few red buoys rolled back and forth in time with the waves.

Ellie stepped over one of the many ropes that were coiled securely at various places along the deck. Up the hill, the sounds of the band drifted down to the water. They would play all day, she knew, and if she were to stop by later this afternoon or even tonight, they would still have the same energy to their songs, which were powerful and brassy and patriotic, the perfect send-off for a sea voyage.

"Ready to go?" she asked Graham, who was examining the many dials at the helm. The key chain that dangled from his hand had a squishy orange float attached, in case it went overboard.

"Sure," he said, holding it out for her.

But Ellie only stared at it. "I thought you were driving."

"What?"

She nodded at the key chain, which was still swaying between them. "Aren't you driving?" she said. "It was your idea."

Graham shook his head. "It's a lobster boat," he said, and when she didn't respond, he widened his eyes, as if it should be obvious. "You're from Maine."

"So you just assume I can drive a lobster boat?"

"Well, yeah," he said. "Can't you?"

"Do I look like a lobsterman?" she asked with a frown. "I thought *you* knew how. I saw you driving the other day."

He looked at her blankly. "When?"

"When you were filming."

"It's a movie," he said and groaned. "I was acting."

Ellie sighed. "Well, why would they lend you a boat if you can't drive it?"

"I never said they lent it to me."

It took a moment for this to register, and when it did, she reached out and punched his shoulder. "Are you kidding me?" she said. "You stole the keys?"

"I told you," he explained, rubbing the spot where she'd hit him. "They won't mind if we borrow it."

Ellie opened her mouth and then closed it again. She turned around and walked to the far end of the boat, where

302

she stood looking up at the town, trying to decide whether it was too late to get to her mother's car.

She was still there when Graham appeared at her side.

"It's okay," he told her. "I know enough."

"How?" she asked, without looking at him.

"They had me take a few lessons before the shoot. It's enough to get us there and back. I just figured you might be more of an expert."

She turned to face him. "Because I'm from Maine."

"Because you're from Maine," he agreed.

"Well, I've been driving Quinn's ski boat for years," she said. "But this looks pretty different."

"We'll figure it out then," he said. "Between the two of us."

"Between the two of us?" she said, and he gave her a sheepish smile.

"Well, mostly you."

She held out a flattened palm, and he dropped the keys into her hand. "That was some pretty good acting the other day, then," she told him, "because you looked like a regular sea captain out there."

"Then you don't need to worry," he said, leading her back to the front of the boat. "If you'd seen my other movies, you'd know that I'm also a magician."

– Uh-oh.

– What?

– I forgot my phone.

– So?

– So how am I supposed to e-mail you now?

– I guess we'll just have to talk.

Once they were out of the harbor—through the precarious maze of buoys and docks—Graham relaxed. The open water stretched out ahead of them, blue-green waves tipped in white, like some great confection coated with powdered sugar, and the thin line where the paler sky met the darker ocean with perfect symmetry. Everything shimmered under the gaze of the sun, and Graham closed his eyes against the wind and the spray of the wake on either side of the boat as they sliced through the water.

Beside him, Ellie stood with one hand on the wheel, moving it back and forth every so often, the tiniest of adjustments that went unfelt as the boat barreled ahead, leaving behind a trail of white foam. At first, they didn't speak; the rush of the wind was too loud in their ears. But even without words, there was a complicity to the moment that felt louder than all the rest of it. Together, they had made their escape.

"See?" Graham shouted over the wind, and Ellie cocked her head in his direction. "You're a pro."

She shrugged. "Turns out it's not all that different from a ski boat."

The last time he'd been out here, Olivia had been the one at his side, and in between takes she'd brushed the flecks of water from her face and scowled. They had only two more days of filming left, and he knew she was excited to get back to L.A. For her, this was nothing but a time-out, an unwelcome break from her regular life, which consisted of photo-ops and fancy parties, manicures and meetings.

But now that Ellie had returned to him, Graham felt the last day approaching with a deep sense of dread. He would miss watching the fishing boats go out in the morning, the way the sun broke across the village green, the sound of the waves that seemed to follow you throughout the town. And, of course, he'd miss Ellie. He didn't feel ready to say good-bye just yet, and the thought of it was something he'd been chasing from his mind with alarming frequency.

"Can I try?" he asked, and Ellie stepped aside, leaving two fingers lightly on the wheel until she was sure he had it. He peered out through the glass, watching the bow of the boat moving up and down like a rocking chair.

"You're a natural," she said, and to his surprise, she leaned against him, coming to rest beneath his free arm, which he looped around her shoulders. He was embarrassed by how tall this made him feel, how adult, with one hand on the wheel and his girl at his side, and he straightened his back and lifted his chin and let out a happy sigh.

"I think I've found my new calling," he told her, and she laughed and slipped away from him again, quick as a minnow. She reached for her backpack and pulled out a water bottle, taking a sip, and then offered it to Graham, who shook his head. "I feel like Ahab," he said. "Off on another quest."

"Hopefully a more successful one this time."

"It will be," he promised.

"And if not, at least we'll have found you a backup career for this whole acting thing," she teased. "Sailing the seven seas."

"That's not the worst idea," he said. "It sure beats L.A."

She sat down on the bench that ran the length of each side of the boat, a place to stow tackle and nets and buoys. "I don't know," she said. "The circus probably never thinks the towns where they stop are boring either."

"Are you saying I'm the circus?"

She grinned. "I'm saying you're a clown, anyway."

"Thanks," he said, laughing as he looked out toward the shore, where enormous houses were perched along the rocky coast. They passed a sailboat, and the couple aboard waved. Graham lifted a hand in return.

"This is going to make things worse, isn't it?" Ellie asked, and he glanced over at her. "Taking the boat."

"It might," he said with a shrug. "But it's not like we're smuggling drugs or anything."

She looked at him sideways. "Does chocolate count?"

"No, I'm pretty sure that's okay."

"Good," she said, pulling a bag of candy from the backpack and tossing it over to him. He caught it with one hand, then held the wheel with his forearm while he opened it. The chocolate was soft from the sun, and it melted on his tongue. He felt a spreading warmth expand in his chest, and he wished they could stay out here all day. But he knew they were on a mission of sorts, and it was there in Ellie's every move: a grim sense of resolve.

"So are you nervous?" he asked, passing the bag back over to her. "To see your dad?"

She nodded, her lips pressed into a straight line.

"Do you have a plan?"

This time, she didn't answer, and Graham wondered if his words had been whipped away by the wind; it almost seemed like she hadn't heard him. But then she pushed her sunglasses up on her head, and he was able to see her green eyes again, focused on him with an intensity that made his heart skip like the bow over the waves.

"Remember that poetry course?" she asked, but she didn't wait for him to respond. "It's a big deal to get in. And I really want to go."

He wrinkled his brow. "I thought you were."

"I am," she said, a bit too fiercely. "But I'm still short. And there are no scholarships."

Graham sucked in a breath as he waited for her to continue, biting back the question he wanted to ask, though he knew it would be the wrong thing to say right now; the moment felt delicate, easily breakable, and so he kept quiet.

"I'm gonna ask him for the rest," she said, and her words came out in a rush. "I can't ask my mom for that much, and it's not like he doesn't have it."

"How much—" he began, unable to help himself, but she cut him off, as if she hadn't heard him.

"And it feels like he owes me at least that," she said, digging at a groove in the wood with her fingernail. "All these years, and nothing. And it's not like I'm using the money for something crazy or frivolous, like a car or a tattoo."

Graham raised his eyebrows. "That's true."

"It's for school," she said. "It's for Harvard."

Against his better judgment, he cleared his throat. "How much do you still need?"

She raised her eyes to meet his. "A thousand dollars," she said quietly, the words almost lost to the breeze, and then she bent her head over the wood again.

A thousand dollars, Graham thought, ashamed at how small the number seemed to him. He was reminded of the money his parents had used to send him to private school, how enormous that had seemed at the time, how much it had cost them to use it. Now things were different. *A thousand dollars.* Just last month, he'd paid a contractor almost twice that to build an indoor pen for Wilbur in the back of the laundry room. He'd seen his costars drop that much on a celebratory meal, and he was sure the many purses strewn around Olivia's trailer added up to at least that, and probably even more.

He looked over at the curve of Ellie's shoulders as she sat there on the bench. For her, a thousand dollars was clearly an insurmountable obstacle, enough to send her off on a stolen boat to seek out her estranged father. How easy it would be to write her a check, to hand her a thick stack of bills, to surprise her by sending the payment to Harvard without saying a word. But this wasn't a movie, and he knew her well enough to guess that she wouldn't consider him a hero, and she wouldn't throw her arms around his neck in gratitude. There was a fragile pride to her that would never allow her to accept that kind of charity. This was something she had to do herself.

"What if..." Graham began to ask, keeping his shoulders square to the windshield. "What if he says no?"

Behind him, Ellie slung a hand over the side of the boat, letting her fingertips catch the spray of the water. "Then I'm not going," she said, her voice flat. "But how could he say no?"

What Graham didn't say—what neither of them said—was that he would almost certainly say no if last night's episode were to land him in the gossip columns just as he was revving up his fund-raising campaign. Graham realized now why she'd been in such a rush to leave. She was trying to outrun the news.

She stood up and sidled around him, reaching out to

take the wheel. He stepped out of the way to let her drive, and she shifted the boat into a higher gear, the nose lifting out of the water as the engine dug in and they picked up speed.

When he looked over the side of the boat, Graham could see the dark shadows of fish beneath the surface. If things had turned out differently, he might be out here with his own father right now, their lines dangling, an easy silence between them as they waited for something to bite.

The shoreline was rougher here, the looming estates had given way to smaller fishing cabins, and he thought of all the other pairs of fathers and sons that might be gathering their gear at this very moment, ready to spend the holiday in quiet company. They all seemed so peaceful, so serene, these homes that dotted the shoreline. How nice it would be to have a house up here—nothing fancy, just a little cabin set back along the coast, a place to visit when he grew tired of the plastic landscape of Los Angeles, a way to keep this particular piece of the world with him even after he was gone.

"Hey," he said, twisting around and pointing toward the shore. "Do you know what town this is?"

Ellie turned to look, then shook her head. "How come?"

"It just looks nice is all."

"Look it up," she suggested, and he felt for his phone in his pocket before remembering that he'd left it back at the hotel. He hadn't done it intentionally, and he'd only realized this as they were gliding out of the harbor, but it wasn't the worst day to lose his tether to the rest of the world. There was nobody he wanted to hear from at the moment, not Harry or Rachel or Mick or anyone else. Without it, he'd thought he might feel unhinged, but all he felt was free.

"I don't have mine, remember?" he said. "Can I borrow yours?"

It was balanced on the dashboard in front of her, and she nudged it in his direction. He pulled up the map feature, waiting for the radar to register, a slow dance of pixels arranging themselves across the screen. The wind lifted the hair from his forehead, and he squinted out at the church steeple that rose from the trees along the coast, the idea of his future home growing more solid in his mind.

He was about to tell Ellie what he was thinking when they cut across the wake of another boat, their own vessel popping up like a skipped rock, and the phone went flying out of his hands in slow motion, pinwheeling end over end until it landed soundlessly in the water. The surface was too busy with foam to see even a ripple, and in seconds they were past it, the little square of metal probably halfway to the sandy bottom.

"Uh," he said, his back still to Ellie.

"What?" she asked from behind him.

"Your phone..."

"Don't tell me."

"I'm afraid it's swimming with the fishes," he said, stepping over to her with what he hoped was a sufficiently apologetic look. "I'm really sorry. It just slipped."

She groaned.

"I'll buy you a new one."

"That's not very helpful at the moment," she told him. "I was using that to navigate."

He looked out the front of the boat. There were a few sailboats in the distance, and a motorboat toting a water-skier, and to the left, nearer to the shore, the harbors were speckled by buoys, each one capped by a resting seagull. The town he'd so desperately wanted to move to only a moment ago had slipped behind them, lost for now.

"We'll be able to see it from here, though, right?"

Ellie shrugged. "It's not like a train stop," she said. "The towns aren't labeled. I'm not sure how we're gonna figure out which one it is."

"I'm sure it'll have a bunch of big houses."

"I guess so," she said, but the corners of her mouth were turned down, and her eyes gave away her worry.

"We can always ask someone."

"How?" she asked. "By smoke signal?"

"We'll wave them down."

She glanced at her watch with a sigh. "It's only eleven," she said. "It'll probably still be a while, anyway."

"Okay," he said. "We'll just keep an eye out, then."

"Okay," she repeated, and above their heads, a seagull let out a long cry. Graham tipped his head back to watch, wondering what they must look like from the sky, dozens of boats spread far along the water, a mirror image of the birds fanned out across the sky. And in the middle of it all, the *Go Fish*, moving steadfastly past a series of identical towns as it carried them farther and farther up the coast, leaving only a trail of foam in its wake, like bread crumbs meant to guide them home again.

– Know any good sailing jokes?

  I've got one about seagulls.

– Okay.

– Why do seagulls fly over the sea?

– Why?

– Because if they flew over the bay, they'd be bagels.

21

The sun followed them like a spotlight, making everything shimmer under the intensity of its glare. Ellie could feel the warmth across her shoulders and on the back of her neck, the tip of her nose, and the pale line of scalp that was visible against her red hair. It had been more than two hours now, and still they were drifting.

Graham scratched at his forehead, which was already starting to burn. He'd forgotten to pick up sunblock earlier, and they were now out of water too. Every so often, they shifted to a lower gear, slowing enough to wave at a passing boat and then shouting their question across the blue space between them. Sometimes, an answer was lobbed back at them—*probably another half hour at most*, or *four more towns, tops*—but other times, they were met with only blank stares or helpless shrugs.

Ellie tried to tamp down the anxiety that rose and fell like a parachute inside her. She wanted to be back in Henley, drinking pink lemonade out of star-spangled plastic cups. But if she was going to do this at all—and she *had* to, not just for the money, but for other reasons too, for all the things that had been left unsaid all these years—then she wanted to do it now.

Behind her, she heard a tapping sound, and she turned to see Graham with one hand on the wheel. He was frowning down at the little dials that dotted the dashboard, and as she watched, he lifted a finger to drum at one of them again. Beneath her feet, Ellie could feel something deep within the boat groan in resistance as they slowed down.

"What's wrong?" she asked, walking over to join him. She put a hand on the throttle and tipped it forward, but rather than the expected surge, there was a soft sputtering, an alarming rattle, and then the engine cut out entirely, and the needle that Graham had been studying so intently—which Ellie now realized, too late, was the gas gauge—fell onto the *E* with a stiff-armed finality.

Graham looked over at her, his mouth forming a little *o* of surprise, and for a brief and fragile moment, Ellie felt a lump rise in her throat. Her eyes stung from the salt and she could feel a sunburn setting in, so hot it made her shiver. Here they were, floating up the coast with not a drop of gas left in their stolen boat. Behind them, there were reporters and photographers and consequences. There was Ellie's mom and Graham's manager and the awful memory of last night. But what lay ahead of them wasn't much better, and now they were stuck somewhere in between, and her eyes burned with tears at the helplessness of the situation.

Beside her, she could feel Graham waiting for her reaction, holding himself perfectly still, like a deer caught between crosshairs. But when she finally gathered herself enough to look back at him, she was astonished to discover 'that he was trying not to laugh.

"It's not funny," she said. He tried to compose his face, but he couldn't help himself, and a laugh escaped him. He looked like a movie star then, with eyes as blue as the water that surrounded them, his head crowned by the sun so that he seemed as wavy and indistinct as all the rest of it. She had a sudden urge to stand on her tiptoes and kiss him, and she could feel her panic melting beneath his gaze. After all, it seemed to be saying, what better excuse was there to stay out here for hours, just the two of them, at the whim of the tides?

"It's a little funny," he said, and she moved closer, taking his hands in hers.

"Maybe a little," she admitted, but just as he lowered his head, just before she could rise up and kiss him, the air was split by the sound of a nearby siren, and they both turned to see a coast guard boat barreling in their direction.

Graham dropped her hands, and Ellie staggered over to lean against the side, her eyes wide as she watched its approach, the prow raised high in the air as the water churned all around it, alarming in its rush.

"What are the odds," Graham said, "that they've realized we're out of gas and are just coming over to help?"

"Slim," Ellie said, her heart thumping hard. She'd never

so much as stolen a pack of gum before, never sneaked a cigarette or cheated on a test, and now here she was, about to get caught stealing a boat. It wouldn't matter that she wasn't the one to have stolen it. She'd gone along with the plan. Because Graham had stolen it *for her*, and she could almost feel the guilt scrawled all over her face as she watched the gap between the two boats grow smaller. Theirs was more of a ship, really, huge and white and angular, with blaring red lights along the top. When they were close enough, a man in dark sunglasses and a bright orange Windbreaker raised a megaphone.

"Please remain where you are," he said, the words crackling. "Do not move your vessel."

"We couldn't if we tried," Graham mumbled.

"This is bad," Ellie whispered. "Isn't it?"

"It's not good," he admitted, but when he saw her face, he forced a cheerfulness into his voice. "It'll be fine, though. It's just a misunderstanding. We'll work it out."

When the coast guard ship drew up alongside theirs, the man lowered the megaphone. "This boat has been reported missing," he called out. "Know anything about that?"

Graham cupped his hands around his mouth to call back. "It's my fault, sir," he said. "I was only borrowing it."

The officer took off his sunglasses and squinted at Graham. "You're that guy," he said, looking perplexed. "From those movies."

"Exactly," Graham said, bobbing his head encouragingly. "I'm up here filming a new one, and we've been using the boat—it was a production guy who called it in, I bet, right?—and I guess I just forgot to let someone know."

Ellie marveled at the ease of his explanation, the nonchalant way in which he chalked the whole thing up to a misunderstanding, and the reaction of the officer, who seemed to be absorbing all this with a thoughtful air. If it had been Ellie, she would have been stumbling through the story, flustered and nervous. Even if she were telling the truth, she would somehow manage to appear guilty.

"Give me a minute," the officer said, holding up a finger. "I just need to verify this."

He disappeared back into the cabin of the boat, and Ellie turned to Graham. Before she could say anything, he gave her shoulder a reassuring squeeze. "It'll be fine," he said. "It *does* come in handy sometimes, this whole being-recognized thing."

Even so, they waited in tense silence. A few Jet Skiers streamed past, their yellow life jackets bright against the water, and a plane flew low overhead. Ellie wasn't wearing a watch, and her phone was now somewhere on the bottom of the Atlantic, so she had no idea what time it was, but the sun had crossed the highest point, and she imagined it must be well after noon by now.

When the man returned, he took off his sunglasses and rubbed the back of his neck. "I spoke with the guy who called it in," he said, then glanced at a piece of paper in his

323

hand. "He didn't realize you were the one who'd taken it. He said it's no trouble at all, just to bring it back in one piece."

Graham flashed a smile and lifted his hand in a little gesture of gratitude. "Thanks, sir," he said. "I'm sorry to have caused any confusion."

The officer nodded, and was about to turn around when Ellie called out to him. "Actually, we're out of gas," she said quickly, and he raised his eyebrows, looking weary at the prospect of another problem from the movie star on the borrowed boat. He didn't offer any suggestions, just stood there looking at her, so she cleared her throat and tried again. "What should we do?"

Forty-five minutes later, the coast guard had towed them into a marine gas station in the small town of Hamilton. The two officers had been cordial about the whole thing—though Ellie suspected that underneath their professional veneers they were both thinking about what an idiot you'd have to be to run out of gas—and Graham even signed an autograph for one of their daughters.

They left them in the hands of a mustached man who set about filling the tank, bidding them good-bye with a smart tip of their coast guard caps. Ellie watched them go back out to sea, relieved to be on dry land, her stomach still flopping around like a beached fish.

"How far to Kennebunkport?" Graham asked while the attendant came around to examine the gauge, his wrinkled face pressed close to the dial.

"Ten minutes by bus," he said without looking over.

"Why would we take a bus?"

"Because your gauge is busted," the man said, straightening up. "I just filled you up and it's still showing you're empty. I need to fix the dial. Shouldn't take more than an hour."

Graham handed over his credit card, and they agreed to return later in the day. There was a local bus that arrived every half hour, stopping at each town along the coast, and the attendant crooked a finger up a tree-lined road to where they could apparently find the stop just in front of the town's tourist center.

Their legs were rubbery after so many hours on the water, and they made their way across the street unsteadily. Ellie was relieved to see that the tourist center wasn't far—a narrow wooden building that looked more like a tree house than any kind of office—and the bus stop was directly in front of it, nothing more than a red plastic bench and a nearly unreadable schedule tacked to the back of a stop sign.

Graham squinted at it. "Twelve minutes," he said, then glanced at the tourist office. "Let's check it out."

Inside, an older woman with a halo of wispy hair was hunched behind the desk, her head bent over a thick book. Ellie began to wander around the periphery of the small space, which was lined with brochures about everything from sailboat rides to whaling trips to blueberry-picking expeditions, but Graham walked right up to the desk.

"Happy Fourth," he said brightly, and the woman glanced

up, her face registering no recognition. If there was an element of the job that required a welcoming demeanor, then she was certainly out of her depth. She made no move to ask if they needed help, only pursed her lips and stared at them over her glasses.

Graham pointed at the computer behind the desk. "We've had kind of a rough morning," he said, his voice a little too saccharine, "and I was just wondering if it might be possible to borrow your computer to check in about something. Just for one quick minute."

From where she was standing before a panel of brochures about lobster-related activities, Ellie smirked. She had no idea what he wanted the computer for, but it was obvious the woman—staring up at him with a befuddled expression—had no clue who he was, and even Ellie didn't believe he could make this happen on charm alone.

But he flashed her a dazzling smile, uttered a somewhat sheepish "please," and just like that, without a word, she was moving aside, tucking the book under her arm and clearing a space for Graham to sit beside the counter, like he was in charge of all tourist-related information for the town of Hamilton.

Afterward, as they walked out to wait for the bus, she rolled her eyes at him.

"What?" he asked. "Didn't think I could pull it off?"

She shook her head in amusement. "What'd you need to look up anyway?"

"I just wanted to make sure there was nothing new," he said. "Before we go see your father."

Ellie blinked at him, impressed that he'd thought of it. "And?"

"Just the same old stuff," he said. "Graham Larkin's a brute, Graham Larkin's a thug. Nothing you didn't already know." He said this jokingly, but there was a tightness to his voice too, and she remembered that he hadn't checked the news before they'd left. That he'd done it for her—to make sure she was fully prepared before approaching her father—touched her deeply, and as the bus came squealing around the corner, she laid a hand on his arm.

"Thanks," she said, and he nodded. As they climbed aboard, Graham produced a few bills for the driver, and they found a seat near the front, far enough away from the few other passengers, who gazed out the windows toward the back.

"So the next time that woman opens her computer," Ellie said, leaning against the window, "her search history is going to say something like 'Graham Larkin punches photographer.' "

He laughed. "I think it was actually 'Graham Larkin clocks the idiot who got too close with his camera.' "

As they wound their way out of town, drawing nearer to Kennebunkport, the houses in the windows grew larger and more imposing, huge beachside mansions with porches that jutted out over the water, all of them topped with

American flags that waved crisply against the cloudless sky.

Before she'd left this morning, Ellie had found the address of the house where her father was staying, a feat that hadn't turned out to be all that difficult. The estate had a long history of being rented by important politicians, and there was a sizable paper trail left behind by the journalists who'd made a habit out of lurking around its edges. She'd sifted through enough images that even now, hours later, she could call up the weathered gray siding and wraparound porch with perfect clarity. But what she couldn't imagine was walking up the flagstone path and knocking on those red double doors. What she couldn't imagine was coming face-to-face with Paul Whitman.

She turned to Graham, who was hiding a yawn behind his hand. "Okay," she said, her voice businesslike. "I need a plan of attack."

"Going to war, are we?"

"I can't just waltz up to his house without knowing how this is gonna work," she said, swiveling to face him more fully. "What if his wife's there? And his sons?"

"Your half brothers," Graham pointed out, and Ellie shrugged.

"I guess."

"Well, have you figured out what you want to say to him?"

"Sort of," she said, which wasn't exactly true. She had no idea what she wanted to say. How could she, when she wasn't even quite sure how she felt? She'd spent years studying his photos and watching his interviews, observing the life he'd built from afar, wondering what it would be like to be part of it. But now that she was this close, the idea that he might not be happy to see her was too devastating to consider.

After all, he hadn't ever denied that he was her father—at least not in any kind of official capacity—but he hadn't ever acknowledged it either. Which meant that in the eyes of the world, she was still fatherless and he was still daughterless. And there was no way of knowing how he'd react when she showed up at his door. Was it possible that he might recognize her? Would she recognize him? And not just in the way she did in the newspapers, but on a deeper level; she wondered if there'd be some spark of familiarity, of belonging, something to indicate that they were more than just two strangers standing on opposite sides of a doorway. That they were family.

Ellie wasn't sure. She was grateful to be armed with the knowledge that he wasn't aware of what had happened last night, that at the very least, she hadn't yet dragged his name through the papers. But there were still so many other unknowns.

"Practice on me," Graham suggested, sitting up taller against the back of the seat and puffing out his chest. He dipped one eyebrow and arranged his mouth into an overly serious frown. "Hello there, young lady," he said, and the imitation of her father was so striking that Ellie gave his arm a little shove.

"Stop," she said. "Too weird."

Graham relaxed again, unfazed. "Okay, then what?"

"I guess I'm just gonna knock on the door and see what happens."

"At least you've got the element of surprise on your side," he said, folding his arms across his chest. "He'll be caught off guard, and it'll give you a chance to figure out how to play it."

"I guess," she said, turning back to the window.

As they neared the edge of the town, the smell of seafood was heavy in the air, wafting through the open windows of the bus. Up ahead, they could see that crowds of people filled the streets, and she felt a pang of regret at missing the celebration back in Henley. Rows of flags were draped above the long picnic tables, and a few curls of smoke twisted in the air above the shops.

Graham inhaled deeply. "Must be a clambake," he said as the bus pulled to a stop in front of a much grander-looking tourist office, presumably with someone far more welcoming inside. Ellie didn't relish the thought of passing through the throngs of people with Graham, who would surely attract unwanted attention, and once she stepped off the bus behind him, she handed over his sunglasses, which he'd left on his seat.

"Not as good as the mustache," he said as he put them on. "But they'll have to do."

There was a map at the bus stop, and Ellie could see that the house wasn't far, set off on a small peninsula just north of the main shopping district. They'd have to cut through town to get there, but once they made it through the busy streets, it shouldn't take long. As she followed Graham in the direction of the party, she pictured the red front door of the house the way a quarterback pictures the end zone, trying to focus in spite of the noise and the music and the smell of food.

"I wouldn't mind a lobster roll first," Graham said as they reached the party, a sea of red, white, and blue shirts. Dozens of picnic tables were arranged end to end, stretching up and down the length of the main street, but the party spilled over onto the sidewalks and into the stores. There were children everywhere, in wagons and on bicycles, carrying water balloons or cookies, left mostly to their own devices as their parents tended the food or just tipped back their bottles of beer with willful obliviousness.

Ellie was trying to remember the last time they'd eaten, and when she realized it was the melted chocolate back on the boat, her stomach growled too.

Graham stopped when they reached the first checkered table. "It's like a mirage," he joked. "Exactly how long were we lost at sea?"

The blue checkered tablecloths were almost completely hidden by trays of food: clams and oysters and shrimp, but also hot dogs and hamburgers and chips, potato salad and corn on the cob and chocolate cupcakes. Graham walked straight down to an enormous tray of lobster rolls, and the man behind the table—who wore a lobster apron they carried back at the shop—raised a pair of tongs and looked at Graham inquiringly.

"Want one?" he asked, and Graham gave Ellie a pleading look.

"Go ahead," she said. "But let's take it to go."

"Don't worry, I can walk and eat at the same time," he told her, then added, "I'm very talented."

"I'm sure you are," she said, but she was distracted by a swell of murmurs that rippled through the knot of people to her left. She stood on her tiptoes to see what was causing the crowd to part, and when she did, her heart began to drill against her chest. She cast a frenzied glance back at Graham, but he was still talking to the guy in the lobster apron as he tried to separate two paper plates.

Ellie whirled back around, her mouth dry. There, not ten feet away, was her father. He smiled as he shook hands, looking more relaxed than usual in a red polo shirt and khakis, his salt-and-pepper hair ruffled by the breeze. He was tall and thin, towering over the crowd as he made his way through, and there was a photographer just behind him, snapping the occasional photo as he paused to admire a baby or pump someone's hand with a sincere smile. But otherwise he was alone: no aides or reporters, no wife or kids.

Ellie's knees locked as the number of people between them dwindled. It was clearly nothing more than a meet and greet, a casual public appearance, and he kept each conversation short, just a quick exchange of pleasantries while he worked his way through the crowd. As he drew closer, her mind whirred frantically, trying to find traction. But suddenly, she found she couldn't remember anything: why she'd come, what to say, how she was supposed to act.

He was only a few feet away now, and the nearness of him was startling; until this moment, he'd seemed almost like a figment of her imagination, perhaps because of the number of times she'd pictured a scenario exactly like this one. But in those daydreams, she always walked right up to him, and they would look at each other with two pairs of identical green eyes, and he would know exactly who she was.

That, she realized, was why she'd come.

Not for the money. Not even just to see him.

It was so that *he* could see *her*.

There was only one person between them now, a man in a Red Sox cap who looked bewildered as the handsome senator clapped him on the shoulder. "What a day, huh?" he said with what seemed to be genuine enthusiasm, and the man raised a drumstick in an awkward salute, his mouth too full of chicken to respond.

The senator laughed, and his eyes shifted to Ellie. She found herself stiffening, bracing herself for—what? She didn't know. Those matching eyes of his, green as sea glass, landed on her with a look of benign interest, and she could see that there was a little fan of wrinkles at the corner of each one, so small you didn't notice them in the photos.

"Happy Fourth," he said, extending a hand, and Ellie stared at it. She waited a beat too long before reaching out, half expecting to feel some kind of jolt. But there was nothing, only the warmth of his hand, which was a little sweaty as he shook hers.

The words died like bubbles inside her, one after another, all the many things she wanted to say. For a moment, she forgot about Mom and she forgot about Harvard; she forgot about his beautiful wife and the two boys he took hunting and fishing; she forgot about politics, his job, the very reasons they were wrenched apart in the first place.

The only thing she was thinking was, *Can't you see?*

But on his face, there was nothing but a polite smile, utterly professional and almost entirely blank. When he pulled his hand back, Ellie's stomach plummeted, and she looked down, vaguely surprised to find herself on solid ground. Out of nowhere, it seemed, Graham was at her side, balancing a paper plate in one hand. The lobster roll rocked like a small boat as he reached out to accept the senator's hand.

"Happy Fourth to you too," he said, and Graham smiled uncertainly, glancing at Ellie. But she was still watching her father. The look he gave Graham could hardly be called recognition—it was more like how you'd consider an old classmate you hadn't seen in years and weren't quite able to place—but even so, it was still something.

It was still more than the way he'd looked at Ellie.

She blinked, feeling dazed, but he only flashed a too-bright smile, looking beyond them to the next people in the endless series of handshakes and greetings. "Enjoy the day," he said, but he was already moving past them. His photographer, a few steps behind, raised his camera to take a picture of them—not just Ellie and Graham, but the man in the Red Sox cap and the chef with his lobster apron and a few others who were standing nearby—but Graham's whole body stiffened, and he threw a hand out in front of him. The photographer shrugged—confused but unbothered—then trotted after the senator into a sea of potential voters.

"Sorry," Graham said, turning to Ellie. "I guess I'm still a little gun-shy after last night."

But she didn't answer. She just stood there, staring after her father, watching as he was swallowed up by a crowd of admirers. She glanced down at her empty hand, which prickled with the memory of his palm, and when she raised her eyes again, he was gone.

– Would it help if I told you another joke?

– Probably not.

– Okay.

– But... thank you.

22

They decided to leave the boat behind.

It was no doubt ready to be picked up by now, but neither of them felt quite up to the job of sailing all the way back to Henley, and though it had been a while since Graham had spent so much time on a bus, it seemed the far preferable option at the moment. It wasn't that he was seasick exactly—if such a thing was even possible on solid ground—but the feel of the ocean was still with him, even after all these hours, a rolling sensation that made him feel shaky and slightly off balance. Even as they walked back toward the bus stop, the noise from the clambake growing distant, the road felt untrustworthy beneath his feet.

"It'll be fine," he was telling Ellie, who kept her eyes straight ahead. "I'm sure the production guys can pick it up tomorrow morning, and besides, they said they wanted it back in one piece, and I think there's a much better chance of that happening if we're not in it."

She nodded in the same blank way she'd been nodding

at him for the past ten minutes, with glassy and unfocused eyes that she refused to turn his way.

Not sure what else to do, he kept up a steady line of chatter that sounded nervous even to his own ears. "And anyway, I'm not sure how that lobster roll would feel about being back at sea," he said, patting his stomach. "I mean, it was good, definitely. But you just never know with those waves—"

"Graham," she said, and he looked over.

"Yeah?"

"Can we not talk about the lobster roll?" she said, though not unkindly.

He laughed. "Sure."

At the bus stop, they sat on the wooden bench on the opposite side of the street from where they'd been dropped off earlier. It seemed like it had been hours ago, but Graham knew it couldn't have been more than an hour, and probably even less. They were still weary and sunburned, but where before the journey had been urged along by a sense of gritty determination, they were now on their way back to Henley, where nothing good could await them.

Graham dreaded having to face Harry, who had been so patient with him last night, and who would surely have been told about the boat by now. He knew he should have stayed in Henley today. He should have faced the consequences and helped deal with the situation himself. But instead, he'd done what he always did: he ran away.

In his real life, it was admittedly more like hiding away,

this specialty of his. It had become the worst kind of habit. He'd started to avoid everything, parties and press events and people in general, tucking himself away with only a pig for company. When his life had changed, the world rushed in and he'd responded in the only way he knew how: by creating a cushion between himself and everyone else, a distance that extended even to his parents.

It was easy to blame them. But the truth was, it was Graham's fault too. He'd told himself they didn't understand his new life, and then, instead of letting them in, he'd shut himself away. He'd mistaken loneliness for independence, and had become so good at closing himself off from the world that it took an e-mail from Ellie to remind him what it was like to have a real conversation.

She'd been so much braver than he ever was, marching into an unknown town to confront a father she didn't remember, and who obviously didn't remember her either. Graham's parents lived only a short drive away, but it wasn't until he'd made it all the way to the other side of the country that he'd finally done something about it, and now, it seemed, it was too late. The geography of the thing wasn't the point; it didn't matter where they were: there was still too much space between them.

But watching Ellie with her father this afternoon had struck at something deep inside him, something hollow and expansive that he hadn't even known was there. Her face had been etched with such undisguised hope that he wished he could have done something to protect her, to shield her from what had unfolded. To look at one of your parents and have them look back at you with complete and utter blankness was unimaginable to Graham. He knew it wasn't the senator's fault—how could he possibly have guessed that this random girl in the crowd was his daughter, of all things?—but still, he'd burned with a quick and sudden anger. No matter how long it's been or how far you've drifted, no matter how unknowable you might be, there were at least two people in the world whose job it was to see you, to find you, to recognize you and reel you back in. No matter what.

Now he inched closer to her on the bench. The silence between them—usually so full—felt empty and brittle, and he wasn't sure exactly how to fix it. Up the street, the bus came into view, and there was a long hiss as it pulled to a stop in front of them. Ellie and Graham were the only two people waiting, and they climbed the steps slowly, weary travelers nearing the end of a long journey.

"Maybe it's for the best," he said once they were in their seats and the bus had lurched forward again. The ocean was on their left now as they headed back south, and Ellie leaned her forehead against the window. Graham wished he were sitting on the other side, wished that she would lean against his shoulder instead, but he knew she needed space right now. He could understand that better than anyone.

"You're probably right," she said, though it was clear her heart wasn't in it. "It's just kind of weird, you know? Ever since I was little, I've always dreamed about what it would be like to be a senator's daughter. But I guess I never really thought about being *his* daughter." She paused and shook her head. "That probably doesn't make any sense."

"Are you kidding?" Graham asked. "Do you know how many girls dream about me—" He hesitated when Ellie rolled her eyes. "I'm serious," he said with a half smile. "But the thing is, it's not me they're actually dreaming about, you know? It's the idea of it. And so the real thing is always a big disappointment."

"In the case of my dad, yes," she said. "But in the case of you..."

"Only a little bit?" he said with a hopeful grin, and she smiled.

"Only a little bit," she agreed. "But you're probably right. It's for the best. Besides, if my mom ever found out I'd asked him for money without even coming to her..."

"You know," Graham said, "I'd be happy to—"

"No," she said, a bit harshly, then caught herself, realizing how it had sounded. "But thank you," she said, her voice softer, and she gave him a rueful smile. "It wasn't really about the money anyway."

"It was about seeing him," he said, and she nodded.

"I've been picturing that moment my whole life," she said. "That wasn't exactly how I thought it would go."

"Really?" Graham said. "You never imagined shaking hands with him at a Fourth of July clambake?"

Ellie laughed, and then—because he couldn't wait any longer—Graham lifted an arm and drew her into it, pulling her against him so that her head was on his shoulder, and they were both angled to the window, the ocean rushing by, a wavering ribbon of blue against the paler sky.

"Do you think I should have asked him anyway?" she said, and Graham shook his head, his chin brushing against her hair. "Or even just told him who I am?"

"It wasn't the right moment," he said. "You did what anyone would do."

"Which was nothing."

"You went there in the first place," he said. "That's something."

"Doesn't feel like it," she said, then let out a hoarse laugh. "I actually believed this time too."

"Believed in what?"

"The quest," she said. "My dad."

Graham's eyes moved to the window, the sun flashing through the trees. He thought again of the way her father had looked at her, the empty greeting and absent smile, and then he pictured his own dad, flipping burgers on a barbeque in someone's backyard in California. Would it have been different if Graham were applying to colleges right now, worrying about the SATs instead of memorizing lines? Or was this just what happened when you got older? Maybe growing up was really nothing more than growing away: from your old life, from your old self, from all those things that kept you tethered to your past.

"I'm sorry," he said, and he felt Ellie go still against his chest.

"About what?"

"About everything," he said. "And about Harvard."

"It's okay," she said with a forced lightness. "I didn't want to go that badly anyway."

"I'm sure your mom would help."

"I'm sure she would," Ellie agreed, "but I can't ask her."

Out the window, the trees opened up so that all they could see was the water, still dotted with boats. "You're lucky," he told her. "You have a great mom."

"I'm sure you do too."

"How do you know?"

"Because she has such a great son," she said, and Graham smiled. "Aside from the whole beating-up-a-photographer thing, of course. Not to mention that one little boat-theft incident."

"You know," he said, "before I left school my friends always joked I'd be voted 'Least Likely to Get Arrested,' and now I've almost done it twice in twenty-four hours."

"Really?" Ellie teased. "I'd have pegged you for 'Most Popular' or 'Best Smile' or something cheesy like that."

He laughed. "What would you be? 'Most Likely to Rebel Against the System by Stealing a Boat One Day'?"

She considered this for a moment. "'Least Likely to Fall for a Movie Star.'"

"Boy," Graham said, pulling her closer, "would they ever be wrong about that."

They rode in silence for a while, the bus stopping every now and then to let someone off. They could feel the vibrations of the tires beneath their feet, and the sway of the

345

bus—a gentle motion that reminded Graham of the boat—made his eyelids heavy. He was halfway to sleep when Ellie's voice broke into his thoughts.

"So what now?" she asked, and he wasn't sure what she meant. The question could have a thousand different meanings. It could mean *What do we do when we get back to Henley?* or *Should I try again with my dad?* It could mean *What happens when you leave in two days?* or *How will this all turn out?* It could mean *Here we are, the two of us wedged together on a bus in the middle of Maine, and even after the worst day ever, which came right on the heels of the worst night ever, there's nowhere else we'd rather be, so can we stay forever?*

"What do you mean?" he asked, his voice hoarse, and she sat up, turning to face him with a serious look. Her green eyes were large and her red hair was tangled from the wind, but she looked beautiful, the kind of beautiful that makes your heart fill like a balloon, so light you worry it might carry you away.

"With us," she said, and Graham felt the words one at a time, each a sharp jab, because he didn't know; he didn't know what would happen, and even more than that, he didn't know what he could offer her. In two days, he'd be leaving Henley. In two weeks, he'd finish filming this movie. And in three weeks, the last installment of the trilogy would be out in the theaters. Graham would be shuttled around the world with a smile pasted on his face to talk into a thousand different microphones about what it all meant, traveling from L.A. to Tokyo to Sydney to London, and back around again. There would be late nights and big crowds, endless talk shows and press junkets.

There would be no more fishing boats or walks along the rocky beach.

There would be no more Ellie.

"I don't know," he said truthfully, because he didn't. It seemed too big a question for a simple answer. Right now, sitting so close, he couldn't imagine being without her. But including her in his real life didn't seem logical either. It was like there were two different Graham Larkins, and even if one of them was truer, more substantial—even if one of them was *happier*—the other one still took up more space, and it wasn't going away.

He looked at her helplessly. "I don't know," he said again, afraid to meet her eyes. But when he finally did, he saw that she was nodding. She didn't seem to be hurt or offended or even surprised at this. There was a thoughtful expression on her face, maybe even expectant, and his stomach churned with doubt. She nodded again.

"Well, we have a couple more days," she said eventually, and it was Graham's turn to nod. "So what should we do?"

He smiled. "We'll go stick our toes in the water."

"I love doing that."

"I know."

"What else?"

"Eat ice cream on a hot day," he said quietly, closing his eyes. "Listen to the waves. Take an evening stroll. Go swimming. Read poetry. Hang out with Bagel."

Ellie was watching him in wonder. "That's my e-mail," she said, shaking her head. "How did you remember all that?"

"How could I not?"

She was smiling now, her eyes bright. "There's too much," she said. "We'll never have time to do all that."

"We'll figure it out," he promised her, and he was certain then that they would.

But as they neared Henley, Graham felt a deep sadness wash over him. Each time someone got off the bus, he found himself growing tenser, their departure a preview to his own. The seats smelled like mold and the windows were streaked with salt and the glare of the sun felt like a furnace, and if you'd asked him what he'd like to be doing on the Fourth of July, this would have been pretty far down on his list. But still, he hated to think of stepping off and back into the real world.

When the bus turned off the main highway that had carried them down the coast, the engine slowing beneath their feet, Ellie sat up and stretched.

"We still have a little while till the fireworks," she said. "I told Quinn I'd meet her at the party." Graham could tell she was weighing something as she bit her lip. She gave him a long look, then seemed to come to a decision. "Do you..."

"What?"

"Do you want to come with me?"

"I love that you're asking," he said, knowing what it

meant, what it could cost her. They both understood that it was more than just a simple invitation. It was a choice she was making. She'd chosen him.

He leaned down and kissed her on the forehead. "But it's probably not such a good idea."

She smiled ruefully. "Photographers?"

"Among other things," he said. "We've gotten this far. No sense ruining your life now."

She nodded. "So I'll just stay 'unidentified girl.'"

"With any luck," he said, then he smiled. "It has a nice ring to it, don't you think?"

The bus turned onto the harbor road, and they could see the crowd up on the green, which spilled out onto the streets in front of the shops. Graham couldn't believe how many people there were; they were everywhere, milling around with hot dogs and hamburgers and lobster rolls, drinking beers and dancing to the band and setting up firecrackers that leaped from the grass and twirled in the air before dying with a whistle. It wasn't all that much different from the clambake just an hour north, only this party held Ellie's mom instead of her dad. And it probably also held Harry.

"I wish you could come with me," Ellie said as the bus slowed to a stop just before the harbor, where there was a green bench and a little sign with the schedule.

"I need to deal with the boat thing anyway, and I should probably see what's going on with the photographer too," he said. "But maybe we'll see each other later?"

349

Ellie grinned. "Under the cloak of darkness."

They stepped outside, shielded from the party by the broad expanse of the bus, but in a moment, it would pull away, leaving them exposed.

"I'll see you soon," Ellie said, leaning in to kiss his cheek, and then she began to walk up toward the party, her chin high as she scanned the crowd.

Graham knew he should be moving too, skirting the back streets to avoid the festival on his way to the hotel, but it took a moment to stir himself into action. He was too busy watching her go, and it wasn't until the door of the bus closed with a pop that he blinked, looking around, and then began to walk.

As he neared the hotel, he could see the balloons that decorated the entrance, huge bunches of red, white, and blue that burst from the front of the building like fireworks. A short distance away, the party carried on, and Graham pulled up the hood of his sweatshirt and then slipped into the quiet lobby without being seen.

He moved straight past the empty chairs and the watercolor paintings that decorated the sitting area, hurrying toward the elevator. Behind him, he heard the concierge call out, but he pretended he hadn't, tugging at his hood and punching at the button impatiently. There was nothing he wanted to hear about right now, not a message from Harry or his lawyer or anyone else. But the voice was insistent.

"Mr. Larkin?"

Finally, Graham spun around to look at him with obvious annoyance. It was a kid about his own age, skinny and nervous, leaning over the front desk and waving a small piece of paper. Graham pulled off his sunglasses with a sigh, raising his eyebrows.

"I'm sorry, sir," the guy said. "But I've got some messages for you." He glanced down at the paper and cleared his throat. "Forty-three, actually."

Graham let out a groan. "All from Harry?"

"Twenty-seven of them, Mr. Larkin."

"Call me Graham," he said, walking over to the desk. "What about the others?"

"Someone named Rachel who wouldn't give me her last name..."

"My publicist."

"A lawyer named—"

"Brian Ascher."

"Yes, sir."

"Graham."

He nodded, holding out the slip of paper, which had a list of names and then a collection of tally marks beside them. Graham scanned it, then looked up again with a frown.

"No calls from my parents?" he asked, and the boy shook his head.

"Sorry, sir."

"That's okay," Graham said, tapping a fist against the desk. "They probably tried my cell. I don't think they even know where I'm staying."

"I can't wait till I can go away without my parents knowing where I am," the boy said with a rueful grin. "That sounds awesome." He coughed, his cheeks reddening, and then added, "Sir."

"Yeah," Graham said, slipping the list of messages into his pocket and turning back toward the elevator. "It's pretty awesome."

From: GDL824@yahoo.com
Sent: Thursday, July 4, 2013 7:38 PM
To: EONeill22@hotmail.com
Subject: (no subject)

I've been officially reunited with my phone. Again, really sorry that yours is on the bottom of the ocean. I'll make sure you have a new one first thing tomorrow. Or you can just take mine, and I'll happily put you in charge of fielding calls from Harry, which has apparently become a full-time job...

The Quinn who awaited Ellie at the edge of the green was not the same one she'd met along the harbor road this morning. And it certainly wasn't the same one she'd been tiptoeing around for the past few weeks. Even from a distance, Ellie could see it in her posture, a mix of anxiety and concern; she stood slightly apart from the rest of the crowd, glancing at her phone, her whole body practically vibrating with impatience.

The sun was starting to slope toward the tops of the trees on the other side of town, and the band had taken a break, the brassy sound of their instruments replaced by the uneven hum of voices. Ellie had been looking for her mom. Her thoughts were still spinning like tires over the events of the day, and she wanted nothing more than for the two of them to fill a couple of paper plates and collapse onto a picnic blanket, to spend the rest of the evening talking about anything but her father, anything but Graham, just eating and laughing until the sky fell dark and the fireworks took the place of the stars.

But there was Quinn—this oddly unsettling version of Quinn—pacing at the edges of the party, and when her eyes found Ellie's, she went still.

And just like that, Ellie knew.

"Want to take a walk?" Quinn asked, and Ellie nodded, allowing herself to be steered away from the many people who fanned out in rings around the gazebo, away from the shops and the food and the noise. She felt oddly numb, her thoughts slow and fumbling as she tried to absorb what she knew to be true. She didn't need to hear Quinn say it; it was there all over her face, her mouth set in a thin line, her eyes full of concern.

To her surprise, they arrived at Sprinkles, having taken the long way around the backs of the shops that bordered the green. Quinn dug a key from the pocket of her shorts and they slipped inside without a word. The shop was officially closed for the day, though for the festivities they'd donated enormous tubs of ice cream, which were lined up along with everything else on the picnic tables outside. But inside, the store was cool and quiet, the sun coming through the windows at a slant, leaving rectangular stamps across the tiled floor. Ellie followed Quinn into the back, where a small table with a few folding chairs was set up in the storage area, surrounded by cardboard boxes like the start of an igloo, all of them filled with ice-cream toppings and various kinds of candy.

They sat down, and Ellie leaned heavily on the table, a wave of exhaustion sweeping over her. "So it's out there?" she asked. "My name?"

"It is," Quinn said with a matter-of-fact nod, and Ellie realized how relieved she was to be hearing this news from her friend. Quinn had always been unflinchingly honest; it was one of the things Ellie loved most about her. Even now, when they hadn't talked for weeks, when Quinn must have a thousand other questions she wanted to ask, a thousand other things she wanted to say, she seemed to instinctively know what part of the equation Ellie would be most worried about, and she was almost businesslike in her assessment of the situation.

"It also mentions your father," she said, and her eyes filled with understanding, though she couldn't possibly have understood any of this. When they were kids, Ellie had told Quinn that her parents were divorced, which somehow sounded better than the truth, even if she'd been allowed to tell it. "He's out of the picture," she'd explained, parroting back the words she'd overheard her mom say in the coffee shop when asked by one of the women in town. And just like that, he really *was* out of the picture, at least between Ellie and Quinn.

Ellie never knew whether Quinn's mother had forbade her highly inquisitive daughter from asking too many questions, or whether Quinn, even when she was little, saw a warning in Ellie's eyes whenever the subject came up. But either way, they'd spent the past twelve years dancing around the idea of

Ellie's father, and now—when Quinn had every right to be angry or confused about this gaping hole in their friendship, this enormous secret between them—she instead emanated a kind of quiet capability. They'd fought about far less, and Ellie wouldn't have blamed her for being upset about this. But that was the thing about best friends; all the petty grievances and minor complaints were left behind as soon as something more important came along, and Ellie was grateful for that.

"It's not as bad as you're probably thinking," Quinn was saying. "Really."

Still, Ellie's heart had plummeted at the mention of her father. She took a deep breath and tried to steady her trembling hands. She'd known this would happen ever since she saw the first article this morning, ever since last night, when she'd watched Graham draw his fist back, maybe even since the moment he walked up the steps of their porch that first night. But she still didn't feel quite prepared.

She thought of her father, with his bright polo and even brighter smile, the feel of his hand as he shook hers, and she was suddenly relieved that she'd lost her nerve earlier. It was better this way. After all, he couldn't be angry with her if he didn't know her. If everything had gone according to plan this morning—if she'd knocked on his door and he'd let her in, ushered her over to a table where they could sit and talk, the years between them melting away, if she'd walked out of there with not just a check but also a phone number and a memory and a promise of something more to come—then it would have all dissolved now anyway, as flimsy and fragile as a soap bubble. This would have been all it took for everything to fall apart again: the moment when an unidentified girl was, quite suddenly, identified.

Maybe later—today or tomorrow or the next day—he'd study one of the pictures that would no doubt accompany the articles, and something in his mind would click with the faintest recognition. He'd puzzle over her face, the face of the daughter he'd never reached out to, wondering whether it was familiar because she belonged to him, or because of something else. He'd try to catalog all the smiles he'd seen and the hands he'd shaken, flipping through the images to locate the girl with the red hair and freckles who had stared back at him with unspoken urgency at the clambake that day, willing him to make the connection, to figure it out, to open his eyes. But even then, he probably wouldn't be able to do it.

"I've been trying to reach you all day," Quinn said, leaning over to open one of the boxes that were strewn all around them. She wrinkled her nose at whatever was inside, and moved on to the next one, pulling out a bag of saltwater taffy. "As soon as I saw the news, I wanted to make sure you knew. Where have you been anyway?"

"My phone's...broken," Ellie mumbled, accepting a piece of green taffy from Quinn, then twisting it in her hands. "My mom. Is she...?" She wanted to say *mad* or *angry* or *upset*, but she was sure that her mother would be all of those things, and she couldn't quite bring herself to

359

complete the sentence. Her stomach lurched when she tried to picture it: her mother picking up a newspaper, or opening up her e-mail, or being stopped by someone on the street in town. They might ask about her daughter, or about the man she'd had an affair with, or they might just ask about Graham and the cameras, the biggest scandal this sleepy town had probably ever seen. There were so many things she could be mad about, it was almost hard to focus on just one.

"I think she's just worried about you," Quinn said. "I was too."

Ellie had closed her eyes, but now she looked up again. "Thanks," she said, biting her lip. She felt her shoulders relax, just slightly; of all the many things she was still toting around with her—the broken news story and all it would mean for her mother, the polite handshake with a father she'd never get to know, the disappointment of missing the Harvard program, the looming and inevitable good-bye to Graham (a thought that squeezed at her heart and took the breath right out of her when she thought about it too hard)—it was a relief to have one of them slip away. Whatever had passed between her and Quinn this summer—the hurt feelings and jealousy and misunderstandings—all of it now seemed to have been forgotten. It was a little bit like the taffy, this friendship of theirs; you could stretch and pull and bend it all out of shape, but it was no easy thing to break it entirely.

"I'm sorry I never told you about my father," Ellie said.

"I wanted to. You have no idea. But Mom was always worried this would happen."

Quinn tilted her head. "What?"

"That the news would get out and everyone would know the truth," she explained. "About who we are. And who he is. And where we came from."

"Ellie, come on," Quinn said with a small smile. "Nobody here cares about that. You've lived here how long? You think anyone who knows you would care about some scandal that happened a million years ago?"

"Well, they do now," Ellie pointed out. "You said the word's out there. All those articles..."

Quinn laughed. "That's practically a footnote," she said. "Really. All anyone cares about is Graham."

Ellie stared at her. "What?"

"Do you think people would rather read about Paul Whitman's daughter or Graham Larkin's girlfriend?"

"I'm not his—"

"Trust me," Quinn said, popping a piece of taffy in her mouth. "You are."

Ellie leaned back in her chair and shook her head in wonderment. Her father had always loomed large against the background of her life, his absence so big it almost felt like a presence. Now, the idea that Graham—who she'd only just met—could somehow turn out to overshadow him struck her as amazing. All this time, she thought Graham's fame would be the thing to tip her off balance. But he'd managed to salvage the whole situation simply by

361

being himself. To almost everyone else in the world, he was far more important than Ellie's father. And it took her only a moment to catch up to them, to realize—with a little shock—that he was more important to her too.

Quinn sent another piece of taffy sailing across the wooden table in her direction, and Ellie reached out to stop it. "My mom's still gonna kill me."

"Maybe," Quinn said merrily, now fully back to her old self. "But once she's done with that, how about we grab some sparklers and head down to the beach? You can even bring your boyfriend, now that you guys have been outed."

"Only if you bring yours too," Ellie said, and Quinn's smile broadened.

They swept the rest of the taffy into the cardboard box, then pushed back their chairs and walked out to the front of the store together. The sky was turning gold at the edges, the waning light glinting off the band's instruments. Ellie could see Meg from the deli making snow cones just beside it, and farther down, Joe from the Lobster Pot was standing beside an oversize grill, a spatula in one hand and a chef's hat perched at an angle on his head.

The whole town seemed to be out tonight, and the invisible boundaries of a dance floor had been loosely arranged, the first few brave couples out for a spin. Behind it all, the ocean was dark and glittery, and Ellie thought of the *Go Fish*, still docked in the town of Hamilton, and of those few quiet moments at the bow with Graham by her side before everything had gone wrong.

When she shifted her gaze back to the party, she saw her mom weaving past a line of children at the ice cream station. Ellie felt a hitch in her chest at the sight of her, and she turned to Quinn, who had fallen uncharacteristically silent.

"I should go talk to her," Ellie said. "But we'll meet up later."

Quinn nodded. "We always do."

Outside, Ellie hurried across the street before she had a chance to lose her nerve. Even as she walked, she found she was bracing herself against the stares that were sure to come her way. She'd seen how far and wide the story about Graham and the photographer had traveled in such a short time, and if her name was now out there too—not to mention the name of her father—then there was no reason not to think everyone in town already knew.

And it was clear that they did, their eyes tracking her progress across the lawn. But there was also something odd about the way they surveyed her as she walked past; it was like they weren't looking *at* her so much as *around* her, their gazes skirting the edges of her, hopeful and searching. They were looking for someone else, she realized. They were looking for Graham.

Ellie felt like laughing. Quinn was right. Nobody cared about who her father was or why they'd come to this town in the first place. All they cared about was that the movie star in their midst had chosen one of them. And now they wanted to see for themselves.

Mom was standing at one of the tables, her back to Ellie as she refilled her glass of lemonade. When she turned around, the hand holding the pitcher trembled a bit, and though Ellie had expected her to be angry—and rightfully so—all she saw was the relief that was scrawled so plainly across her face.

"Where have you been?" she asked, setting down the pitcher. "I've been looking for you everywhere." Her eyes seemed to hold another question, but she didn't ask it. Instead, she turned and peeled a star-spangled paper plate from the pile on the table. "Grab some food," she said, handing it to Ellie. "We've got some catching up to do."

Ellie's stomach grumbled as she filled her plate with huge spoonfuls of potato salad and macaroni, topping it off with a hot dog and a cupcake, and then she balanced a glass of lemonade in the crook of her arm and followed her mother across the green to where she'd laid out the same plaid blanket they used every year.

"Where's Bagel?" Ellie asked, sitting cross-legged, the food spread out in front of her.

"I took him home after he stole his second hamburger."

Ellie laughed, picking up her cupcake, which had a tiny flag drawn on top of the white frosting. "Have you been here all day?"

Mom didn't answer. She settled down across from Ellie,

364

holding her blue cup of lemonade with two hands. "Have you checked your phone at all?" she asked, her expression serious.

Ellie shook her head. "I lost it." She knew what was coming next, and she knew what she should say, but somehow *I'm sorry* didn't seem like nearly enough. She'd given away the secret that had run like a thread throughout their lives. And now the whole thing had unraveled in exactly the way that Mom had said it would, and there was nothing that Ellie could do to change it. Maybe it would help that the focus seemed to be on Graham, and maybe it wouldn't. But she knew that wasn't the point, and she swallowed hard as she waited for Mom to continue, still holding the cupcake in midair.

"What happened last night," she began, choosing her words carefully, "with Graham and the photographer. You know that's been in the news, right?"

Ellie couldn't look at her, but she nodded, her eyes on the cupcake, the smudged corner of the little frosted flag. She didn't know exactly how to answer, but a flood of words had welled up inside of her anyway, and she felt exhausted by the effort of holding them back.

"I'm sorry, Mom," she whispered, and then a lump rose in her throat, and the rest of it came out thick and choked. "It's my fault. You told me this would happen, but I just couldn't—I couldn't help it. It's not like I was seeing him this whole time. I stopped. But it was awful, not seeing him. I was completely miserable. And then it just happened

365

again. But the thing with the photographer wasn't really his fault. He was trying to keep them away from me, and they were horrible. Just like you said they'd be."

She was half crying now, fueled as much by exhaustion as emotion. Mom was sitting across from her, watching the words tumble out with a strained expression, and Ellie couldn't tell if it was anger or worry or something else entirely. She sucked in a breath of air before continuing. "It was awful," she told her. "He had no choice. And this morning, they still hadn't figured out that it was me who was with him, and I thought it would be okay, but now it's obviously not, and I'm sorry. I know this is a huge mess, and I've probably ruined everything, but I didn't mean to, and I'm just so, so sorry."

For a moment, there was no reaction at all. Mom simply sat there, staring at Ellie, the untouched plates of food on the blanket between them. Then she leaned forward. "You haven't ruined anything," she said quietly, and Ellie opened her mouth to protest, but Mom shook her head. "Would I rather this hadn't gotten out? Of course. It's a chapter of my life that I'm not particularly proud of, and when I left D.C.—when I left your father—I felt like I was running away, which is never a good thing."

She paused, looking thoughtful. The sky had darkened several shades, and the orange streetlamps that lined the edges of the green winked on behind her.

"But look what happened," she said, sweeping an arm

366

out. "We landed here. And much more important, I got *you* out of the deal. How could I ever regret that?"

Ellie bit her lip. She'd spent the day in search of her father, like Ahab going after the whale. But she realized now that she'd been on the wrong quest all along. In the end, she was much more like Dorothy. In the end, what she'd been searching for was simply this: home.

She lowered her eyes, wondering whether she should admit where she'd been today; it would be so easy to pretend it had never happened, to block out the memory of her father entirely. It was painful to think about even now, and talking about it—being forced to examine it and analyze it and argue about it—was the last thing she wanted.

But there'd been so many lies already—about Graham and about Harvard and about the boat—and this one was far too big to hide, far too important to keep quiet. She ducked her head, examining the forgotten plate of food.

"I saw him today," she said quietly. She was about to continue, to say who she meant by *him*, but it was clear by the look on Mom's face that this wasn't necessary. She was sitting cross-legged across from Ellie, a paper plate with a cob of corn on her lap, and it rolled onto the blanket as she straightened, her whole body going tense. When she made no move to pick it up, Ellie reached out and did it herself, brushing off the fuzz from the blanket and then putting it back onto Mom's plate with an apologetic shrug.

"You saw him?" she repeated, her eyes glassy.

"That's where I was today."

"In Kennebunkport?"

Ellie sat back, stunned. She hadn't ever considered the fact that Mom might keep tabs on him too, follow his progress the same way Ellie always had. She'd always assumed they never spoke of him because Mom didn't want to talk about it. But now, for the first time, she realized she might have been wrong. Maybe it was because she *did* want to talk about him; maybe all the silence was just a way to stanch the flow of memories like a bandage.

Maybe she left him all those years ago not because she hated him, but because she loved him.

After a moment, Ellie nodded. "Graham went up there with me," she said, leaving out the part about the boat for now. "I don't know what I was thinking. I just wanted to see him."

Mom's face was still oddly blank. "And you did?"

Ellie nodded again. "He was in town, meeting people for the campaign," she said, and then, to her surprise, her voice broke. "He didn't know it was me. He didn't recognize me."

"Oh, El," Mom said, scooting closer, so that they were side by side. "I didn't know. I had no idea you wanted to meet him."

"I didn't either," Ellie said, feeling suddenly miserable. "Not really. I guess it was stupid to think he might know who I was."

Across the lawn, the band finished their song with a trilling crescendo and then fell silent. There was an air of anticipation as people found their blankets. Pretty much everyone here had been coming to the festival for enough years to know that when the sky turned a soft denim blue, and the band finished their last number, and the clapping petered out in the warm evening air, the fireworks would soon begin.

"Do you know how I first started talking to him all those years ago?" Mom asked, and Ellie nodded.

"You were his waitress."

"Right, and I always just took his order, and that was it," she said. "But there was this one week when it rained every single day. He'd come in each morning with his coat dripping and his hair soaking wet, and slide into that booth that never seemed like it was big enough to fit those long legs of his. And then one morning, it just stopped."

"The rain?"

She nodded. "As I was taking his order, I looked out the window and said something about how it was a miracle. And you know what he said?"

Ellie shook her head.

"He said, 'There will be no miracles here.' I remember we both looked around the table, and I was thinking he was right. I mean, it was a diner, and kind of a crummy one at that. We were surrounded by overcooked eggs and water stains and torn plastic seats and pies that had been sitting out for way too long. But when I asked what he meant, he told me a story about this town in France in the seventeenth century that was supposedly the site of all these miracles. When too many people started flocking there, all of them filled with hope, the authorities posted a sign: THERE WILL BE NO MIRACLES HERE."

Overhead, the first firework went whistling past the roof of the hotel and into the night sky, a tiny bead of light; as it sailed higher, it grew quieter, and Ellie lost sight of it entirely. But a moment later it exploded into the air with a fizzle, its spidery golden legs arcing down toward the ground again.

"But that's the thing," Mom said, her voice soft amid the noise. "There *was* a miracle. We just didn't know it yet." She smiled. "The miracle was you."

"Mom—" Ellie said, but she was cut off.

"He might not have recognized you today," she said, shaking her head. "But he loves you. I saw the way he looked at you when you were little. He always wanted a daughter." She reached out and gave Ellie's hand a squeeze. "And staying out of our lives? That wasn't easy for him either. You have to know that. It was my decision— I was the one who cut it off. He was ready to go public about you, even though it might have ruined his career. But I wouldn't let him do it."

"Why not?"

"That wasn't what I wanted for us," she said. "Him with his wife and kids in Delaware, sending us checks while we were stuck in D.C. with all the press. I wanted you to have a real life. This kind of life." She swept an arm around at their friends and neighbors, all of them cheering, and Ellie felt her chest swell at the sight of this town that she loved, and that she'd never trade for anything, especially life as a senator's daughter.

All this time, she'd wondered if things would have been better if she were part of his family, but she understood now that it was the other way around. She wasn't the one who'd missed out. Maybe she hadn't grown up with money for summer camp or trips to Europe or a new car every year. But he'd never watched the sunset from the cove near their house. He'd never spent a winter's morning at Happy Thoughts, warming his socks by the radiator. He'd never eaten at the Lobster Pot or tried the orange sherbet at Sprinkles. He'd never seen her win a soccer game or a spelling bee, and he'd never met Bagel. He'd never had dinner at Chez O'Neill.

"He didn't abandon us," Mom said. "He gave us a gift."

"He let us go," Ellie said quietly.

Mom nodded. "And we've been fine," she said. "But believe me: he still loves you. I don't have to be in touch with him to know something like that."

It was getting harder to see, and the people still looking for places to sit were silhouetted against the streetlamps. A few kids with glow necklaces ran past, laughing, and Ellie squinted to make out the solitary form settling onto the grass not far from their own blanket. Her heart gave a little thump as she recognized him.

It was Graham.

He sat down alone on the grass, folding his legs beneath

him and tipping his head back to look up at the sky, and she realized he had a phone pressed to his ear. She hoped he wasn't talking to his manager or his lawyer or his publicist. Something about his posture, the relaxed expression on his face, made it seem like maybe he wasn't. He was alone, as usual; he had a way of being in a crowd of people and still somehow apart from them, and tonight was no different.

As each firework exploded and then disappeared, she closed her eyes, preserving the memory in glowing lines on the backs of her eyelids, thinking about the day behind her, the memory of her dad's hand in hers, the comfort of her mother's presence, and mostly—mostly—the boy sitting not ten feet away, watching the very same sky.

She thought of the words her father had spoken all those years ago: *There will be no miracles here.*

He was wrong, she was thinking, the words arriving with a fierceness that surprised her. Even in that diner, there must have been a sense of possibility. You just had to know where to look. Even a dirty window or stale apple pie could be a kind of miracle.

"So what happens now?" Ellie asked. "If it's all over the news, he has to know we're here. Do you think he'll try to find us?"

"Do you want him to?"

"I don't know," she said honestly. "Maybe someday. Or maybe not. I don't know."

"That's okay," Mom said. "We've got time to figure it out."

"I'm really sorry," Ellie said again. This time, she wasn't exactly sure what she was apologizing for; there were so many things to choose from.

"Hey," Mom said, reaching over to cup her chin. "It'll be fine."

"How?" Ellie asked, her voice very small.

"We're lucky," she said. "It seems like everyone's more interested in the other part of the story. Apparently Graham Larkin's a lot more fascinating than Paul Whitman." She shook her head with a smile. "I definitely didn't see that coming."

Ellie's eyes trailed over to Graham's back again. He'd hung up the phone and his face was now angled toward the sky.

"It's a good thing," she said. "It takes away the focus."

"Not while he's in town, it doesn't," Mom said, leaning back. "But he'll be gone in a couple of days, and then that will be that."

Another firework exploded overhead, this one a ring of green and purple, but Ellie didn't see it. She was too busy watching Graham, and when he turned around, his eyes caught hers immediately. They stayed there like that for a long moment while the sparks rained down overhead. Another explosion colored the night sky, and Ellie felt this one down to her toes, the heat and flame of it, like a candle, like a fever, like a burn.

That will be that, she was thinking, but she didn't stop looking at Graham.

"Hi," he mouthed from across the lawn.

"Hi," she said right back.

By morning, it was as if none of it had happened: the band and the fireworks, the food and the games. As Graham walked to the set beneath an orange sky, the village green looked as it always did, a thumbprint of grass in the center of town, empty and quiet and covered in dew. There were no paper cups left to be batted around by the wind, no singed firecrackers or sparklers strewn on the sidewalks, not even squares of flattened grass where the blankets had been spread out like an enormous patchwork quilt.

Graham took a sip of the coffee he'd gotten in the hotel lobby, careful not to spill it as the sidewalk began to slope down toward the water. Up ahead, he saw Mick crossing the street, looking tired and unshaven and holding a cup of coffee at least twice the size of Graham's.

"Well, if it isn't our very own prizefighter," he said, stopping to wait for Graham, who braced himself for what was to come. But to his surprise, Mick didn't seem angry. Instead, he was trying not to laugh. "It's always the quiet ones," he said, shaking his head. "But from what I've read, you got the bad guy *and* the girl in one punch, huh?"

"I'm really sorry, Mick," Graham said. "I didn't mean to screw things up for—"

Mick waved him away as they walked down the hill. "It's fine," he said. "I talked to Harry already this morning. The guy's a magician. He's made it all disappear."

Graham stared at him. "How?"

"Like I said," Mick told him with a shrug, "magic. He turned the whole thing on its head. I guess he didn't even need the lawyers."

For the first time in two days, Graham felt the muscles around his jaw unclench, and he let out a long breath, shaking his head in relief. "But all that publicity?" he said. "It can't be good for—"

"It's always good for something," Mick said. "First rule of the business. Besides, it never hurts for the lead to be seen as a bit more of a tough guy."

Graham glanced down at his hand, which still ached this morning. "I guess," he said. "But I *am* sorry. Really."

Mick groaned. "Two minutes with you, Larkin."

"Huh?"

"That's all it took to undo your new image."

"Sorry," he said again, and Mick rolled his eyes.

"Look, as long as we get that kind of fire out of you today on set, we're still in good shape," he said, giving him a pat on the shoulder before peeling off toward the catering truck.

On the set, a production assistant was waving to Graham, already herding him in the direction of the makeup trailer. There was a sense of urgency to the shoot today, everyone trying to get this portion of the filming wrapped on schedule, and the frenzied atmosphere made it feel like the last day of summer camp. On Monday, they'd all be meeting again in L.A., and there would be two more weeks of production there. But that didn't make today feel like any less of an ending. And like every ending, it was a strange mix of exuberance and sorrow.

Graham was already seated on a canvas chair, a woman with a powder puff stooped before him—peering at his sunburned nose with a dissatisfied expression—when he noticed Harry crossing the lot. He was on the phone, gesturing with his free hand, and he wore his exhaustion like a heavy coat, his shoulders rounded as he trudged across the set. But when he glanced over and saw Graham, his face broke into a smile. He paused just long enough to give him a thumbs-up, and when Graham started to stand, Harry waved him back down and pointed to his phone. He stood there for another moment, grinning broadly and producing yet another thumbs-up, and then he continued on his way.

Olivia had arranged herself on the chair beside Graham, who sneezed as the woman whisked the powder puff across his face. She drew back, frowning at him, and then started again with a disapproving shake of her head.

"I heard he bailed you out," Olivia said, waving in Harry's direction as the big man disappeared around the side of a trailer. "Even I have to admit that was some impressive spin. He managed to make you look like some sort of hero, defending the love of your life from the big, bad paparazzi." She raised her eyebrows. "Not bad."

"It's why I pay him the big bucks," Graham said with a smile.

"Think he's got any extra room on his roster?"

"Nobody has enough room for you," he teased her.

"Well, you certainly got yourself some headlines," she said, rolling her eyes, though he could hear a hint of admiration in her voice. "Your girlfriend too. I feel like this place is some kind of alternate reality where you're the interesting one."

"Don't worry," Graham said with a laugh. "A few days from now you'll be back in the clubs, where you belong."

"And you'll be back at home with your pig."

"Yes, well, if you need any tips on getting yourself some extra media attention in the meantime…" he said, lifting his hands. "I'm happy to help."

"Your technique leaves something to be desired," she said, but he could tell she was amused, and as the makeup artist stepped back to examine her work, he took in a deep breath. Around them, the production crew was preparing for today's scene, and the hum of activity made the day before them seem full of promise. It was always in these moments, away from the fans, before the cameras were pointed in his direction, when he felt an odd energy coursing through him, and he knew with an unshakable certainty that it was going to be a good day.

As he walked from the makeup trailer over to where Mick was waiting for him, Graham glanced up at the sky, which was pale and pocked with birds, the whole thing like a negative of yesterday's fireworks display. When he lowered his gaze to the hotel, he found himself thinking back to last night, when he'd stood in that very spot, watching a herd of children weave through the crowds, holding out sparklers like magic wands.

It was exactly as he'd imagined the Fourth of July here, exactly as it was where he'd grown up, but still, a part of him had wanted to walk past it all, to just start moving and see where he ended up. It had been a day of journeys, of boat trips and bus rides, and it seemed a fitting end to his time in Henley to head off in no particular direction, north or south, up or down, until he'd gotten himself good and lost.

There'd been a lull as the band lowered their instruments, and an expectant hush fell over the crowd. From where he was standing, Graham had looked up at the sky, though there was nothing but the first faint glow of the stars. When his phone buzzed in his hand, he glanced down again. He'd grabbed it on his way out the door, but he hadn't been able to bring himself to return any of the missed calls. He simply wasn't in the mood to talk to lawyers or agents or publicists just yet. Those were all things that belonged in L.A. And for the moment, at least, he was still in Henley.

But just as he was about to shut off the phone entirely, he realized that it was his mom.

"Hi," he said, bringing it to his ear. It wasn't until he'd already answered that he realized she might be calling because she'd seen him on the news. It hadn't even occurred to him; his mother and his acting career were about as far apart as was possible on the spectrum of his life, and trying to account for them within the space of the same thought was like trying to bring something blurry into focus.

"Hi," she said, and then there was the sound of whispering. "Hold on," she told Graham, who began walking over to the sea of blankets that checkered the green. It was too dark for most people to tell who he was, though a few tracked his progress with squinted eyes. On the phone, he heard laughter and a tapping sound, and then suddenly everything was amplified as she put him on speaker. "Your dad's here too."

Graham cupped a hand over his free ear so he could hear better, sinking down onto the cool grass at the far edge of the park. "Is everything okay?" he asked, not sure he wanted to hear the answer. But to his surprise, his mom only laughed again.

"Are there fireworks?" she said, half yelling over the noise in the background, the barbeque at their neighbor's house. He could picture them there, Dad in his traditional blue polo and Mom wearing a red-and-white-striped T-shirt, both of them huddled around the phone.

"Where?" Graham asked, confused. "By you?"

"No," Dad said. "By you. We checked this morning to see what time the sun was setting in Maine. Are there fireworks yet?"

"Not yet," Graham said, but just as he did, the first one streamed overheard like a shooting star. "Actually, yeah. They just started."

"They're not on for another few hours here," Mom said. "But we wanted to watch them with you."

Graham smiled, unsure what to say. The thought of them looking up the time of the sunset, waiting until they were sure it was dark, and then sneaking off to call him was so unexpected that he didn't know how to respond.

"Remember that one year when we watched from the park?" Dad said. "And you burned your finger on one of the bug candles?"

Graham laughed. "Remember that time we watched from the beach?"

"And your father dropped our watermelon off the rocks?" Mom said, her voice full of amusement.

"Hey," Dad said, but he was laughing. "That seagull snuck up on me."

Overhead, two more fireworks went off with a crackle, each sparking a different color. "I wish you guys were here," Graham said quietly, but even this, even the muffled sound of their breathing, was a comfort. He watched the fireworks go off one at a time, each one different, but each a kind of echo too, a memory of all the ones they'd seen in the past, all the many times they'd watched together as a family. Graham cleared his throat. "The last few days have been—"

"We know," Mom said. "We tried calling earlier when we saw the papers."

"I'm sorry," Graham told her. "I just—"

"Those guys are vultures," Dad said in the same tone he used to talk about things like Republicans and opposing baseball teams. "They had it coming."

"Thanks," Graham said. "But I feel pretty awful about it."

"You're working too hard," said Mom. "All this filming, and as soon as you get back, they have you doing the interior scenes, and then there's the publicity tour coming up..."

Graham laughed. "How do you know all that?"

"We subscribe to *Variety*," she said, a note of pride in her voice. "And the *Hollywood Reporter*."

"You do?" Graham asked, unsuccessfully trying to picture his mother reading through the daily entertainment news.

"Of course," she said, like it was the most natural thing in the world. "We like to know what you're up to."

"And it's always interesting to keep tabs on the world of colorized films," Dad joked, and Graham laughed.

"We usually just call them movies."

"Colorized movies then," Dad said. "Your name's been bandied about quite a lot lately. All sorts of interesting roles..."

"Don't believe any of it," Graham said. "I haven't decided what I'm doing next."

"Well, I think you'd be good in anything," Mom said. "Remember how great he was in *Guys and Dolls*?" This was directed at his father, who grunted in acknowledgment. "We're so proud of you."

Graham swallowed hard. "Thanks, Mom."

"When exactly are you getting back?"

"Day after tomorrow," he said, his eyes on the sky. "It went by fast."

"Has it been good otherwise?"

He nodded, knowing they couldn't see him. But he was surprised to feel his throat go thick at the thought of leaving this place, and he blinked fast. "Yeah," he said. "It's been really good."

"I made key lime pie for today," Mom said. "I'm saving you a piece, so you'll have to come over when you get back."

"Okay," he said. "I will."

"Sounds like you could use a break," Dad said. "We should go do something this weekend. Are you working Sunday? Maybe bowling, or the batting cages..."

A firework exploded in the shape of a star, and the pattern lingered long after it had died out, like a stamp across the sky.

"Or fishing," Graham said, and Dad let out a soft laugh.

"I guess it's been a while since we've done that," he said. "We didn't have much luck last time."

"Sure we did," said Graham, feeling a prickle on the

385

back of his neck. He half turned, and as the shadowy figures on a nearby blanket came into focus, he was surprised to see Ellie. He adjusted the phone in his hand, distracted. "We caught a ton, remember?"

Beside Ellie, her mom was saying something, making broad gestures with her hands, and Graham's father continued to talk in his ear, reminiscing about their fishing trip while the fireworks exploded overhead.

But Graham was still watching Ellie, and it was as if a great quiet had fallen between them, as if there was nothing and nobody else around.

"We were just about to give up," Dad was saying. "We didn't catch a single thing until the last day."

Graham had smiled. "That," he'd said, his eyes still on Ellie, "is the only one that counts."

From: GDL824@yahoo.com
Sent: Friday, July 5, 2013 8:18 AM
To: EONeill22@hotmail.com
Subject: do over

Let's try this again . . .

Would you like to have dinner with me at the Lobster Pot tonight?

He was already there when she arrived, waiting beneath the wooden sign. The evening had turned unexpectedly cool for early July, and he was wearing a long-sleeved button-down with khakis, his hair still damp from the shower. He hadn't seen her yet, and so Ellie took her time, walking slowly, trying her best to memorize him, as if that alone would make it last.

Already the crews were breaking down the set from today's shoot. Behind them, the fishing boats were coming in for the evening, and the clatter of lobster traps mixed with the scrape of metal as the trailers were loaded. There was still one more day of shooting, but Graham would be done in the morning, and Ellie knew he'd be flying back right afterward. By this time tomorrow night, the street would be cleared, the barriers gone, the trucks driven off, and it would be like the whole thing had never happened.

Earlier today, she'd walked down to the water to watch them filming along the pier. It was less exciting than she might have expected, mostly just a whole lot of starting and stopping as they played out the same moments over and over, each time seemingly the same as the last. Graham would say something to Olivia, palms up in a conciliatory gesture, and she would bow her head, then turn and walk away, leaving him standing on the edge of the dock again and again.

Ellie was too far away to hear what they were saying, but even from a distance, there was something striking about seeing Graham like that, all focus and intensity. It reminded her of that day on the beach, when she'd emerged from the grove to see him with new eyes, when Graham Larkin the movie star fell away, and all that was left was the boy with a smile that seemed intended only for her.

It was that way now too; he'd shed something of himself, become someone else entirely, even if only for the space of a moment. And Ellie could see for the first time just what it meant to be an actor, that it was more than red carpets and paparazzi, that it was a kind of art. And that he was good at it.

She stayed there for a long time, unable to pull herself away. A production assistant recognized her from the papers and waved a hand to invite her past the metal barricades, but Ellie just smiled and shook her head. She didn't mind observing him from afar, was in fact steeling herself for that very thing. Tomorrow he'd be gone, and there would be no other choice but to see him in the same way everyone else did: in movies and magazines, online and in the newspapers.

Standing there among the rest of his fans, she felt something well up inside her, and she realized that she was saying good-bye. There would be other opportunities, of course, at dinner tonight and maybe even tomorrow before he left, a proper farewell where they would say all the usual things: *We'll keep in touch* and *I'll miss you* and *Thanks for everything.*

But this right here was Ellie's version, and she stayed there long past the time she was supposed to be at Sprinkles, knowing that Quinn would cover for her. Last night, after the fireworks, they'd walked down to the beach together, emptying a bag of firecrackers onto the sand and then setting them off one at a time, the two of them watching as they pinwheeled out over the black water.

It was the same as it had been every year. It was better.

Now, as she approached the Lobster Pot and Graham turned around, Ellie's heart picked up speed, and she realized she wasn't ready to say good-bye after all. Not nearly. She was reminded of the words she'd written to him during their very first e-mail exchange: *I'm not sure I'm quite finished saying hello yet.* She felt that way again now, more than she ever imagined possible.

"You look nice," he said, and she glanced down at her green sundress.

"It's the same one I wore—"

"I know," he said, interrupting her with a kiss on the cheek. He'd just shaved, and his skin was soft against hers. "It looks even nicer this time around."

"Thanks," she said, then waved at his shirt. "You look nice too."

There was an awkward moment as they regarded each other. For all the hours they'd spent together, this was the first time they'd been on anything resembling a real date, and they were suddenly weighed down in the niceties, the things you say to people when you're meeting them for dinner, as opposed to the things you say when you're rescuing them from photographers or stealing lobster boats or just walking on a beach.

The door to the Lobster Pot swung open from the inside, and Joe appeared in the doorway. "You're all set," he said to Graham, then looked over their heads at the street, the people strolling by in the falling dusk. "Nobody for me to get rid of?"

Graham shrugged. "Guess not."

"You must've scared them all away," Joe said with barely concealed delight, then ushered them inside with a sweep of his arm.

Graham stepped in first, followed by Ellie, but they both paused just beside the coat rack that was shaped like a giant fishhook. Every single pair of eyes in the restaurant had snapped up at their entrance; forks were lowered and lobsters forgotten as they collectively stared at the pair by the door. Ellie's first instinct was to duck behind the hostess stand, or to turn and walk back outside; after so much time spent worrying about this exact scenario, it was odd to stand here before a crowd of faces—some familiar, others not—and let herself be seen with Graham. But it was no longer a secret, this thing between them, and there was no longer a reason to hide.

Joe was motioning to their table, in the far corner, in an area he'd left otherwise open so that they'd have plenty of space to talk. But it wasn't until Graham reached for her hand that she felt herself come unstuck, and she followed him to the back of the room, her eyes on the floor. At their table, Graham pulled out her chair and then sat down across from her, and Joe produced a matchbook from his pocket to light the candles, winking once at Ellie before leaving them on their own.

"So," Graham said, leaning forward, and Ellie couldn't help smiling.

"So."

"You still holding up okay?"

Last night, as soon as the fireworks were finished, Ellie had walked over to where Graham was sitting. All around them, families were packing up their blankets and picking up their sleepy children. She sat down beside him in the grass, and the two of them had stayed there like that for a long time without speaking.

"You heard, right?" she'd asked eventually, and he nodded. "I guess everyone knows about us now."

Beside her, a slow smile had bloomed across Graham's face, and he crooked a finger into the darkness. "That guy?" he asked, pointing at a random man dragging a cooler across the lawn. He scanned the crowd for more.

393

"And her?" he said, nodding at a pregnant woman before shifting his gaze to an elderly man with a cane. "And him?"

Ellie laughed. "Yes," she said with mock exasperation. "Probably him too."

Graham leaned toward her, so that their faces were only inches apart. "So that means we can do this now?" he asked, and then he kissed her, a kiss that seemed to go on forever.

She grinned as they finally broke apart. "I guess so."

"That's not such bad news then."

"No, I guess not, when you put it that way."

"As long as you're okay," he added, and she nodded.

"I am," she said. "You?"

"I'm great," he said. "Strange, isn't it?"

She'd smiled. "Not a bit."

Now he was leaning across the table, his face framed by the nautical map on the wall behind him, looking at her with concern.

"I'm fine," she said. "Really. Though I still haven't read any of the articles. I'm just operating under the assumption that every teen girl in the country probably wants to kill me. But it could have been a lot worse."

"How's that?"

"Your scandalous behavior managed to overshadow all the stuff about my dad," she said, picking up her menu and smiling at him over the top of it. "Imagine that."

"So that means your mom's okay with everything?"

"She will be," Ellie said. "We both will."

Graham nodded. "I'm glad."

"She took it better than expected. If you'd asked me yesterday, I would've guessed I'd be locked in my room tonight."

He waved this away. "I'd have come to rescue you," he told her. "I might not have a white horse, but I do have a very portly pig."

"How romantic," Ellie said, and Graham straightened his menu.

"So what's good here?" he asked. "I didn't end up staying for dinner last time. There was this girl I had to go find..."

"So this is kind of like take two?"

"No," he said, suddenly serious. "This is definitely a first."

Ellie looked down at the menu in her hands, but her stomach had dropped. They'd known each other for only a few weeks, but it felt like they'd already said good-bye so many times, and she wasn't sure she had it in her to do it again.

She laid the menu aside. "I know this is awful," she said, "but I'm actually not that hungry."

To her surprise, Graham nodded. "I was sort of hoping you'd say that."

"You were?"

He nodded again. "I think we should skip right to dessert," he said with an enormous smile, the kind that started in his eyes and lit up his entire face. "I think I'll have a whoopie pie."

Ellie rolled her eyes. "Very funny."

"I'm serious."

"I've been coming to this place since I was a kid," she said, reaching for the menu. "Trust me, they don't have them here."

Graham was leaning back in his chair, looking pleased with himself. "You think you know this place better than me?"

"I *know* I do," she said, eyeing him suspiciously. "Unless..."

It had been a long time since she'd actually looked at the menu before ordering, but she opened it now, and the tiny print swam before her in the dimly lit room. She pulled a votive candle closer, the pool of wax sloshing in the little glass holder.

"Unless what?"

"Unless you did something," she said. "Which would explain why you're acting so weird." She sat back in her chair and folded her arms. "Now I'm thinking maybe you worked something out with Joe..."

"Me?" he asked in his best innocent tone. "Do you really think that in between filming a movie and traipsing around the state of Maine with you I've had time to figure out where to get whoopie pies, then make sure to have them here on this particular night, on the off chance that you were still speaking to me after everything that happened, and would agree to have dinner here together?"

Ellie looked at him levelly. "Yes."

"Wanna bet?"

"Definitely," she said. "But I'm betting on you."

He raised his eyebrows. "Meaning?"

"I think you *did* do all that," she said. "I think I'm about to have my first-ever whoopie pie."

"Even though it's not on the menu?"

She nodded, though a little less certainly. "Even though it's not on the menu."

"Okay," he said, putting his elbows on the table and giving her a long look. "Then I'll bet you a thousand dollars."

For a moment, Ellie didn't move. She simply stared at him, her eyes wide.

"Deal?"

"No," she said, her voice hoarse. She set the menu back on the table in front of her, shaking her head. "Graham..."

He was still smiling. "It's just a bet."

"I can't."

"Yes, you can," he said quietly, the candlelight flickering against his face.

She knew what he was doing; of course she did. And all of a sudden, she understood that it *had* happened, all of it; that he'd figured out a place to buy whoopie pies, had them sent to the Lobster Pot; he must have talked it all out with Joe ahead of time, orchestrated the whole thing so that she'd bet the right way. And he'd done it all for her.

Her heart was loud in her ears as she looked at him across the table, and she didn't notice that Joe was at her side again until he cleared his throat.

"And what will we be having?" he asked, ready with a

397

pen and a notepad. But neither of them answered. Graham was still focused on Ellie.

"Deal?" he said again, and she found the word *no* was lodged in her throat so that all she could do was blink back at him. Taking this as a sign, he turned back to Joe, beaming. "I think we're gonna skip right to dessert."

"Of course," Joe said, and Ellie saw his mustache twitch. "Anything in particular?"

Graham could hardly contain his enthusiasm. "We'll have two whoopie pies," he said a bit too loudly, and all Ellie could do was watch with slightly widened eyes as Joe bobbed his head, snapped his notepad shut, and whisked the menus away from them.

When he was gone, Graham turned back to Ellie. "Well, look at that," he said with an expression of mock despair. "I guess I must have lost."

She shook her head. "You're a horrible actor."

"Hey," he said, but he was grinning. "I'm just trying to be a good sport."

"Graham," Ellie said, looking down at her plate. "I can't."

"You can't eat a whoopie pie?"

"You know what I mean."

"I don't, actually," he said. "I have the money. You need the money. It's as simple as that."

"I can't let you do that," she said, shaking her head.

"I'll tell you what," he said. "Throw in a poem and we've got a deal."

She looked at him blankly.

"At the end of the course, I want one of your poems."

"I don't *write* poetry," she said. "I just like to read it."

"Okay," he said cheerfully. "Then I'll take one by a dead guy. In one of those frames. How's that?"

"Graham," she said, her voice cracking. "This isn't your problem."

"It's about you," he said with a little smile, as if that were reason enough, as if that explained everything.

She felt a rush of gratitude then, a slow yielding of the most stubborn parts of her. No matter how hard she tried to steer her thoughts elsewhere, they kept circling back to the pictures she'd seen of Harvard, the redbrick buildings and leafy sidewalks, the classrooms where she'd learn about her favorite poets. It was easy, in a way, to imagine herself there, and she could feel herself giving in to the pull of it.

"And a bet's a bet," Graham was saying, "so it's only fair."

Once again, Joe arrived at the table, but this time, he was carrying two plates. On each one, there were three whoopie pies stacked in artistic fashion, and Ellie sat up in her chair to get a better view. They were like oversize Oreos, two enormous chocolate cookies sandwiched on either side of a layer of thick white frosting. As Joe set a plate down in front of each of them, Ellie tried to imagine the lengths to which Graham must have gone to get them here. He'd made her a promise, and he'd delivered. Just as he said he would.

399

"So," Joe asked. "Who won the bet?"

"She did," Graham said, and Joe gave Ellie's shoulder a little squeeze before heading back toward the kitchen. When he was gone, she glanced up again.

"Graham," she said, and he looked back at her with such intensity that she felt her breath catch in her throat.

"It's already done," he said. "I had it all arranged this morning."

"You did?"

"I did," he said. "You're going to Harvard."

She smiled. "For a couple of weeks anyway."

"At least to start."

"Thank you," she said, feeling that the words weren't big enough to contain all that she really wanted to say. But it seemed to her right then that he understood, and that somehow, it was enough.

"Now eat," he said, picking up one of his whoopie pies. "You can't properly call yourself a Mainer until you've at least sampled the state treat."

Afterward, they stepped out of the restaurant and into the darkened street together. It wasn't yet nine, but the sidewalks were mostly empty, everyone still worn out from last night's celebration. Even so, it was unexpectedly thrilling, being out in public together, and when Graham extended his hand, Ellie took it in hers, and they began to walk.

"I bet you'll be happy to get back to Middle-of-Everything, California," she said as they wove across the green.

"Maybe a little," he said. "But I'll miss Middle-of-Nowhere, Maine."

"Maybe you'll come back one day," she said, looking at him sideways. She half expected him to make some kind of joke, but he seemed to consider this for a moment before nodding, his face serious.

"Maybe," he said. They passed the spot where they'd been sitting last night, watching each other as if there were nothing else around them, no exploding lights or booming music. "Or maybe we'll see each other somewhere else."

"Any chance your world tour is taking you to Boston?"

"It would probably help if I actually checked my schedule," he said. "But it's possible."

"I'm sure there's plenty of trouble we could get into down there."

Graham grinned. "I've always wanted to steal a swan boat."

"And we'll write," Ellie said, without looking over at him.

"And we'll write," he agreed.

"Just don't screw up my e-mail address."

"That," he said, still smiling, "doesn't sound like me at all."

They continued to walk, passing place after familiar place as if to rewind the past weeks: the spot near the gazebo where they'd stood after Graham chased her in only his swim trunks, the shuttered window of the deli where she'd spilled the candy, the place where she'd seen him on that very first day, looking distant and surprisingly

401

sad, a sorrow so deep that it seemed to hold her there, just watching him.

That was gone now, that look in his eyes.

It had been replaced by something lighter, something more peaceful.

Their destination was never discussed, but even so, there was an understanding between them, no less certain for being unspoken, and when they reached the grove of trees that led down to the beach—not just any beach, but *their* beach—they veered toward it together. At the entrance, Graham hesitated. But only for a moment, and then Ellie tugged gently on his hand, leading him across the threshold where the road turned to trees, and then the trees to stones, and then, finally, the stones disappeared into the water.

Ellie felt her heart swell at the sight of the ocean, the reflection of the moon streaked across it like the wake of a boat. The wind carried the scent of it, briny and thick, and the stars were bright overhead. They kicked off their sandals and walked down to the water, standing at the edge of the surf, which was black as the sky.

"I love this," Ellie said, wiggling her toes, and Graham smiled.

"I know," he said. "It was on your list."

In the dark, it was hard to find the rock where they'd sat the other day, the one that jutted out over the water, flat and wide and level, as if it were meant for this alone. They dangled their legs over the side, the bottoms of their feet catching the spray from the waves, looking out over the moon and the navy expanse of water, the wash of stars in the ink-stained sky.

"So what now?" Ellie asked, and Graham looked over at her. She held her breath, waiting for him to say what they both knew to be true: that he would leave tomorrow. That they would have to say good-bye.

"Now," he said, taking her hand. "Now, we wait."

"For what?"

"Tomorrow."

She gave him a sideways glance, and he grinned.

"It's not as scary if you see it coming."

"That's true," Ellie said with a smile. They fell silent again, and after a moment, she turned to look at him. "Are we really waiting here till tomorrow?"

Graham didn't shift his gaze from the water. He looked completely untroubled, sitting there with the breeze ruffling the hair on his forehead.

"You said you always sleep through the sunrises," he told her. "This way, there's no chance you'll miss it."

She laughed. "You're serious?"

He nodded.

"But you have to work in the morning."

"So do you," he pointed out.

"Yeah, but I don't have to look pretty."

"You'll look pretty anyway," he said, pulling her over to him. There was a chill in the air, and she was grateful to be in his arms, listening to his steady breaths.

"It's a long time," she said, "till the sun comes up."

"About eight hours."

"I guess when you put it that way, it almost doesn't seem like long enough."

"Think you can stay awake?"

She nodded against his chest. "You?"

"Yes," he promised.

But already her eyelids felt heavy, the waves a kind of lullaby. She blinked a few times, thinking of the hours ahead of them on this rock that felt like an island, small enough for only the two of them, but large enough to keep the rest of the world at bay.

When she yawned, Graham gave her a little nudge so that her eyes flickered open again. "I'm awake," she murmured, though she wasn't, not really.

Together, they waited for the sky to flip over like the turning of a page, the bone-colored moon giving way to a brilliant sun, the promise of a new day, and Ellie was surprised to find herself thinking of the little town in France, the one with all the miracles. She could only hope that in a place filled with so many wonders, it would have still been possible to appreciate something as remarkable and ordinary as all this.

"Salutations," he said, and she smiled.

"Good morning."

"Yeah," he said. "It really is."

ACKNOWLEDGMENTS

Many thanks to JENNIFER JOEL, ELIZABETH BEWLEY, STEPHANIE THWAITES, HANNAH SHEPPARD, BINKY URBAN, MEGAN TINGLEY, PAM GRUBER, LIZ CASAL, SAM EADES, JOSIE FREEDMAN, CATHERINE SAUNDERS, CLAY EZELL, JENNIFER HERSHEY, RYAN DOHERTY, and everyone at LBYR, ICM, Headline, Curtis Brown, and Random House. And, of course, to my family: MOM, DAD, KELLY, and ERROL.